HISTORY OF ZIMBABWE

BLACK KINGS, WHITE OVERLORDS

History of Zimbabwe
Black Kings, White Overlords

John Macquarrie-Collins

Pentland Books
Durham · Edinburgh · Oxford

First published in 2001 by
Pentland Books
1 Hutton Close
South Church
Bishop Auckland
Durham

British Library Cataloguing in Publication Data.
A catalogue record for this book is available
from the British Library.

ISBN 1 85821 857 8

Typeset by George Wishart & Associates, Whitley Bay.
Printed and bound by Antony Rowe Ltd., Chippenham.

In memory of my parents,
who were early settlers.

Introduction

The author was a senior professional officer of long service in the departments of agriculture in both Southern Rhodesia, now known as Zimbabwe, and Northern Rhodesia, now Zambia. He was also in close touch with the Rhodesia Defence Force. In consequence, his duties brought him into close contact with both black and white inhabitants.

The book is in two parts. Part I, Black Kings, is an historical account compiled from government archives in both Rhodesia and South Africa and from the reminiscences of an old black soldier, who had actually served in King Lobengula's army against the invading force of Cecil Rhodes.

It shows how different the Zulus, the first colonists of Rhodesia, were from all other tribes in Southern Africa; of their high standard of hygiene, their mastery in warfare, and their sagacity in establishing a stable form of government, in many respects, similar to Britain's two houses of parliament.

It describes the trials and adventures of the great Zulu Chieftain Mziligazi during a thousand-mile track of blood across wild and undeveloped Africa. Of a lifelong bond of friendship between two such disparate personalities as Mziligazi and the brave and godly missionary, the Reverend Doctor Moffatt – a contemporary of David Livingstone.

It stresses the importance and trust which a black king and adventurer placed in his pact of friendship with Queen Victoria, and of how his son and successor, King Lobengula, honoured that treaty in the face of his own downfall.

Part II describes the hardship encountered by white settlers, particularly the womenfolk, in converting wild bush land and forest into farms; of training Africans who had never even seen a spoon or known the basic rudiments of hygiene into house servants; or

Africans who had never seen a wheel or a plough or done any manual work being turned into farmhands.

Many of the funny, unusual and sometimes bloody experiences encountered on farms are described. As well as the dreadful outcome which resulted from Harold Macmillan's unpropitious declaration of 'Winds of Change' as he raced across the length of Africa. It led to UDI, Unilateral Declaration of Independence, and that, in turn, to civil war and Southern Rhodesia becoming Zimbabwe, Northern Rhodesia becoming Zambia and Nyasaland becoming Malawi.

During those troubled times it was comforting to hear of kind deeds being performed by blacks for whites and by whites for blacks.

The book also touches on the flight of Belgians from the Belgian Congo and, once again, of reciprocal kind and brave deeds by members of both races.

It concludes with an account of the troubles besetting the country under the presidency of Robert Mugabe in the year 2000.

Southern Africa.

Part I

Black Kings

Chapter I

'Go north young man! Go north!' was the advice being proclaimed across South Africa by an Englishman, Cecil John Rhodes in 1890. He was encouraging young whites to settle on the vast stretch of land north of the Limpopo river, which he had acquired recently by deception and by conquest, from Lobengula, King of Matabeleland and Paramount Chief of adjoining Mashonaland. This new addition in pink, on maps depicting the British Empire, took the name of Rhodisia, after its founder.

Donald Mackenzie was one of those who took that advice. He bought a scotchcart, the oxen to draw it, a few essential supplies, and then faced the ardours of a very long trek of several hundred miles, with only tracks for roads and little or no indication of where to find the next supply of water.

African villages were miles apart. The round thatched huts of pole and dagga, with just the one small entrance to each, were always set apart at random. The silos for the storage of grain were built on platforms to keep the contents dry and to protect them from the pigs, goats and poultry which wandered freely. As no thought was given to sanitation, flies bred in profusion. The inhabitants were always shy and wary of the whites now hurrying northwards. They were seldom, if ever, antagonistic, but never hesitant at being light fingered wherever opportunity offered.

Less frequently and, much to his delight, Donald came across small and isolated settlements of white Boer (Afrikaner) farmers – the descendants of the original settlers from the Netherlands, France and Germany. They had been arriving in South Africa at the same time as the Bantu migration was heading south from northern Africa.

When I first met Mackenzie, he was the proud owner of 2,000 acres of farmland a few miles from Salisbury, the capital of this new country. By dint of perseverance, coupled with sheer determination, he had battled successfully against the immense adversities of severe drought, of his crops being destroyed by dense swarms of locusts, and his cattle dying from that most dreaded of all cattle diseases – rinderpest.

He was married to a girl he had met on the long journey north. They had two daughters, Kathleen and Betty. Kathleen was married to Harry who had come out to Africa in the hope that the warm sunny climate would cure the tuberculosis from which he was suffering. He was an accountant by profession and knew little about farming, but Mr Mackenzie had nominated him manager because of his marriage to Kathleen. It was she who was manager in reality, and so it was with her that I had most of my dealings.

In my capacity as Agricultural Adviser in the Department of Agriculture, I visited the Mackenzie property quite often and so saw quite a lot of Kathleen. On one occasion, when we had had an exhausting few hours treating cattle grazing at a distant part of the farm and were heading homewards, we drew rein at a kopje (stony outcrop) to rest the horses. There was not a soul in sight – just wide open grassy veld.

The only sounds were the cooing of Namaqua doves and the shrill noises made by crickets. Obviously the brisk gallop had stirred emotions in Kathy, for she peeled off her shirt-blouse and bra, threw herself down on her back with her knees drawn up and legs stretched wide apart most invitingly. Her sweaty breasts glistened in the bright sunlight; her nipples stood up hard and erect, a come-hither gleam shone in her big blue eyes. I just couldn't resist, and had bent over and was smothering her mouth with kisses, when a voice called out '*Sakabona*'.

In the wide open veld in Africa, you can imagine yourself to be the only person for miles around, then suddenly and unexpectedly, a black head pops up. The greeting had come from a very old man, a Mashona, with a mop of grisly grey hair and sparkling black eyes. He showed neither shock nor surprise at what he was seeing.

Kathy returned the greeting quite calmly while stretching for her blouse. Since she returned the greeting in his own language, he exclaimed with delight: 'Fancy! How wonderful to meet a white lady who speaks my tongue! All the Europeans I have met speak only kitchen kaffir, which is not a language at all.'

Kathy asked him what he was doing so far from any habitation. He explained he was on his way to attend a wedding some 10 miles away. 'But surely you are too old to be going on such a long journey all on your own?' she exclaimed. 'Yes,' he replied proudly, 'I am old. I am very old, but I was given good training as a youth. When I was still a young boy I was taken captive in one of the Matabele raids on the Mashonas and was made the slave of a Matabele general. He trained me to become a warrior and enlisted me in the black shield regiment.'

While Kathleen was interpreting the conversation for my benefit, I grew more and more intrigued, because for months I had been greatly interested in studying the early history of Rhodesia. If the old veteran was speaking the truth, and there was no reason to doubt him, this would be a golden opportunity for me to learn from a man who must have been in the forefront when Cecil Rhodes's force entered the country.

However, to make sure he was genuine and not just bragging, I put some pertinent questions to him, the answers to which he could know only from personal experience. His replies satisfied me that he was telling the truth. So I asked Kathy to persuade him to break his journey and to stay to talk. Realising how much this meant to me, she invited him to go to the house for rest and refreshment.

With a toothy grin of delight he accepted the invitation readily, but explained he couldn't stop for long as he didn't want to miss the wedding ceremonies. However, he agreed to break journey on his return trip.

About a month later the old man returned and informed Mr Mackenzie he was there at the invitation of his daughter and that his name was Mosheshe; Kathy had told her father about him. He had appeared disinterested, but now, to her surprise, he had taken Mosheshe by the hand and had offered him accommodation and even gave him a plot of land on which to grow his crops.

It was from what I learned from Mosheshe, together with the time spent studying government archives in Cape Town, Pretoria and Salisbury that I have been able to compile the following story which I believe to be a true one.

Chapter II

The whole village was in a flutter of apprehension: a messenger had arrived, hot foot and dusty. His uniform of a brief leopard-skin kilt, an orange-coloured eagle feather worn in his hair, and anklets of zebra hide, revealed him as a messenger from the great, feared and respected Chaka, King of the Zulus. He had delivered his message and had then left without even resting or partaking of any hospitality.

Men and women looked anxiously at each other, and then tried to study the reaction of their clan chieftain. If he looked worried, so should they be. That was one of the many ways in which the astute Chaka kept control of his subjects. A chieftain was responsible for the misdeeds of his clan, and the clan was responsible for the misdeeds of their chieftain.

Mziligazi was a tall, broad-shouldered man with a scar running the full length of one cheek. He looked every inch a warrior, and his clan, the Kumalos, was a big one numbering some 2,000 men, women and children. He was regarded as being one of the most senior and most successful of Chaka's generals.

To discuss the message he had just received, he summoned to his hut the two men he most trusted – his uncle Kalipi and his nephew Mnombate. The message had merely ordered him to report to the King, but had given no reason for the summons. They went over all the events of the recent past, but couldn't recall having offended the King in any way whatsoever.

Chaka was not only the King of the Zulus, but he was also the greatest military tactician in the whole of southern central Africa. His ambition was to create a great Zulu nation, and, to do this he had set about conquering all the tribes for miles around and compelling them to become his vassals. They were required to pay for his protection and patronage by annual contributions of slaves, cattle and grain.

Instead of fighting as an undisciplined rabble as did all other tribes, Chaka had formed his warriors into district regiments, each under the command of a gallant and trusted commander. Intensive training and strict discipline were enforced. Each regiment was recognised by the colour of its shields: all black, or all white, or all red, or black and white or red and white. So also by the different types of head plumes worn by each regiment.

It was Chaka who had introduced the long shield, the short stabbing assegai (spear) and the pincer movement in attack.

While the enemy used small shields which protected only the face and upper part of the body, Chaka provided his men with long shields, which protected most of the body. The enemy hurled long spears, which, once thrown, were lost; Chaka's men used short stabbing spears which they held on to throughout the battle. That was where the pincer movement proved his genius: when the enemy had lost their spears and tried to escape, they were horrified to find themselves completely encircled, for while part of Chaka's force fought the enemy face to face, as was the custom, he deployed other units to move forward fast on each flank so as to completely encircle them. Then would start the slaughter in real earnest – stabbing with spears and bludgeoning with knobkerries. Generally he would allow a few men to escape to advertise what happened to anyone who dared to oppose the Zulus.

The royal kraal was quite an edifice; virtually a town on its own covering several acres of ground. The huts were sited in serried rows, were well maintained, and special areas were demarcated for the disposal of garbage – unlike the kraals of other tribes where the refuse was thrown outside the huts for dogs and pigs to snuffle through and for flies to breed in their millions. This was one reason why the Zulus were fairly free from eye infections, while the members of most other tribes went about with their eyes and faces covered in a thick black layer of flies.

The town was protected by three rows of stout palisades surrounding it completely. Between the outer two were the bomas (pens) for the livestock and the huts of the ordinary folk. Between the second two dwelt the indunas (councillors) and senior government officials. Beyond the second palisade, and in the very heart of the town were the royal dwellings. The King's house was circular and of pole and dagga (mud plaster) construction; it differed from all the others only in size and in having the thatch roof decorated in colour. Like all others, it had only the one low door compelling those entering to stoop double; there were no windows. Surrounding his house were the huts of his large harem of wives and concubines, with the largest of these belonging to his first wife who lorded it over all the other women.

Within the precincts of each palisade lived the witch doctors. They were appointed directly by the king and were always selected from other tribes so that they did not owe allegiance to any of his sub-chiefs. Their prime duty was to act as the King's spies. They were hated and feared by all, as they exercised great power by virtue of their spying activities, and they used that same information to become consummate blackmailers.

As Mziligazi approached the gate to the royal kraal, he realised he was in trouble, for even old friends ignored him and looked away. He told himself he would have to watch his step and be careful not to show any sign of the fear he was feeling, because nothing annoyed the King more than to see any sign of fear in any of his commanders.

Chaka was of medium height, broad-shouldered and barrel-chested. His personality was overpowering. He was a commander in every sense of the word, but he was self-conscious of one particular weakness – that his skin was darker than that of other Zulu chieftains. This made him fear he might not be considered a full-blooded Zulu. In general, Zulus were fairer than other Bantu tribes; they were colour conscious as well as status conscious.

Nobody could be certain of what was in Chaka's mind; much depended on his mood at the moment. He could be benign and generous one minute and an absolute fiend the next.

The King was seated on his favourite three-legged stool outside the royal hut. A fine leopard skin was draped over his broad shoulders; the only other garment was a brief kilt, also of leopard skin. A crown of ostrich feathers adorned his head.

The chief indunas (councillors) squatted on the ground each side of him. Behind him stood a bodyguard of four warriors and, well behind them, two executioners, armed with heavy knobkerries and with long *rimpis* (ropes) made from the sun-dried hide of giraffes or zebras wound around their waists. They came in useful, when needed, to bind the arms and legs of persons sentenced to death or to some other form of vicious punishment.

Mziligazi, with steeled nerves and in bent posture, approached the royal presence, knowing that the slightest breach of etiquette or the slightest sign of fear would spur the King to savage fury. He squatted on the ground in front of his royal master, making sure that at all times his head remained well below the level of Chaka's.

He felt his heart thump as he heard Chaka say, 'I have heard that you have been comparing yourself with me, but I have dismissed that report as being untrue, for I know you are far too intelligent to indulge in such thoughts. However, always remember, Mziligazi, that you have become a good commander only because all you know of warfare you have learned from me.'

Mziligazi was about to speak, but was ordered to be silent as Chaka went on to say, 'A far more serious story is in circulation: you have been boasting that you are descended from Kumalo, son of Zulu, and are therefore the paramount chief or our nation and that I am a usurper!'

Before Mziligazi could protest, he was told to go home and think deeply about who was the real ruler of the Zulus.

He left the royal presence considering himself lucky, but lucky for how long he wondered? When he had described to Kalipi and to Mnombate all that had transpired, they too were equally depressed, for the seed of suspicion had been sown in the King's mind. There was only one solution: the whole clan would have to escape from Chaka's clutches, for the punishment of a chief meant the punishment of all members of the clan. If their lives happened to be spared, the best they could hope for was to be dispersed among other clans as citizens, always under suspicion.

The scheme they decided on was for Mziligazi to appease the King's anger with a gift of really fine cattle, and then to induce him into believing in his loyalty by seeking authority to undertake an herculean task somewhere very far from Zululand. In that way, they envisaged, they could get the Kumalo regiment well away from Chaka's vengeance. To avoid his suspicions being aroused, they would, of course, send back the usual proportion of plunder they gained from fighting tribes en route to their distant destination. Then, at some future date, when Chaka's attention was directed elsewhere, they would return speedily to collect their families.

'What happens if the King doesn't fall into the trap?' Mziligazi had enquired. 'You know the answer to that,' replied Kalipi. 'Your head will be the first to be bludgeoned and ours will follow in quick succession. All will depend on how well you play your part.'

They recognised the absolute necessity to keep the plan to themselves. That was vital because Chaka had been astute enough to infiltrate men from other tribes into all his Zulu regiments, and they were made to realise that their future lay in observing greater loyalty to the King than to their regimental commanders. Similarly, all witch doctors owed their allegiance, first to the king, and only then to the clan chieftain.

A few days later the three men carried out a meticulous inspection of the cattle that were to be presented. They made sure there was not a single poor beast among them, for Chaka would be even more than usually critical, and would be looking for any excuse to accuse Mziligazi of insulting behaviour. When they were entirely satisfied, they set out with herd boys driving the cattle before them.

The commander of the guard at the outer palisade was surprised and perturbed to see Mziligazi back so soon. He went inside to seek instructions. Chaka's first reaction was one of wariness, for he knew Mziligazi to be a brave man who would not take a threat lightly. Then he smiled broadly and asked, 'Has he come bearing a gift?'

'My king, he has come bearing many gifts. He has brought a large herd of very fine cattle.'

Reverting to suspicion, Chaka asked, 'What is to be his request?'

'My lord, he says he only wishes to pledge, once again, his loyalty and that of his whole clan.'

Chaka pondered over that for a while and then ordered that

Mziligazi be made to wait outside the walls of the town, and not to be shown any hospitality.

After a nerve-wracking wait of several hours, permission was given for him to enter, but not for his two companions; with steeled nerves and bent posture, he approached the royal presence. The silence was suddenly broken by a witch doctor calling out curses, insults and obscenities at him. The King yelled, 'Shut up you filthy, despicable creature. How dare you insult a Zulu chieftain.' Turning to the two executioners he commanded, 'Take him away and bludgeon him if he so much as utters another word.' All present smiled to themselves, knowing with what wide latitude the executioners would interpret that order. The witch doctor was already dead or as good as dead for the executioners would be rewarded with all the deceased's possessions, including his wives, concubines and children. No feelings of sorrow were felt for the wretched creature, because his false accusations had often led to the execution of many an innocent person.

'What brings you here again, so soon?' asked the King, 'Is it that a guilty conscience is troubling you?'

'No, my lord,' came the answer, 'I have come with a gift of the very best animals in my herd, to prove to you my feelings of absolute loyalty. What is more, I have a request to make in order to prove, even further, my loyalty to you – the great bull elephant at whose trumpeting the whole world shakes.'

In a petulant voice bordering on impatience, Chaka ordered, 'Get on with it and don't waste any more of my time.'

'My lord, please let me carry out some really difficult and dangerous tasks so as to prove to you the fealty of myself and of every member of the Kumalo clan. Please, I pray you, give me permission to punish that renegade who has dared to set up his own kingdom in distant Gazaland.'

After a moment of hesitation the King said, 'Lift up your head, I want to look into your eyes.' Mziligazi obeyed with beating heart and hoping the fear he was feeling would not show in his face. All the indunas and guards waited anxiously for the King's reaction. 'Alright, your request is granted, but it is not that scoundrel in Gazaland whom you will punish, but that other renegade Shoshangan.' Then he added, 'Of course, you know full well what happens to a commander who fails a mission! Just make sure you don't! When you have dealt with Shoshangan, I might consider sending you even further north.'

Mziligazi could hardly believe his ears. Chaka had walked into the trap! However, as he was leaving the royal presence, Chaka called out in a voice for all to hear: 'Of course, you won't be taking your families with you, nor your livestock. Have no fear, I shall take great care of them.' He smiled broadly, wickedly.

The menace hidden in that kindly undertaking was not lost on Mziligazi: Chaka was exacting a maximum premium against trickery.

As soon as he reached home, he sent messengers to all the military kraals under his command, ordering the men to prepare for war in a far-off country, and to report at his headquarters by the third day. They were warned they would be away for a long time, but were not to worry about their families, as the King had undertaken to give them his personal protection.

The basic plan was to send messengers ahead to warn all those villages on the route they would travel to be ready to supply the Kumalo force with food and water. Then, on entering new territory, they would, whenever it became necessary, fight for essential supplies, cattle and slaves. In accordance with traditional practice, each victory would be followed by brutal carnage, so as to serve as warning to persons in neighbouring areas, what would happen if they were foolish enough to resist Zulu demands.

The persons to be taken into slavery were youths who had shown bravery and were not too black in colour, and young girls who were fair enough skinned to pass for Zulus.

The Zulu practice of slavery was quite different to our concept of the word. Persons taken as slaves were not maltreated or abused; they merely became unpaid labour and were treated as members of the owner's family. Girl slaves relieved wives and concubines of the more onerous duties in the house and field. Boy slaves tended the livestock, or, if they were brave, they were enlisted into the army as soon as they could speak the Zulu dialect and had learned Zulu traditions. All slaves, both boys and girls, had their ear lobes slit so that they would be easily recognisable as foreigners, and so were not to be trusted to the same extent as pure-blooded Zulus.

The further north the impi went, the sparser became the population and more distant apart the settlements. That, of course, meant that without having to spend time in battles they could cover more ground more quickly, which would have suited the rank and file because the sooner they accomplished the mission set them by Chaka the sooner they would be home. However, that was completely contrary to the most basic element in Mziligazi's scheme; which was always to be within easily returnable distance to home to collect, and to escape, with their families. In order to slow down the pace of advance, he dispersed his force over a much wider frontage to encompass more settlements for attack.

His reputation as a great general grew in direct ratio to the increase in cattle and slaves taken as booty. After each successful raid a murmur was raised that it was a pity to send such valuable booty back to Chaka and to retain only a relatively small share for themselves. Gradually, as the seeds of discontent germinated, the murmurings gave way to outright complaint against Chaka and even to demands for freedom from his tyrannical rule.

It was not long before the men were pleading with Mziligazi to become their king, but he remained uncertain of Chaka's spies and of the loyalty he could expect from the men belonging to other clans and tribes who the King had enrolled in the regiment under his command. However, he and those leaders he fully trusted, began to watch, very carefully, the reactions of their men each time a call was made for independence from Chaka.

Those notions of freedom were heightened by the stories of how successfully Shoshangan, the man they were to attack, had established himself as the paramount chief of a new tribe. He had been one of Chaka's military commanders, who, having failed in a mission, had dared not return home for fear of the humiliation and the punishment he and his men would receive.

The pleadings for Mziligazi to become king increased day by day, but he remained uncertain of Chaka's spies. Anyone who appeared shocked by the suggestion of breaking their loyalty to Chaka lost their lives mysteriously in the next battle. The number of such casualties rose to quite a high level.

When it was felt that no more hard-core dissidents were left among the fighting men, apart from witch doctors, the stage was set for the last scene in the drama. After a particularly successful raid against a weak tribe, the impi (regiment) paraded in review order.

Victory parades in the Zulu army were the only occasions when warriors were allowed to voice their opinions and criticisms without fear of punishment. Mziligazi's nephew, Mnombate, shouted, 'Freedom. Let the Kumalos be free.' Another shouted, 'Yes, let Chaka find others to raid cattle for him. We shall keep whatever we win with our assegais.' That was followed by a tumult of shouts declaring Mziligazi to be their king. Assegais were rattled against shields and then, the most enthralling sound of all, hundreds of male voices, in perfect unison, chanted Mziligazi's praises and ended with: 'Oh! Mziligazi, be our king!'

Kalipi, Mziligazi's uncle, stepped forward and in a loud voice declared: 'Oh! Mziligazi, son of Matshobane, son of Ngulu, direct descendant of Zulu, you have heard the voice of your warriors and their demand that you become our king, so lead us to freedom and to a place where we can become a nation as great, nay greater than that of the dreaded Chaka. Our ears have heard with great interest how Shoshangan has become king of all the country for many days march around him. We call on you to do the same for us.'

Mziligazi then addressed them: 'Warriors, I am proud of you! Of every single one of you! Your words have reached my ears and I am prepared to heed them. Before we left home, the great Chaka had threatened my life and, in consequence, the lives of all men, women and children in our clan, and that is why by subterfuge and secrecy you are here, in this particular place today. What we have heard of Shoshangan is true, and I intend not to fight him, as is Chaka's intention, but to make him an ally and, in doing so, to make him a barrier between Chaka and the homeland I intend to make for us much further north. The nation I intend to build must be a nation of Zulu blood and not like the tribe of mixed blood which

Shoshangan has created by inter-marriage. As soon as I deem the time ripe, we will return home, at speed, to rescue our families. To achieve all this, untold hardship and great danger lies ahead of us. I now ask you, are you, with women and children, prepared to face moon after moon of drought, flood, famine and severe loss of life? Are you truly prepared to stand firm and to obey me implicitly when times are really bad?'

Shouts went up. 'We are prepared to do all you command. We will obey and fight for you to the death. We are now your dogs to obey your commands.'

There came the words he had been longing to hear – the royal salute given only to Zulu kings – 'Bhayete Inkosi Baba! Bhayete Mziligazi son of Zulu! Bhayete devourer of Nations!'

Even after that outburst of adulation, Mziligazi still entertained doubts about the complete loyalty of some of the foreigners left in the regiment and, as always, he knew the witch doctors to be Chaka's spies. Success depended entirely upon every man being bound to him by an oath, so terrible, that he would never break it. Such an oath could only be administered by a seer of great renown. Enquiries made locally revealed that there was such a man living in Swaziland, whose power was known and feared far and wide.

An *indaba* (conference) was held with all men of senior rank being present at which that subject and the future itinerary was discussed openly. It was decided their best route ahead lay straight through Shoshangan's territory, and, as they had no wish to war with him, so a delegation would have to assure him of their new king's goodwill, evidenced by a gift of fine cattle. If that were not enough, they were authorised to negotiate a treaty which would be sealed by the marriage of one of the Swazi king's daughters to Mziligazi. They were then to ask permission for the Kumalos to pass through Swaziland rather than circumvent it, and for the famous wizard to be allowed to carry out a special ceremony for Mziligazi. The delegates selected were Kalipi, Mnombate and two others.

Shoshangan had known for some considerable time, through the grapevine, that Chaka had sent Mziligazi to punish him for disloyalty and desertion, so his impi, trained in the Zulu tradition, was well prepared for combat. It was, therefore, with surprise and considerable suspicion that he received the delegation.

It was only after several calabashes of beer had gone the rounds that the atmosphere mellowed. Young Mnombate had set out from camp inwardly hoping more for battle than friendship, but was now embracing peace and goodwill: Inesha, the King's favourite daughter was a lovely girl in her early twenties. She was dressed like all the other women in just a small – in her case, a very small – leather flap dangling in front and, behind, a flap long enough to protect her bottom when seated on the ground. Her long well-shaped legs glistened in the sun with the oil she had rubbed into them, and she kept ogling Mnombate with her big bright eyes. Each time she approached him, to top up his beer bowl, she gave an extra waggle with her hips and made sure her lovely firm breasts dangled enticingly near his face as she bent over the bowl.

Just as the *indaba* was drawing to a close, and she could see his thoughts were centred more on her than on what was being said, she gave an extra swirl to her front flap so that it disclosed a better glimpse of her femininity.

When the delegates were shown the daughter destined to be Mziligazi's wife they were rather taken aback. Doubtless she was pretty and young (in her teens) but her complexion was darker than desirable. Without doubt she was of mixed blood: Zulu and some other tribe. They gave each other worried looks for had not Mziligazi promised the impi that the nation he was going to build 'must be a nation of Zulu blood, and not like the tribe of mixed blood which Shoshangan has created by inter-marriage'. Kalipi asked, as tactfully as he could for Inesha and offered a very much bigger dowry for her. But Shoshangan was adamant. Shoshangan also refused permission for the Kumalos to pass through the centre of his region but would allow them to cut across the south-west corner.

He was quite content to allow the seer to officiate, knowing full-well that the old man would reveal to him all that Mziligazi had in mind.

When the others were busy bidding goodbye to their host,

Mnombate managed to whisper in Inesha's ear that he would arrange, somehow, for them to meet again.

A large area of open vlei land (meadow) adjoining a river, in which crocodiles and hippos enjoyed life, was selected for the ceremony.

Maseru, the seer was indeed an old man. He was believed to have celebrated more than a hundred birthdays. His grizzled hair was covered by a mixture of ashes and animal fat; his eyes were large, and despite his age, were bright and watchful. His tiny shrivelled face was a mass of deep lines and wrinkles. A filthy *kaross* (cape) was draped over his skinny shoulders and from his neck hung a necklace of the claws and beaks of wild animals and birds. Around his waist he wore a kilt of civet cat tails and over them hung a variety of small leather pouches containing the muti (literally medicines) used in the performance of his trade. All of it was designed to inspire mysticism, loathing and fear, fear most of all – and it certainly did!

The old witch had been brought to the site on a litter carried by four young acolytes, who placed it carefully under the shade of one of the few trees. He remained seated. Mziligazi, Kalipi and other chief indunas approached him. The silence was pregnant! Who was to speak first? The little wizard continued to stare. His body might be skinny and shrivelled, but his personality was so strong that even the hardened warriors stood back in awe.

Eventually he broke the silence, calling out in a shrill and penetrating voice: 'Greetings, oh king! Father of an impi which is destined to grow into a nation. Your parents possessed great foresight when, at your birth, they called you Mziligazi: a path of blood; for indeed you are destined to blaze a bloody trail through Africa. Great will be the trials and tribulations your followers will have to endure, but in the end you will become a nation to be feared and respected by all your neighbours.'

After he had feasted on beef and beer, he sought a private audience with Mziligazi, well out of the hearing of all others. What was said and discussed has never been known, but it is presumed that the wizard forecast the future, for, in the years to come, when most unusual and unexpected events occurred, Mziligazi seemed to have been expecting them.

The men were ordered to sit in a large circle, well apart from each other, so that those in the back rows were not concealed by those in front. A close watch was kept on those who tried to keep out of sight. Mziligazi then explained that success in the venture ahead depended on absolute loyalty to him and to each other. That meant that men who were not full-blooded Kumalos had the choice of either returning home without fear of persecution and with no loss of goodwill, or taking a life-binding oath on the lives of their sons. Not a single man declined.

One report of what then occurred was that goats were driven into the circle. The regimental witchdoctors ripped open the stomachs of the live animals and pulled out their hearts; other goats had their eyes gouged out. The poor mutilated animals were left to drag themselves around, or to run around blindly, till death came to their rescue. The organs were handed over to Maseru who incorporated them into the 'muti' he was preparing out of a mixture of herbs, toads, dried lizards and snakes.

When all was ready, Maseru called on each non-Kumalo to take an oath made on the spirits of his family by drinking a cupful of the horrible concoction.

Another version of the proceedings was that the vaginas were cut out of living goats, and the individuals taking the oath had to have intercourse through them into a bowl of menstrual fluid mixed with girl's urine and drink the disgusting mixture. (How very similar to what is believed to have been the seventh oath taken by rebels in the Mau Mau rebellion in Kenya in the 1950s!)

To appreciate the full significance of the binding effect such an oath had, it must be realised that warriors, such as those men, had little fear of death as long as they had sons to succeed them or sons yet to be born. They believed that the germ of a man's life lived on in his sons, so the sin of dishonouring an oath would be inherited by the boys, and the man's soul would remain in limbo and never find rest.

The very purpose of making the concoction so obnoxious was that the participant could never, throughout his life, forget the undertaking he had made.

Oath-taking over, Mzilikagi ordered Maseru to smell out any persons disloyal to him. The regimental witchdoctors had expected the privilege of doing just that, but the King ordered them to be quiet and to sit on the ground alongside all the others. They looked mystified and very nervous.

From out of a dirty leather bag, Maseru extracted a snake. It looked alive, but it wasn't. It was a stuffed and dried cobra in coiled state ready to strike. He commanded absolute silence while he conversed with it in a language not known to any of those present. Then, in a loud voice he ordered it to smell out all persons disloyal to the King. He caused the disc on which it was placed to spin around. It stopped facing the principal witchdoctor. 'Seize him!' the seer shrieked out. 'He has been sending reports back to Chaka on all your activities. Cut out his tongue and send that to Chaka!'

Mziligazi ordered him to do it himself, for he knew none of his men would like even to touch the despicably filthy creature, let alone grab his tongue. Maseru ordered his acolytes to do it. One held the struggling man down, while another forced his mouth open and a third grabbed and sliced through the tongue.

'Are there any more traitors?' Mziligazi enquired. Maseru once again talked to the cobra, spun it around. This time it stopped at another regimental witchdoctor. Mziligazi ordered him to be bound and to be thrown, while alive, to the crocodiles in the nearby river. The Kumalos were now free of the spies infiltrated by Chaka.

A few days later, while they were on their way once again, Mziligazi received the news he had been longing to hear: the Zulus had attacked the Pondos, a powerful tribe of good fighting men who had stood up well in the past to Zulu attacks and had now adopted Zulu tactics. The seriousness of the fighting was reflected by the fact that Chaka was commanding his troops in person. It had the prospect of being a long-drawn-out battle.

The fleetest warrior was sent back, post haste, to Zululand to warn the families to be ready to leave their homes the moment their men arrived. No one was to breathe a word to outsiders, and there were to be no goodbyes to friends in other clans. Absolute secrecy had to be maintained.

There was no need for commanders to chivvy their men, for all realised that speed was essential, and they covered well over 50 miles a day. By the time they arrived, their families were ready to move – an exodus similar to that of the Israelites fleeing from the Pharohs had begun.

There was one sad note: anyone too old to travel long distances at speed was required to stay at home. Many of them sought death at the hands of each other or of their friends, rather than face Chaka's wrath when he found that the Kumalo had fled.

The impi spread out over a wide front with patrols fore, aft, and on each flank. Within that protective force moved the women carrying on their heads the household possessions of cooking pots, calabashes and as much grain as they could carry; to their backs were strapped the infants. Press on, press on was the theme, short rests and long marches was the order. Anyone unable to keep pace was left behind. The dust created by hundreds of feet trampling on dry soil was suffocating; there was no relief from it; babies were almost smothered by it.

Black bodies were turned red by the dust. Often they had to trek for days on end without coming to water and, when they did arrive at a village, there was no food and no livestock because of the burnt-earth policy the troops had employed on their previous march forward.

With the Swazi king's permission they travelled across the deserted south-west corner of his territory and headed for the lofty Drakensberg mountains. The difficulties they had faced so far were insignificant to what lay ahead. Bitterly cold winds swept down on them from ice-cooled peaks several thousand feet high. The nights and early mornings were particularly cold. The rain beat down on them; the dense mist affected their throats and chests. The older people and the children were the ones who suffered most. Every day members would fall by the wayside, too ill or too weak to carry on.

Some would beg their friends to end their sufferings quickly with assegai or knobkerry.

By the time the column had crossed the mountain range their position was desperate. Stocks of corn were completely exhausted, and a dearth of cattle to be raided meant a shortage of meat. Mziligazi realised that if he were to continue to command allegiance, he must show some proof of the benefits they were to receive from running away from Chaka. So he headed for Basutoland where he had heard that large herds of cattle existed. He hadn't realised that they would be faced with problems they had never encountered before. Zulus were completely unfamiliar with horses and wondered what sort of people the Basutos were – people who had succeeded in training zebras; and what strange zebras at that – without stripes, and differing in colour from each other! Surely such people must be protected by very powerful witchcraft, they thought.

The Basutos were very wary. As soon as they were attacked they fled on their sturdy little ponies into the hills, taking their cattle with them. Once they were within the protection of the hills they became a formidable army, much to the chagrin of the Kumalo, who soon found that the hunters were becoming the hunted. Quietly, in the dead of night, parties of Basutos raided the Matabele outposts, killed the unsuspecting warriors and then fled back into the hills with the livestock. The Kumalos were completely unfamiliar with guerrilla warfare of this type.

Try as hard as they might, Mziligazi and Kalipi were unsuccessful in drawing out the Basutos to fight in the open, army to army, so in the end they decided to storm the stronghold of Mosheshe, King of the Basuto. In doing this they realised that their own casualties would be heavy, but considered it to be the only way in which they could seize livestock.

Attack after attack was repulsed with heavy losses. The Basutos, secure in their fortified position on the summits of the hills, suffered very few casualties, being masters at this type of warfare. As parties of Kumalos charged a position they would suddenly find an avalanche of boulders hurtling down on top of them. After a time Mziligazi realised the futility of continuing with a type of warfare at which he was no master. Mosheshe also realised that an impasse had been reached as his stocks of food and water were not standing up to a prolonged siege. Accordingly a truce was arranged between the two kings. Mosheshe undertook to pay Mziligazi several hundred head of cattle and the latter promised to leave Basutoland immediately.

During the fighting a party of Kumalos had succeeded in overrunning a Basuto strong point. They had killed all the occupants barring two, father and son, who were putting up a desperate fight with their backs to the cliff. Soon the father fell with an assegai thrust through his chest, but the boy continued to fight on. Left on his own he was no match for three Kumalo warriors, one of whom was poised to spear him, when an authoritative voice rang out 'stop'. The man spun round in surprise to find Mziligazi standing there. 'Leave the boy alone,' he commanded. 'He has fought well. He is as fierce as a leopard cub and deserves to live.'

That evening, Mziligazi sent for the boy to be brought from among the prisoners. Turning to Kuruman, his young son and heir, he said, 'I give you this little Basuto boy as a slave; but I want you to regard him as a companion.' Turning to the Basuto, the King said, 'Here is your master. You will fight for him as you fought for your father.'

On leaving Basutoland, the column headed in the general direction of the Vaal river. They attacked Moroka, chief of the Baralong tribe and overcame him without much difficulty. A large number of cattle were seized and many young boys and girls were taken as slaves. The concerted two-horned formation in attack, learned by Mziligazi from Chaka, was too much for the undisciplined local tribesmen. They were completely unaccustomed to this new method of fighting. They could not face up to the terrifying well-disciplined assegai charges of the Kumalo and would hurl their spears at them in panic. When the supply of their spears was exhausted they would try to run, but would find themselves encircled as the flanking horns of the enemy's attack closed in on them. They were then completely at the mercy of their opponents, and in battle, men of Zulu blood neither expected nor showed any mercy. The slaughter was terrible.

* * *

Some two years after leaving Zululand, the Kumalos arrived in the country to the north of the Vaal river which is now known as the Transvaal. The wide open country appealed to them and as the grazing was good and the climate was admirable, they decided to make it their home. It was far enough away from Chaka, and the local inhabitants were timid and disorganised, offering no serious resistance. The Kumalos were tired and were longing to settle down after their long trek. It was with relief that the families at long last received the order to build their kraals. They called the town 'Eku-pum Kweni' (The Place of Rest). Unfortunately, it did not remain a place of rest for long, because a very severe drought compelled them to move further north in search of better grazing.

Plundering as they went, they arrived in the beautiful, fertile and well-watered valley of the Marico. Without doubt this was the promised land, so they immediately set to with a will to build their homes. It was here that they became known as the Amandabele or Matabele, 'the people with long shields'.

That was the first occasion since he was elected king, that Mziligazi had been able to take stock of his position and that of his people. Until then it had been impossible to devote sufficient time to organise and administer the civil life of the community, or to formulate the rules and procedure by which he was to govern. The clan had now become an independent tribe and it was up to him to make it into a free and powerful nation.

In consultation with his tribal councillors and elders, he decided they would adopt the name of Matabele and that their laws and customs should continue to be based on the Zulu pattern. On all matters of importance which affected the welfare and future of the tribe, the King was to consult the tribal council of his indunas. He would not be compelled to act according to their advice, but if he deviated from it, he would have to accept full responsibility for his action.

The King and his people were to be regarded as one; the land and their wealth was to be invested in the King for the common good of the people. In framing their laws they were to pay due regard to the customs and practices of their ancestors. The King was to be head of state, judge and commander-in-chief, and was to be regarded as trustee of the tribe.

Looking back in time, one wonders how it was that the early Zulus were so advanced in discipline, culture, organisation and planning compared with the other tribes in Southern Africa, the vast majority of whom were disorganised, ill-disciplined savages, not far removed from the animals with whom they shared the veld.

Chapter III

During those early days, very few Africans, with the exception of Hottentots and Bushmen, had much knowledge of Europeans other than of the Dutch Boers (farmers) who had been settled for very many years at the Cape. Gradually they began to hear of the Portuguese who were colonising the eastern coast and tales reached them of a strange white man, named Livingstone, who, much further north in Nyasaland (Malawi), was preaching about a strange god, was healing illnesses with strange mutis and was opposed to slavery and to witchcraft.

At about the same time, the Matabele were receiving news of another white man by the name of Moffat, who was doing similar things much closer to home in Bechuanaland (Botswana). He was living among the Batlapin and was of the same tribe as Livingstone. He was teaching about the same God and that it was wrong to lie and to commit murder and to steal. Indeed he was going so far as to say that all tribes should live in peace with each other, that it was better to forgive an insult than to avenge it and that it was wrong to raid cattle. He was even declaring that it was wrong for a man to have more than one wife or to have concubines and slaves.

The more Mziligazi heard of the Reverend Dr Robert Moffat, the more interested he became. In his mind's eye he pictured Moffat as being an exceptionally brave man, for who else but a very brave man would wander about and live completely alone among absolute strangers, and strangers of a totally different colour to himself. It was even being said that he thought nothing of sleeping out under the stars completely alone and without any protection from men and from wild animals! Surely, he thought, this man must possess the greatest of magical powers.

The more he heard about him the more he thought about him, the more he wished to meet him, but he considered it was beneath the dignity of a king to call on a strange individual. So, on a day in 1830, he sent a deputation headed by Mnombate to call on the Reverend Doctor Moffat at his headquarters in Kuruman. They were to convey the King's greetings and to bring back a detailed and unvarnished report about this strange being.

Moffat, of the London Missionary Society, the first missionary to establish a mission station in that remote part of Africa, received the deputation with great courtesy, and was interested in hearing all they had to say about this king whose fame was spreading far and wide and whose name as a destroyer of tribes was being used as a threat by mothers to naughty children.

What most impressed Moffat about the delegates was their cleanliness, orderly and polite behaviour, and their manliness and proud bearing; so vastly different to the squalor, filth and furtive bearing of all the other Africans he had met in his wanderings. The local people were terrified of the delegates and kept well out of their way unless Moffat was nearby to protect them should the need arise.

Moffat noticed that the Matabele commenced each day by going down to the river to bathe. He found it difficult to get the locals to wash even occasionally; they went about unperturbed by scores of flies crawling all over their faces and bodies, whereas the Matabele were spotlessly clean. The skins from which their brief kilts were made had been properly cured, whereas the locals wore sporrans of grass or of leaves or of smelly half-cured hide. The visitors' head rings were neat works of art, so different from the dirt-encrusted, vermin-infested heads of the Batlapin.

Exactly how the poor missionary felt at times about the local tribes with whom he had come into contact is recorded in his diary:

> There is nothing naturally engaging; their extreme selfishness, filthiness, obstinate stupidity and want of sensibility, have a tendency to disgust and, sometimes, cause the mind to shrink from spending [one's] whole life among them, far from every tender and endearing circle.

The more he saw of the Matabele delegates, the more he wished to learn what the tribe was really like. Perhaps, he wondered, the delegates had been hand-picked for appearance and that the majority of the tribe were not much better than the locals. His curiosity was also roused by all they told him about their king – an extraordinary man by all accounts.

He was in two minds whether to undertake a long, arduous and dangerous trek of some 250 miles across the dangerous veld by slow-moving ox-wagon, or to stay at home. In the end, curiosity overcame prudence and he accompanied the delegation on its return journey to Mziligazi.

News travelled fast. Long before the little party reached Mziligazi's headquarters, people had gathered along the track to see the members of the deputation returning with a white man travelling in a strange-looking contraption drawn by sixteen oxen. Never before had they seen cattle being used in such a way! By the time the group reached the royal kraal, the whole town had turned out in cheerful and inquisitive greeting. The King received the missionary with great warmth and courtesy and greatly appreciated him having undertaken such a long and tiring journey.

Moffat had expected so see a giant of a man with a booming voice in keeping with the many stories in circulation. Instead, he was to find a man of medium height, thick of neck and of stocky build. The King spoke in a soft but manly voice, and it was easy to see that he was possessed of great personality and that his word was law, not to be contradicted or questioned by his subjects.

It was strange that two men who differed so much in upbringing and character should immediately take to each other. From the very start a strong bond of friendship and trust was forged between them. A bond that lasted over the years to come.

Moffat was given the honour of being invited to the King's own house where the head wife served him with roast beef, garnished with greens and herbs freshly picked by the women, and washed down by a panikin of beer brewed from sorghum.

It was not until he was refreshed that conversation commenced in accordance with protocol. Mziligazi was keen to know why Moffat had left his home and his own people, people of different colour, to wander about and to live among such uncouth people as the Batlapins, Baralongs, and others like them. His guest explained that he had two important duties to perform: one was to teach people about the one and only God who created and ruled the universe; and the other was to apply his knowledge of medicine among people who were very much in need of such help.

'I am told,' said his host, 'that very often you sleep in the veld at night, right out in the open, alone, and not even bothering to make a zareeba of bushes, or arranging for someone to keep watch. Aren't you afraid of being alone in a strange and dangerous land?'

Moffat explained that he trusted in God; that his life was in God's hands; that as he harmed no one and did only good, why should anyone wish to harm him?

Mziligazi wished to know something about Britain and of Moffat's background, so the missionary obliged him and found the King to be particularly interested in what he had to tell him about Queen Victoria and of how she ruled over an ever-expanding empire of white, black, brown and yellow people. He tried to explain how widespread that empire was, of how Pax Britannica succeeded in keeping people of different religions and ideas within a country, from fighting and destroying each other. It was difficult to explain all this to a man who had never even seen a map and, until recently, had not even known that human beings were of any colour other than shades of black.

Later on an induna conducted Moffat to a large hut which had been made ready for him, complete with a buxom matron to take care of his meals, and a very comely young virgin to share his bed. The girl found Moffat most kind and considerate, but when he made it clear that he had no intention of deflowering her, she felt dejected and humiliated.

Naturally, the missionary was keen to learn as much as he could of Matabele laws and practices, and the King was delighted that Moffat showed such interest; he invited him to be present when he was listening to petitions and hearing court cases. On one such occasion an induna was brought before him and found guilty of having committed a very serious and unpardonable crime. Before passing sentence, Mziligazi turned to Moffat and said: 'The sentence for such a crime is death, by knobkerry or assegai for a councillor, and by a less honourable means for a commoner. What would you like me to do?'

Moffat requested that the man's life be spared. The King paused for a moment or two then said, 'Alright, in deference to you as my honoured guest, I shall spare his life; no blood shall be spilled.' He ordered the culprit to renounce his indunaship and banished him from the tribe. However, rather than suffer such dishonour, the induna pleaded for death. Consequently the death sentence was awarded without the shedding of blood. The man was led away to the river nearby, his hands were bound and he was then cast over the cliff to be devoured by crocodiles below.

Moffat found that the King dealt summarily with cases of petty crime by ordering flogging or seizure of livestock. But on one occasion, a very serious case, and an unusual one among the Matabele, came up for hearing: it was of incest between father and daughter. Moffat was interested to see how the Matabele would deal with this, because among some of the other tribes with whom he had had dealings, incest was far from uncommon between parents and children, or between brothers and sisters and other close relatives. In fact, in some rain-making ceremonies, or in ceremonies to invoke a fruitful harvest, the most shocking forms of incest were carried out in public and formed a major part of the orgy.

The missionary learnt that among the Matabele incest was abhorrent. The girl was sentenced to death by a blow from a knobkerry. Her father had his hands tied securely behind his back and a wooden wedge, with the bark still on, was shoved up his bottom, and he was expelled from society. That meant that he could only eat by lying face down on the ground, for not even his family were allowed to feed him. Nor, of course, could he lie on his back or sit down. He had become an outcast faced with a lingering and painful death – either from starvation or becoming a meal for hyenas or wild dogs. A similar sentence was handed out for men found guilty of homosexuality.

Mziligazi was very interested in all that the missionary had to tell him of Christianity. He found no difficulty in believing the existence of only one true and spiritual god, and of Jesus Christ, but he was not prepared to accept the doctrine. He considered it to be too contrary to his way of life, and that it would be a fundamental obstacle to his ambition to make his people into a powerful nation by conquering and subjugating all the tribes far and wide. He began to imagine a similarity between himself and Queen Victoria as he felt both were destined to wield great authority. He made a promise to himself that one day he would go to England to see her – the only person to whom he would pay such an honour!

When Moffat was leaving to return to his mission station, Mziligazi expressed disappointment at his departure and extracted a promise that he would return as soon as his duties permitted. In honour of his departing guest, the King renamed his heir-apparent 'Kuruman', after the name of Moffat's mission station.

The year following the meeting between the King and Moffat, the Matabele received another visit, but nowhere near such a welcome one. Barend Berends, chief of the Griquas, a half-caste breed of Dutch Boers and Hottentots, had mustered a strong mixed force of his own people and of Korrannas and Baralongs, who had already suffered badly at the hands of the Matabele. With these he made a surprise attack on Mziligazi's kraal. This time it was the Matabele who were to be initiated with a new form of warfare for the Griquas were armed with rifles. The Matabele were taken completely by surprise; many lost their lives and Barend Berends got away with a very large herd of cattle.

However, two nights later, Kalipi crept up on Barend's party and quietly surrounded them with a strong force of his own. The Matabele had lain in the long grass quietly watching the Griquas and their allies gormandising on the meat they had purloined. At dawn, while their enemy slept, Kalipi gave the signal for his men to close in. The slaughter was terrible. Berend's sister was the only survivor, a very beautiful girl who was taken as a present for the King. The Matabele had suffered no casualties and had recovered all the cattle, barring of course those that had been eaten. What was more important, face had been saved and an example given of what would happen to those who were foolish enough to attack the Matabele.

Four years later, Moffat again visited Mziligazi. This time he was accompanied by another missionary, Dr Andrew Smith. When the King learned that Smith would later be going south to Cape Town, he requested permission for his nephew Mnombate to accompany him. Mnombate was to convey the King's greetings to the Great Queen's representative, the Governor of the Cape Province.

Mnombate, and the indunas who accompanied him, were much impressed by all they saw en route on the long ox-wagon journey of several hundred miles to Cape Town. The Governor arranged for them to be shown the sights of Cape Town and particularly to watch British troops on parade and in their barracks, doubtless so as to impress upon the delegates the power of the British Army. The visit ended with a treaty of friendship being concluded between the British and the Matabele, whereby King Mziligazi was pledged to act as a faithful friend and ally of the Cape Colony, to maintain peace with the British Government, to give his protection to white people visiting his country, to encourage missionaries and to generally promote civilisation.

The King was delighted at learning that a treaty of friendship had been negotiated for he felt it was as well for him to have such powerful people as the British as his friends and ally. He had heard from Moffat and Andrew Smith how scrupulous they were in honouring their obligations so he was determined they would find him equally honourable.

Mziligazi and his council of indunas closely questioned the delegates on all they had seen and heard. They were impressed by the stories of how the British were mainly the business people and kept more to the towns, while the Boers concentrated more on farming. Of particularly interest to them was the enormous size of the estates which each white farmer owned, and of how he was virtually a chief in his own right with large numbers of black men working for him. Apparently there was trouble brewing between the two white tribes over the question of slaves. The British were saying that all slaves should be released and be made free men, but the Boers were strongly opposed to this.

The King intervened, to say that on this point he was in agreement with the Boers. But one of the delegates explained that there was a great difference between slavery as practised by the Matabele and by the white man. 'With us the slaves become part of the family which owns them, but with the whites this is far from being the case. They have to work very hard from morning till night. They get paid something called money and they get far less consideration than their owner's dogs. They do not live in the houses of their masters and are not allowed to wander about freely at night.'

Mziligazi expressed fear about the future if Europeans were gaining such a hold on the country. That fear was reinforced when Mnombate asserted that many many more whites were arriving at Cape Town every week in enormous ships fitted with large white sails.

As the delegates went on describing the large houses built in stone and brick, the shops selling all manner of things never before seen or imagined by Zulus, and of white men and women riding in rickshaws drawn by natives, the more Mziligazi began to fear for the future. He wished his trusted friend Dr Moffat was nearer at hand to explain and to advise.

Those doubts and fears had increased rapidly when the bush telegraph revealed that a large convoy of Boer farmers was approaching the Vaal. Little did he know that the great Boer trek of 1836 to get away from British influence was already well on its way. He had come to regard the river, not only as stout protection from Chaka, but also as his southern boundary; so he dispatched impi units to patrol the northern bank and to deter people from crossing without his sanction.

A week or so later, the scout of a Matabele patrol stopped short in his tracks when he saw smoke rising from cooking fires ahead. He crept forward to investigate and then hurried back to report to his commander the presence of – believe it or not – white persons! He could only guess they were women because their bodies were not exposed like those of black women, but were covered by a strange material hanging from their shoulders right down to their ankles. There were also little girls and boys in strange clothes playing about among great big wagons parked several paces apart in the shade of trees. Smallish black men dressed in clothes (shirts and shorts) like those of the white boys, were moving about cleaning the area and washing pots and pans by the river. Others were working among the livestock. Dogs were running about everywhere.

At first the commander was perplexed about what he should do – these were not blacks but whites; he had never seen white women. In fact the only white person he had ever seen was Moffat. Should he return to headquarters for instructions from an induna? On second thoughts, he decided against doing that fearing criticism and possible punishment. His orders were to stop entry to all visitors coming across the Vaal, so that he must do.

He rejoined the members of his patrol and led them forward cautiously into positions overlooking the Boer camp. His men lay motionless in the grass, and were ordered not to move an inch or a muscle until the order was given to attack. Then they were to charge using the two-horn formation to encircle the camp completely. The killing was to be straight and clean with knobkerry or assegai – no torturing, no mutilation.

Once he was satisfied the campers were unaware of the danger surrounding them, he gave the order to charge. The raid was over in minutes. No one was left alive. The wagons, and the oxen trained to draw them, made suitable gifts for the King.

When the Boer menfolk had returned from the hunt and had seen with absolute horror and disbelief what had befallen their loved ones, they rode post-haste to warn other Boer trekkers to be on the lookout as they would be entering hostile territory. Right until then there had been no need for the trekkers to take precautionary measures, because at no time on their long trek northwards had they met with any opposition. For most of the long journey of several days and weeks, they had only seen the odd native or small groups of natives and they had scampered into the bush at the mere sight of strangers.

* * *

That episode made King Mziligazi reinforce his impi along the banks of the Vaal; the force was placed under the command of his most experienced general, and uncle, Kalipi. Kalipi had not long to wait before a Boer convoy of about thirty long ox-wagons were seen approaching the river. He sent a warrior to inform the leader that they must not attempt to cross until they had obtained the permission of the King of the Matabele. The response was curt and dismissive – they would fight their way across if they had to do so. With that, they set about making a defensive laager with their large cumbersome wagons, by hauling them head to tail to form a rectangle. Gaps between the wagons were blocked with branches and any other obstacles they could lay hands on. Access to the laager from beneath the wagons was denied by throwing up ramparts of earth. Horses, cattle and goats were herded into zarebas of bushes and branches; the white men and boys took up their positions armed with muzzle-loading blunderbusses; the women and girls got busy filling powder flasks and melting down lead for cartridge moulds; Hottentots were posted at vantage points to give warning of enemy approaching. 'Keep careful watch,' they were ordered, 'for your own lives depend upon it.' The Boer farmer was always considered to be an excellent hunter with keen eyesight, but the Hottentot was second only to the pigmy bushmen for keenness of eye and hearing.

The atmosphere in the laager was tense and the tension increased as hour passed hour and there was neither sign nor sound of the enemy. Time and again a Boer would slip out to espy the land, but not a soul was to be seen. Then, just as the defenders were beginning to relax, the silence was shattered by a deep hissing sound of breath being forced through clenched teeth, followed by a nerve-wracking sound of spears and knobkerries being struck against rawhide shields in rhythmic unison. Then, and only then, did they see plumed warriors emerge from the cover of grass and bush. The Boers were flabbergasted; they had never expected anything like this. In past encounters with natives, the enemy had been wild hooligans hurling spears and insults from a distance. But this was quite different. They were being opposed now by a well-disciplined force advancing in order, shield against shield. All of a sudden the ranks parted and with wild, blood-curdling yells, the Matabele charged down upon them. The defenders held their rifle fire until the warriors were sufficiently close and then, with devastating accuracy, shot right into them.

The attackers, stunned by surprise, stopped for a moment and then bolted for cover. They reformed immediately and again they attacked and again their casualties were heavy. Once more they reformed their ranks and again they charged, but with no greater success.

Time and again they repeated the attack courageously but their numbers had been so depleted that they had to withdraw and lie concealed in the bush hoping that some of the Boers would be tempted out of the laager. This they didn't do, so, under cover of darkness, Kalipi sent a detachment to open up the zarebas and drive out the livestock as quietly as possible. They knew how angry the King would be that the Boers had not been destroyed, but they hoped that so large a gift of prime livestock would abate his displeasure. They felt sure the gift of horses would be welcomed, particularly as they would be the first for him to own.

The King was furious about the Boers' attitude and regarded it as a breach of the agreement of friendship signed with the Governor of the Cape. With great difficulty, Mnombate succeeded in getting him to understand that the Boers had broken away from British influence and had acted on their own initiative, and certainly not with the approval of the Queen. He explained that the situation was similar to their own history – just as they had escaped from Chaka, so the Boers were moving away from the British.

The Boers, smarting from their loss of horses and cattle and from the impudence of black kaffirs (unbelievers) daring to attack white men, formed a powerful mounted commando, and using half-breed Griquas as guides they attached Mziligazi's capital town. The King happened to be away on a raiding expedition, and those left behind were so taken by surprise that they offered little opposition. The Boers and Griquas mounted on horseback chased the Matabele as they fled and shot down several hundred.

The Matabele proverb 'They come carrying the enemy on their backs', meaning that one feud leads to another, was soon proved true. In a matter of months, the Boers launched another and even more formidable mounted commando raid. Mziligazi's men were no match for mounted troops armed with rifles. Their losses were very heavy indeed. The situation had become worse than serious.

A council of indunas was convened, and it was decided that to stay where they were was suicidal – they must move on. This time their course lay through Bechuanaland (Botswana). They raided and plundered far and wide over a radius of hundreds of miles to recoup their losses in cattle and slaves. The Batlapin were the only tribe in Botswana not to be harassed, in deference to Dr Moffat's mission station being sited among them.

So, at long last, after trudging some 2,000 miles on foot, raiding, plundering and warring, they arrived at the Limpopo. They crossed the river into very sparsely populated, splendid pastoral country, ideally suited to their lifestyle. It was to be the land of the Matabele, the Amandabele – Matabeleland, as it is still known today – though now a province of Zimbabwe.

Chapter IV

Mziligazi wasted no time in putting his plans and ambitions into action. Patrols were dispatched in north-easterly and north-westerly directions, to report back on the suitability of the land and on the numbers and morale of the inhabitants. Gundwane, a very senior and highly respected induna was entrusted with the care of all the women, children and livestock, and to head in the direction of the Matopos Hills and there, if the country was as good as it was reported to be, to establish a royal kraal – the capital of the new Matabeleland.

With a strong body of warriors, the King himself carried out an intensive study of the countryside. The main tribes living in the very large tract of land between the Limpopo and Zambezi rivers were the Mashona and Ma-kalanga. They were still suffering from maulings received from previous raids by Zulu and Swazi hordes passing through their territory and were too dispirited to offer serious opposition to the new invaders.

Mziligazi once more showed his wisdom and astuteness. To destroy such scum – as they were in his eyes – would be very simple, but would serve no useful purpose in the long term. Instead, it would be far more sensible to make use of them. They were agriculturists and gatherers, the Matabele were pastoralists, so let them be the purveyors of cattle, corn and slaves. As they were knowledgeable in working iron, they would also be required to make assegais for their new overlords.

First he must make them realise what opposition to the Matabele would mean, so he sent a raiding party to destroy a particularly large Mashona village with utmost savagery and ferocity, in order to 'turn hearts to water' of all other kraals for miles around. Those not killed in fighting were rounded up, the healthy young boys and girls were seized as slaves, the men were assegaied or had their brains knocked out with knobkerries, and the young married women were violated before being ripped open.

The old men and women were made into human torches by binding them to trees, covering them with grass soaked in fat and then setting them alight. As the village was close to a main track leading to other villages, the infants were suspended from the branches of trees by their feet and left to their fate, so that passers-by would be left in no doubt as to what happened when the Matabele went on the rampage.

It hadn't taken long for the lesson to be learnt. In a matter of days, Mashona chiefs were undertaking to pay tribute and to acknowledge Matabele kings as their overlords. Mziligazi was scrupulous in honouring his promise of protection to all who fulfilled their undertaking. The slightest breach met with severe punishment.

While the King was away taking stock of his new domain, Gundwane was busy establishing the royal kraal. Water was fairly plentiful in the area, the grazing was good and the plains were rich in game.

Month after month passed without news of the King. He hadn't bothered to keep in touch by runner. Patrols had been sent out in search of him but invariably they returned none the wiser. A year elapsed, two years and still no sign or news of him. The people grew restless and feared that either he and the warriors who had accompanied him had been 'swallowed up', or had deserted them. According to their traditions, the King and State were inseparable; they were one, and so his absence was felt even more than it would have been in a differently organised community.

With prolonged absence the cry went up: 'How can we live without a fire?' Meaning, of course, that life without a king was insufferable. Soon it was suggested that Kuruman, the heir-apparent (named after Moffat's mission station in Botswana) should be installed in place of his father. All had been thinking along these lines but once the idea had been voiced many became perturbed. No one was in any doubt that if Mziligazi were to turn up suddenly, he would regard the installation of his son as an act of treachery and would exact terrible retribution.

More patrols were sent in every direction, but when these returned without word of the King, Gundwane openly proposed that there was no point in waiting any longer. He reasoned that undoubtedly some grave misfortune must have befallen the King and so Kuruman should be installed as his successor. Induna Mkitka Tebe rose and said, 'A son cannot reign while his father is still alive. Let one brave man join me and we will search for our King.' Many volunteered but one, a warrior of great renown, was chosen.

The two men duly set out. After several days of searching, they were informed by a party of Ma-kalanga tribesmen that the King was encamped by the next river.

They hastened to him and, after greeting him warmly and loyally, gave him all their news. They extolled the advantages of the area in which they had settled and begged him to come and see the town they had built in his honour. Care was taken that not a word was breathed about the Kuruman incident.

When he arrived at the town, the King was duly impressed by all he saw and commended Gundwane and his councillors on the choice of site and on their stewardship in his absence. He had brought presents of slaves and cattle for all and, to celebrate the reunion of the tribe, he ordered hundreds of head of oxen to be slaughtered.

Great was the joy of all, but within a few days it was to be shattered. Troublemakers, in the hope of currying favour with the King and in settling old scores with Gundwane, informed Mziligazi of the 'plot' to make Kuruman king in his stead. Mziligazi was furious. 'Have I not governed you well?' he raged. 'It is seventeen years since we left Zululand and covered and fought over hundreds of miles. In all that long time have I not led you to victory over dozens of tribes? Have I not punished the Griquas for daring to attack us? Have I not repulsed the Ama-Bula [Boers]? Is this how you express your gratitude – to replace me by my son?' He summoned every single induna and all members of the royal family to attend an *indaba* (conference) on a flat-topped hill where, he said, he would enquire into all the details of 'that treacherous act'.

The *indaba* was long-drawn out because the King was determined that every detail of the plot should be made known to him. Much to Gundwane's chagrin and anxiety, false witnesses testified that at the time he had proposed Kuruman being made king, he was well aware that Mziligazi was alive. It was alleged he had been receiving regular reports from Ma-kalanga spies about the king's movements. They went on to suggest that Gundwane had gained a strong influence over Kuruman, so that when the latter became king, Gundwane would be his principal induna and exercise the real power in the land.

In light of that evidence, false though it was, there could be only one verdict. Gundwane and every other councillor who had supported him or was alleged to have supported him, was to be put to death. Not only they, but their families too. In Matabele parlance, the councillors and their families had 'ceased to walk'. The hill on which the trial had been held came to be called 'Inthaba yez Induna' or 'The hill of the Indunas'.

The trial had developed a terrible phobia in the King's mind about disloyalty and treachery. He ordered witchdoctors to 'smell out' all his enemies. They went about the task with great gusto, because part of every condemned person's possessions went to them in payment for their services.

Two of the King's sons and their mothers also ceased to walk, so, also, the Swazi princess, but her son Lobengula, who was only a small boy at the time, had an amazing escape thanks to the outstanding courage and cunning of Gwabalanda, a senior induna. When soldiers, directed by the witchdoctors, were searching for the boy to kill him, Gwabalanda, at the risk of his own life and that of his family, managed to conceal the lad. Then, on an occasion when the King was in a convivial mood, the boy was brought in to serve the guests. As he entered shyly, Gwabalanda called out ecstatically: 'Who is this boy? Surely he carries the blood of Kumalo, son of Matshobane,, son of Zulu! See how like our king he is!'

The King was completely taken aback by surprise at the outburst. He turned to Mnombate and asked him what he thought. 'My lord, I have always thought how like you he is. Truly your spirit lives in him.'

The King was delighted. He called the boy over to him, made him sit beside him and patted him on the shoulder (it was impolite to tap a person on the head). Gwabalanda and Mnombate looked across at each other and heaved sighs of relief.

In future the boy was to stay near him and learn from him. All was well! The dreaded moment had passed.

Once Mziligazi was satisfied that all troublemakers and aspirants to kingship had been dealt with, he set about framing a proper constitution for the new state.

The Matabeles had rather an old-fashioned Prussian officer's outlook on life. They regarded themselves as the elite or as herrenvolk whom others should be prepared to serve as serfs. It was that outlook which dominated their behaviour to all other tribes with whom they came in contact. They always remained proud of their Zulu blood.

The army was every man's profession, every boy knew that as soon as he reached manhood or puberty he would be drafted to a regiment. He would not be granted permission to get married until such time as he, personally, had distinguished himself in battle, or at least until his regiment had gained that distinction and it had been recognised as bravery by the King. For this reason there were separate regiments of either *matjaha* or unmarried warriors and of *amadoda* or married men. The latter were distinguished from the former by their much-coveted head rings or *isidhlodhlas.*

The link between soldiery and marriage was an interesting one and directly associated with maintaining a high standard of martial powers throughout the nation; the word nation being used deliberately to show that the rule applied equally to Matabele and to slave.

Firstly, by prohibiting a man from getting married until such time as he had proved himself in battle, was one method of ensuring the characteristics of virility and bravery being transmitted from one generation to the next.

Secondly, withholding marriage, and therefore the opportunity of having sons to follow in a man's footsteps, created an incentive to be courageous. There the connection was a religious one: the Matabele believed in life being eternal through the spirit or soul of a person living on in a child, and it was that intense desire to ensure continuity of the germ of life – so distressing to a barren woman – that made a young man most anxious to obtain the necessary sanction to get married and rear a family. He would willingly face very great risks in order to receive recognition of his bravery and so gain the opportunity of having a son before he died. The *matjaha*, young warriors, were a reckless, bloodthirsty lot of youngsters always on the lookout for an opportunity to 'blood' their spears.

Mziligazi was a strict disciplinarian, always intent on maintaining the morals and stamina of his troops at a very high pitch. For that reason, promiscuity in sexual relationships was severely frowned upon. While the tribe was living in Zululand, pre-marital intercourse was considered wrong; but once a couple were betrothed, the parents of the young girl would permit a certain amount of familiarity with their daughter. The young couple could go through the actions of lovemaking but without intercourse occurring. The more prudent mothers would take the precaution of tying the girl's legs together about the knees! For an unmarried woman to have a child was a social disgrace to the family.

During the exodus from Zululand, the constant fighting and moving from place to place had meant a slackening in supervision and parental control. The result was a loosening of moral behaviour; but if the attention of the King or his indunas was drawn to excessive promiscuity by either boy or girl, the offender would be severely punished. Generally punishment took the form of ridicule. For instance, a young man would be required to associate solely with older married men, which, of course, would make him a butt for jibes and taunts from the girls and women.

The Matabele did not go in for male circumcision as is practised by most African tribes of Bantu origin, but they had a ceremony to mark the occasion of puberty or entrance to manhood. One of its purposes was to develop the traits of manliness, self-sufficiency and toughness. Upon the first appearance of puberty, the boy had to rise early before others were awake and go completely naked to the nearest river or stream. After he had bathed, he had to stand naked by the gate of the kraal waiting for the rest of the community to awaken. As soon as the other boys saw him they armed themselves with sticks and absolutely belaboured him. On no account was he to cry out in pain or defend himself in any way. The more stoically be bore the punishment, the prouder became his parents and relatives.

The boys then drove him away from home into the open veld, where, for three or four days he survived on what he could find. He was not allowed to light a fire or carry arms, and, although he was supposed to be entirely on his own, he soon found that many young eyes were watching him. Whenever he went to eat or to drink water, youngsters rushed out and prevented him from doing so. At the end of three or four days he returned home but for a while there was no comfort awaiting him. The war-doctor appeared and mixed the most loathsome and foul-tasting 'muti' (medicine) into the first cooked food which the boy would have tasted for days. The youth was not allowed to feed himself, but he had to sit with his mouth open while the doctor jabbed large blobs of it in on the end of a stick. Friends and relatives sat around greatly amused by the performance, particularly when the doctor led the ravenous boy on by withdrawing the stick at the crucial moment, or made an unexpected parry at his lips or palate with intent to hurt.

When the last of the revolting mess had been consumed, the doctor gave him three or four really sharp blows across the bare back and pronounced that he was now on the way to becoming a man. The ceremony ended with the boy's parents and relatives giving him presents of small livestock which were intended to serve as the nucleus for a future herd.

No sooner had Botswana been declared a British Protectorate, than a stream of white men began to flow into Matabeleland. The first to come was the Reverend Robert Moffat with a request for permission to send two missionaries to establish a mission station. The council of indunas was very much against the proposal, because they feared the missionaries would be followed by other white persons.

Mnombate, and the other indunas, who had been members of the goodwill mission to the Governor of Cape Town, reminded the King of the huge blocks of land the white settlers farmed in South Africa, each as a lord in his own right, and begged the King not to agree, but Mziligazi declined to accept their advice. He could not bring himself to refuse a request from his revered friend and also because he intended to honour to full extent the terms of the peace treaty signed with the Great White Queen's representative, whereby he undertook to encourage missionaries and to promote civilisation.

In due course the two missionaries, the Reverend Sykes and the Reverend T.M. Thomas arrived. Not only were they to be the introducers of a white culture, but also, most regrettably, of the dreaded highly contagious cattle disease, lung sickness – the trek oxen that hauled their wagons had contracted it en route. Before the missionaries reached the royal kraal, there were not enough animals left alive to haul the heavy wagons. As soon as the King heard of their discomfiture he sent a band of warriors to manhandle the vehicles.

Thomas and Sykes were received with courtesy by the King, but many of his indunas eyed them askance. They were granted permission to camp outside the royal kraal and were provided with food and drink. Mziligazi, realising the resentment of his people to the presence of the white men, decided against widening the breach by showing too much of a welcome, and left the missionaries to their own devices for several days.

The poor men had entered the country full of enthusiasm and they were counting on the direct and active support of the King. He had certainly been helpful in bringing in their wagons and had received them courteously enough, but since that first meeting, he seemed studiously bent on avoiding them. They were obviously being cold-shouldered.

The ordinary people and even some of the indunas would visit the missionary camp out of curiosity. Beneath any show of friendliness by the Matabele, the white men sensed a feeling of mistrust, so they set about hoping to overcome this by treating the sick and injured, but progress was slow. The number of persons turning up for medical attention was rapidly increasing each day, but there was no real sign of appreciation or of gratitude for what was being done for them.

At the end of a fortnight or so the King summoned them to his royal kraal at Inyate and gave them permission to build huts and develop a station. It was made clear that they were in the country on sufferance and as the King's guests. They were to understand that the natural resources belonged to the state and were not conferred on the white men by virtue of them having been granted permission to build huts and reside in Matabeleland. Food stuffs would be supplied to them by the King and they were not to hunt or fish without obtaining his permission.

Other white visitors soon followed. They were traders and hunters coming in from the south. When it was found that many of them were sneaking in without permission, the King established a definite port of entry. All were to report to the induna in charge of the entry post, and must remain in camp there until the induna had obtained instruction from his royal master as to whether or not they were to be allowed to enter.

Persons entering the country through this authorised route were assured of the King's protection, but he would not hold himself responsible for the life and property of anyone who entered surreptitiously.

As the numbers of white men coming in increased, so did suspicion in the minds of many of the indunas, but the King was determined to abide by the terms of the Cape Town agreement. To avoid forcing an issue with his council, he met them halfway, by agreeing to restrict permission for residence only to any particular individual whose presence would be of real and direct value to the Matabele. Each white man's activities were to be kept under strict surveillance and he would be required to leave the country as soon as the purpose of his visit had been completed.

Every white man was interviewed by the King, personally, before he was allowed to transact any business. Fortunately the first visitors were of a good type; they might have been rough and ready but they were straight-dealing men who set a fairly high standard of decency. Mziligazi was much impressed by them and developed a very high regard for the British. This is how he described them to his subjects:

'These are masters of the world. Don't you take notice how they sleep in the open country, alone and unprotected, and are not afraid? They are in my country one day; they pass on to the towns of other chiefs; they go fearlessly for they bear no malice and are the friends of all. And when the great men in the white man's country send traders for my ivory, do you think they give me beautiful things in exchange because they could not take the ivory by force? They could come and take it by force and all my cattle also. And yet look at them! They are humble and quiet and easily pleased. The British are the friends of Mziligazi and they are the masters of the world.'

Unfortunately these high ideas of British bravery and integrity must have suffered a setback by the deceiving actions of a newcomer. Hartley came as a big-game hunter after elephant tusks, rhino horns and hippo teeth. With so much activity going on in Matabeleland itself, the wild animals were retreating northwards and eastwards, seeking refuge in the King's domain of Mashonaland.

Time and again Hartley sought permission to shoot in Mashonaland, but each time this was refused. He was so persistent, however, that in the end the King gave way on the strict undertaking that Hartley would neither supply nor trade guns to the Mashonas.

While he was hunting in that part of the country, Hartley came across abandoned open-pit workings which excited his interest. According to the local Mashona, gold had been extracted from them many years ago for sale to the Portuguese on the lower Zambezi. Mining, however, had been brought to an abrupt end through the invasion of the country by previous Zulu and Swazi hordes.

Hartley was a hunter and knew nothing about mining, so he kept the information to himself until he could obtain the co-operation of someone with the necessary knowledge. When his hunting expedition was over and he was back in South Africa, he straight away busied himself in finding a geologist. In the end he came across a German, Carl Mauch, and obtained permission from Mziligazi to re-enter the country and bring with him another hunter and friend, Mauch. Surreptitiously Mauch set to work examining the rocks, taking good care not to arouse any suspicion in the minds of their Matabele guides. He confirmed that the yellow specks appearing in the quartz were gold. Hurriedly both men gave up further pretence at hunting and returned to South Africa to work out a plan for the future. Unfortunately for them, Mauch was a heavy drinker who talked in his cups and soon the rumour spread that Matabeleland was fabulously rich in precious metals which could be had by the mere act of picking up.

The day the King gave in to Hartley's repeated requests to be allowed to hunt in Mashonaland, he had signed, unwittingly, the death sentence of his kingdom. He was now being besieged by concession hunters of all nationalities pouring in from South Africa. Many of them would come begging and cringing to the black potentate for permission to prospect. Others would seek entry as traders and hunters, but once they were in it was the search for gold which took up most of their time. The King and his indunas were seeing a very different type of white man to the first visitors!

Mziligazi soon began to realise the limitations of his own knowledge and that of his indunas when dealing with such crafty white men, so he began to seek the advice and guidance of the two missionaries. They may not have gained any converts, but the wonderful example they set of honesty, impartiality and morality, could not help but impress those around them and especially the King. The very indunas who had originally suspected them of being spies now had to admit to themselves that they had been wrong.

Unfortunately missionaries are not of much help in this sort of dilemma, but they did what they could. However, there were two other white men present, both big-game hunters and traders, whom the King admired. He felt he could trust them and be guided by them in his dealings with Hartley and the other greedy whites. These were Sam Edwards and John Lee. The King appointed them to be his agents to watch that the hunters and miners did not infringe the conditions under which they had gained entry to his territory, nor exceed the terms of their licences to prospect or dig. Edwards carried out his duties so loyally and satisfactorily that he was made an induna of the tribe.

The King was becoming an old man. He had dedicated his life to the well-being of his people. Just as Moses had led the Israelites away from the domination of the Pharaohs, so Mziligazi had led his clan away from the ruthless rule of Chaka. He had lived a hard and tough life and now it was catching up with him. He developed gout so badly that there were days when he could not move a step, and had to be carried in a chair by four of his wives.

Moffat called again when he heard how ill the King was and was greatly shocked by the change in Mziligazi's condition. In addition to the gout, he had developed dropsy and was partially paralysed down one side. The tough old warrior wept at his white friend seeing him in this piteous condition. In writing of this episode, Moffat said, 'He grasped my hand, gave one earnest look, and then drew his mantle over his face.'

The missionary remained with him for three months and during that time he obtained the release of Troi, the Griqua girl who had been captured some twenty years earlier, during the massacre of her brother Barend Berends and his gang of marauders. Troi had adopted Matabele customs and had become one of Mziligazi's most favoured concubines. She had been well-treated but was longing to go back to her own people.

The King survived another nine years of ill health but during all that time his brain remained active and he continued to govern his country and mete out justice according to the laws of the land.

He was carefully doctored and nursed by the missionary Thomas Morgan Thomas. Like old soldiers, Matabele kings do not die but 'the mountain fell'. The body was sewn up in the hides of two freshly slaughtered oxen and, according to custom, remained in the royal apartments until the odour was too much for even his most devoted widows. It was then placed in his favourite wagon, while all his most used and cherished possessions were packed into a second vehicle. Both were hauled by warriors high up into the Matopo Hills where the King had expressed a desire to be buried.

His body was placed in an upright position inside a cave. His favourite wagon was broken up and all the pieces of it, together with his possessions, were deposited in an adjoining cave. The entrances to both were sealed by large boulders.

Seventy-three years later, on 1 June 1941, the white government of Southern Rhodesia erected a monument under the tree in whose shade he had held court for so many years. The inscription reads: 'Mziligazi, son of Shobana, the Matabele hail you. The mountain fell down on September 9th, 1868. All nations acclaim the Son of Shobana. Hayete.'

Chapter V

According to Zulu tradition, the next in line of descent was Kuruman, named after Moffat's mission station in Botswana, but he was nowhere to be found. In his absence, Lobengula was next in line of descent, but he was loath to accept kingship until it was proved that his half-brother was not alive. The search for Kuruman was entrusted to the Zwong Endaba regiment with which he had been closely associated.

While the search was in progress Lobengula kept as far away from politics as it was possible for him to do so. Whenever there was any fear of being entrapped, he would disappear quietly on a hunting expedition. As often as not, his companions were professional white hunters, and it was from the lessons learnt from them that he became a proficient rider and a remarkably good marksman with a gun.

For the professional hunter, elephant ivory, rhino horns and hippo teeth were the principal attraction. As soon as fresh elephant spoor was discovered it would be followed up and the moment the herd was sighted, the white hunter and his team of Hottentots, all mounted on horseback, would gallop after the quarry and shoot into them pretty well indiscriminately. The intention was to incapacitate as many animals as possible and finish them off later. It was by no means uncommon for an elephant to have half a dozen, a dozen, or even more bullets peppered into it. No mercy was shown; even cow elephants were shot in cold blood while trying to help along their babies with the aid of trunks and tusks.

Poor rhinos suffered the same fate. There was little or no risk to the hunter so long as he remained seated on a fast and nimble horse. The havoc wrought among hippo was indescribable. The pools they frequented would be surrounded by men armed with guns and they would shoot at every animal visible. At the first shot the great cumbersome creatures would submerge. Gradually, as they were compelled to surface for air and the head or nostrils or eyes would show above the waterline, a volley of bullets would be directed at it. Often the dead beasts would float too far from the waters edge to be hauled in. Many would die a lingering death from their wounds, or be savaged by crocodiles attracted by the blood.

Even in the shooting of game for their tables, and as meat rations for their camp followers, the Europeans slaughtered an unwarranted number of animals.

When hunting the big, graceful eland, the intention would be to drive it as close as possible to the camp before giving the coup de grace; the idea, of course, was to avoid having to haul the heavy carcass any great distance. The technique was to wound the animal in a non-vital spot, just severely enough to reduce its speed and then, for men mounted on horseback, to head it in the desired direction. Let alone the shots which would be fired to keep it from deviating, the wild shouts and yells of the men were enough to terrify the poor creature! Sometimes it would fall from sheer exhaustion and terror, and then attempts would be made to goad it to its feet in order to get it a little closer to camp.

Giraffes were hunted in similar fashion. When wounded they would sometimes shed tears. The hunter Hartley had admitted that on occasions he would be so deeply touched by the big tear-drops rolling down the animal's face, that he would be loath to press it any further, and would put it out of its misery with a well-directed shot.

It was not unusual for a hunter at the end of a few months of shooting, to be able to leave the country with the bed of his twenty-foot long wagon full of elephant tusks, rhino horns and hippo teeth. Small wonder that the wild life of Matabeleland was rapidly disappearing and the hunters were having to seek permission to shoot in Mashonaland.

The only animals safe from destruction were crocodiles. The Matabele regarded the killing of one of these saurians as a most heinous and unpardonable offence. The reason was that the liver is supposed to be deadly poisonous. Even if the hunter did not make use of it himself, there was always the possibility that someone else may come across it – or even disinter it if the carcass had been buried

– and wreak havoc among his fellow humans. The penalty for a Matabele to kill a crocodile was death. For a white man to do so, the King would be likely to forbid him from hunting any more game and order him to leave the country.

When the Zwong Endaba reported their failure to find news of Kuruman, and no one else had seen or heard from him, Mnombate proceeded to address the full tribal council:

'Hear my words, councillors and wise men of the Matabele nation. Knowing what I do, there was no need to send men to search for Kuruman, but I raised no objection to the proposal, because I know Umbeko and other indunas of the Zwong Endaba would not accept my word without first making sure for themselves that Kuruman is not alive. The men who went to seek for him have told you clearly that they found no trace of him, but still the Zwong Endaba remain dissatisfied. So I am going to describe to you now what happened, one fateful day, after Gundwane and the other councillors condemned by the late Mziligazi had been put to death, for their part, in the supposed plot to make Kuruman king in the absence of his father.

'The Great One sent for me in the middle of the night and said that his heart was sore at the decision his mind had taken. Kuruman and all members of his branch of the royal family were to be put away, and it was to be my task to see that it was done immediately. My heart was equally sore, but I had received my orders and I would have to carry them out. I summoned twenty of my most trusted warriors, and long before the sun had risen, Kuruman's family had ceased to walk. It was all done so quickly that the victims hardly had time to realise what was happening. The King had ordered that there was to be no brutality, and there was none; each one was killed at the first blow. There was only one hitch, Kuruman was not to be found. His mother laughed at us and refused to disclose his presence, but we learned from a slave that he was in hiding at a village some miles away.

'Several days later he was found. It was in my heart that the Great One should spare the young prince's life, but he would not. He ordered Kuruman's Basuto slave to kill his royal master quietly. He was neither to stab him, nor strangle him, nor bruise him, but was to kill him by twisting his neck in such a way as to dislocate it. By this means royal blood was not spilt.'

In spite of this statement by the regent, the Zwong Endaba still remained unconvinced. The issue between the two factions was becoming so heated that there was a very real danger of it developing into a permanent split, sufficiently wide to cause the disintegration of the tribe.

When the seriousness of the situation was explained to Lobengula, and it was made abundantly clear that the vast majority of the people were in favour of him, he agreed to become king. Reluctant though he was, he realised that if he did not accept the responsibility, his late father's whole life-work of making his people into a free and independent nation would be wrecked.

The medicine men now devoted themselves to purifying the sovereign elect. On a day in 1870, nearly sixteen months after the death of his father, Lobengula was installed as king of the Matabele nation.

The ceremony was a most spectacular one. Between 9,000 and 10,000 warriors in full war panoply assembled to proclaim Lobengula, son of Mziligazi, as their rightful king, and to swear allegiance to him. They wore headdresses of long ostrich plumes or of beautiful long crane feathers; full capes of ostrich feathers adorned their bare shoulders, and around the middle they wore very short kilts of slitted leopard skin. Around their biceps and below their knees, they wore fringes of white ox-tails; castanets of dried fruit pods with seeds rattling inside were fastened around the ankles. In his left hand, each man carried a long war shield of the colour appropriate to his regiment; in his right hand was held the short stabbing assegai.

With perfect precision, and chanting national songs, they marched on to the parade ground at the double. Regiment by regiment, they took up their position forming a large semicircle around their new king.

Lobengula was dressed in similar fashion to his warriors, except that his kilt was deeper than theirs and was made of blue monkey tails. His face and limbs had been smeared by the doctors with black paint and charcoal. His tall, massive figure, with head held high and proud, made him look every inch a king.

Mnombate, as regent, announced in the hearing of the assembled warriors, that despite his own knowledge of the affair and the sworn testimony of the Basuto slave that they had killed his master Kuruman, the tribal council had deemed it wise to institute a search for the prince. That had been done, and there being no news whatsoever of Kuruman, it was now taken as most definite that he was 'no longer walking'. In consequence of this, they were now assembled to install Lobengula, son of Mziligazi, the next in line of descent, as their king. Ten thousand voices gave the royal salute of 'Ba lete' ('let them bring tribute'). The commander of each regiment then came forward and swore that he and his men would fight to the death for their king.

War songs were chanted in full deep chorus in time to the thunderous stamping of bare fee on hard earth. At intervals, warriors of renown would break from the ranks and describe in pantomime their most daring deeds; at the top of their voices they would declare their readiness to die for Lobengula. Immediately the troops would take up the response in chant, and rattle their spears against their shields.

It was a spectacle of barbaric magnificence, as regiment by regiment marched past their new king, hailing him with the royal salute.

What immense problems faced the young newly elected king! His councillors were demanding that no more whites be allowed into the country, and that the number of those already there should be greatly reduced by ordering them to leave. The army, too, was insistent on this same subject. The *matjaha* (young warriors with unblooded spears) were crying out for the blood of white intruders.

He did not know that in far away Europe, politicians, at that very time, were casting covetous glances in the direction of the African continent. Belgium was showing interest in the region of the Congo;

German help was being sought by the Boers against British 'intrusion'; the British themselves were busy in the east, west and south, and the Portuguese were aiming to get the Delegoa Bay railway into their own hands.

No sooner had its southern neighbour, Botswana, been declared a British protectorate, than the stream of white visitors to Matabeleland became a flood, with concession seekers for gold pouring in from the Cape, the Transvaal, the Orange Free State, Natal, Britain and even Germany. To top it all, the Portuguese were infiltrating into Lobengula's domain of Mashonaland from Mozambique, their colony on the east coast.

In desperation, he decided to seek the help of the Great White Queen, the friend of the black people, and with whom he already had an agreement of friendship. A deputation was to be sent to Britain comprising Maund, a white concession hunter, and two very senior indunas. Johann Colenbrander, a trader and hunter from Natal Colony, was to accompany it as interpreter. They carried a letter from Lobengula written to his dictation by one of the Europeans:

> Lobengula desires to know that there is a Queen. Some of the people who come into this land tell him there is a Queen, some of them tell him there is not.
>
> Lobengula can only find out the truth by sending eyes to see whether there is a Queen. The Indunas are his eyes.
>
> Lobengula desires, if there is a Queen, to ask her to advise and help him, as he is much troubled by white men who come into his country and ask to dig gold.
>
> There is no one with him upon whom he can trust and he asks that the Queen will send someone from herself.

Ironically, while this delegation was on its way, another, consisting of Thomas Baines and two men, arrived at the official entry post to Matabeleland, where they were confronted by Lee in his capacity as the King's representative. In his subsequent report back to the Governor of Natal, Baines wrote:

> I told him (Lee) we had come from London in the service of a company of gentlemen interested in South Africa for the purpose of

testing the truth of reports concerning the existence of gold by actual exploration; that for this purpose we required leave to enter the Matabele country and to travel there and that if we found gold we would purchase the right of way and the privilege of working it from the chief for one thousand head of cattle or such other payment as might be agreed on. I also told him that neither our Queen nor nation desired to take from the Matabele any of their land but merely to obtain on fair terms the privilege of working the unoccupied portions, paying them fairly for any provisions they might sell or service they might render.

To Lee's surprise Baines had also come armed with a letter from the Governor of Natal:

ON HER MAJESTY'S SERVICE

To all native chiefs etc. whom it may concern.

From the Secretary for Native Affairs, Natal.

The Lieutenant Governor of Natal to all chiefs of native tribes and their people residing northwards and eastwards of the Colony of Natal,

Greetings.

It had been voiced abroad that Gold, the metal of which the highest money is made, exists in territories northward and eastward of this Colony, which are inhabited by native chiefs and tribes, and the consequence of this report is that many people from over the great waters have arrived in Natal on their way to those territories to search for gold and from them we learn that many more are coming.

If gold exists where it is said to exist, no power can stop the stream of those who seek for it, however much it may be wished to do so; and it is the way of a wise man to guide what he cannot prevent.

Knowledge is the first step towards the application of every effective remedy and, before any action can be taken either to regulate the conduct of the seekers for gold or to protect the interests of those in whose territories it is said to be, positive information of its existence and locality must be forthcoming.

Mr Baines, the bearer of this letter, is on his way with two companions to seek for this information. He is an old traveller of this country and knows many of the chiefs and people: and the Lieutenant Governor of Natal hopes to be assisted by the information Mr Baines may collect and send him, to form a correct opinion of the truth or falsehood of the rumours which are now disturbing the minds of so many people in so many different countries.

The Lieutenant Governor commends Mr Baines and his party to the friendly protection and care of all native chiefs and people with whom they may come in contact and trusts that the knowledge they will be able to acquire will hereafter prove to be of great benefit not only to the white people but to the natives themselves and to all concerned.

By Command,
(signed) Th. Shepstone
Secretary for Native Affairs,
Natal.

Given under my hand and the seal of my office the 12th day of March, 1869.

Understandably this imposing document caused the King and his Council of State much consternation, dismay and desperation. While they were asking the Queen for help in stemming the human tide, here was her representative asking them to throw the doors wide open. Lee and Sam Edwards were kept busy for the next few days interpreting and explaining over and over again what was implied and intended.

The indunas, to a man, implored the King to take instant action in stopping all further entry, and to expel all whites who were already in the country. Some feared that inaction might result in the Matabele army taking the law into their own hands. Some feared an individual Matabele might vent his pent-up resentment by attacking a white man searching for gold in some remote spot, and so trigger hostilities between black and white.

Mnombate begged the King to bear in mind what he, Mnombate, had seen with his own eyes on his mission to Cape Town. Of how the white man invariably ended up by seizing the land. He recalled the very large acreage's each farmer owned, and how he was virtually a chief in his own right with the black man forced to work from sunrise to sunset.

The King knew only too well the truth of what was being said, but he declared that he intended to stand by the undertaking given in the agreement of friendship negotiated in Cape Town. In an endeavour to instil a spirit of optimism and of hope in his indunas, he spoke of his confidence in the integrity of Baines. In his opinion Baines was a man of far superior type to the other whites. He also felt sure that the request he had made for assistance from the Great White Queen would bring a favourable response in due time.

In his heart of hearts, Lobengula must often have wished Kuruman could be found, so as to relieve him of his worries and responsibilities. It was at such moments that he was comforted and encouraged by his sister Ling En. She was younger than him and was his favourite relative and confidante. He placed much reliance on her wisdom and shrewd judgement. Come what may, the one thing he was determined to do was to stand by the Agreement. His word was his bond.

Then came the day when a group of white miners actually had the audacity to obstruct the King's officials from obeying his orders to punish his own subjects proven to be traitors. Immediately there were demands from all quarters for whites to be expelled from the country if they were thwarting the King's command and were behaving as though they owned Matabeleland. Lobengula had to exert all his powers of diplomacy in settling peacefully what had become a very delicate issue.

He got John Lee, the Englishman in whom he had implicit trust, to make it clear to all miners that permission to dig for gold did not confer any other power or right. No white person was to interfere in matters between the King and his subjects.

Chapter VI

Lobengula had a very soft spot for the British and he had many friends among the small white community. Whenever he could get away from the affairs of state, he would enjoy riding down to the white settlement on the outskirts of the capital for an informal chat, or else he would invite his white friends to the royal kraal.

He was almost as good a judge of the white man's character as he was of the black. While he did not expect a European to kowtow to him in the same manner as it was etiquette for his black subjects to do, he nevertheless expected them to treat him with the respect due to the king of an independent country. Excessive familiarity soon met with a polite snub, just as excessive humility immediately became suspect.

The number of black subjects who were permitted to converse directly with the King were so small that they would be counted on the fingers of one hand. Normally a conversation had to be conducted through the King's 'mouthpiece', who was always a most trusted officer of the royal entourage. A Matabele person, seeking audience of the King, was required to leave his weapons outside the gate of the royal kraal and then approach in a humble and crouching manner. As soon as he was fairly close to the King, he was required to crawl on hands and knees to an empty spot among the rest of the audience, and then await the King's attention. It was a gross breach of etiquette for a man to remain standing. In fact, in all spheres of life, politeness required a person of inferior station to remain seated before a superior.

White visitors were also required to leave their arms outside the gate, but they were permitted to approach the royal presence upright, with head uncovered, and give the Zulu greeting of *saku bona, inkosi* (I see you, king). Usually they would bring a stool with them on which they could sit, provided their heads would be at the same level or lower than that of the King, otherwise they would have to squat on the floor.

In the early days of his reign the royal canteen of cutlery comprised only a knife, fork and spoon for the King's own use. His white guests were expected to make full use of their pocket knives.

The King was a most hospitable host and good manners required the guests to show their appreciation by feasting and drinking to absolute capacity. Few white men could keep pace with Lobengula's powerful appetite for both solids and liquids. Refreshments normally consisted of either roasted or steamed beef accompanied by calabash after calabash of beer brewed from maize or soghum. The beer was brought in by women of the royal household and each calabash was taken straight to the King. Then the woman had to take a sip from it before it was handed round, in order to make sure that it had not been poisoned.

Beer and the brewing of it played a most important part in the religious and social rituals of the nation. They were so complicated that it was difficult for Europeans to comprehend their full purport. On one occasion, a girl attendant placed the calabash by accident on a piece of straw which had fallen from the roof of the King's house. Immediately, she had to throw away the beer and purify herself by bathing in the river.

Whenever the King was entertaining inside the royal house, it was considered a breach of etiquette to obstruct the entrance in any way. When visitors were taking their departure they were required to leave with their backs to those remaining inside as a mark of trust. Before the King took up his abode in the house of European style, he entertained his more special friends inside his Matabele hut, which meant they had to crouch to get through the low door. If by any chance a person happened to touch the centre pole supporting the root he was required to go outside and wash his hands. Usually he was more than ready to do so, for it was smeared by the witchdoctor with a concoction of cow manure and other unpleasant ingredients.

All Matabele huts were round in shape and were made of poles driven into the ground close together and braced to each other by straps made from the inner bark of certain trees. The straps were soaked in water for a few hours and then applied while still sappy and green. As they dried out they shrank and so became an extremely effective bonding material. The poles were then plastered inside and out with clay, or preferably, a mixture of clay and termite anthill. The floors were just beaten down earth, usually polished with cow manure; the roofs were of thatch; there was only one low door and no window. The huts were cosy in winter and cool in summer. Most Matabele women took great pride in keeping their huts clean and tidy; not a difficult task, as there was no furniture.

The King's favourite sister Ling En was usually present at the most important social functions, and was a great favourite with the white community who nicknamed her Lina. She was several years younger than her royal brother and, like him, her features were not negroid; both their noses were somewhat aquiline. Her black curly hair was adorned with beads of various colours, and her eyes were always sparkling with fun and good humour. Her ready smile revealed a set of beautiful even teeth, their dazzling whiteness being in sharp contrast to the deep copper tint of her complexion.

Occasionally she wore a loose mantle of brightly coloured cloth draped over her shoulders, but more often her beautifully moulded bosom was completely bare. Her sole garment was a brief kilt of shiny black goat skin or of royal leopard, while for special occasions, she wore a kilt of multi-coloured beads sewn together closely in an intricate and attractive design.

There was nothing gross about Ling En. Her figure was full and firm; her limbs long and shapely. She was the apple of her brother's eye and his most trusted companion, but she was hated by most of the royal wives and concubines. They were jealous of the attention shown her by the King and the popularity she enjoyed among the white visitors to the royal kraal. It was a source of constant amusement to Lobengula to see how astute she was in amassing a veritable horde of treasures given her, or perhaps more accurately, extracted by her, from whites desirous of obtaining a concession, or some favour from him.

Concession hunters were becoming more and more numerous and many were abusing the privileges granted to them. There was the case of Sir John Swinburne, who had been granted permission by Mziligazi to mine gold in the Tati district, but elsewhere he was to confine his activities to prospecting only. When Lobengula became king, he confirmed the privilege, but was soon receiving complaints from his council of elders that Swinburne was grossly abusing the privilege.

The King was disappointed to hear this for the baronet was a particular favourite of his. At first he thought that perhaps Swinburne had fallen foul of some of the indunas and that this was their way of getting their own back at him, but unfortunately, when Swinburne's Matabele guides were questioned, they admitted that Swinburne had ordered two pits to be dug and had extracted stones from them.

The wretched guides were petrified by what was going to happen to them. It was Mnombate who did the questioning on behalf of the King. 'Were you not told to see that the white men only looked for gold in that area but did not dig for any?'

'Yes', they replied, 'that is true. When we heard him give instructions to his Ma-kalanga servants to dig, we remonstrated with him, but he became angry and said that he had found signs of gold in some of the stones on the surface, but how could he tell whether there was much of it deeper down without digging to see? We threatened to leave him and come back and report the matter, but he assured us there was no need to be perturbed for everything would be all right with the Great One. If he found gold lower down he would take only a few stones as a sample, but would not start to mine. We thought that this would be alright. We watched carefully, but he did no more than he said he would.'

Some indunas took a serious view of the matter and reasoned that if one white man was allowed to exceed the rights granted him, others would do likewise. They turned on Mnombate and blamed him for having allowed white men to prospect outside the Tati district during the time of his regency.

Lobengula saw that his councillors regarded the matter as a serious one; in their eyes this could be the thin edge of the wedge. Many of them were most distrustful of whites, not from first-hand experience, but from the stories which were becoming more and more frequent of how the whites were steadily creeping northwards, seizing all the land as they went.

The King settled the issue for the time being by undertaking to warn Swinburne that there must be no recurrence of the episode. Also, an example was to be made of the guides, so that all others entrusted with that duty would realise that it was not for them to deviate one iota from the terms of their instructions.

While the King was deciding what their punishment should be, the poor wretches sat tense with fear. To what sort of dreadful torture would they be subjected? It was their eyes that had seen the wrong done, so perhaps they would be gouged out or burned out? They hadn't reported the wrong, so perhaps it would be their tongues that would be cut out or torn out and be fed to the dogs.

When the sentence was pronounced, the leniency of it was too much for their distraught nerves. Their ears could hardly take it in. They were to be tied for two days to trees by the edge of the most important thoroughfare, where all passers-by could see how they had failed in the responsibility entrusted to them. During that time they were to receive no food or water, nor were they to be protected from insults.

The first two hours were not bad, but then as the green leather *rimips* (thongs) around their chests, arms and legs began to shrink in the sun, the bonds began to bite deeply and excruciatingly into the flesh. The jibes and taunts of passers-by that they had sold their country to the white man began to sear their souls and minds. In the evening, when the cattle were being brought home and kraaled for the night, the herd boys gathered round to torment them with insults and to jab them with pointed sticks and even to spit with derision in their faces. The leaves of the trees had sheltered them from the direct rays of the sun, but the heat had been intense so that by dusk they had developed a maddening thirst. Women carrying gourds of cool water from the river nearby would tormentingly place their loads within sight of the wretched thirst-crazed men. As darkness crept on, myriads of mosquitoes and other insects of all shapes and sizes began to feast on them. With the coming of the dew, the straps of green leather began to shrink even more. Both men knew what that meant. They would be lucky if they saw the sun rise, let alone live through another day and another dreadful night. Soon both were uttering agonised moans and calling to each other piteously.

It was well before dawn when one of them realised that someone was loosening his bonds. The pain in his chest was excruciating, but as soon as he could take a free breath he croaked 'Who is it?' A hand was clapped over his mouth and a voice whispered in his ear 'Keep absolutely quiet. Shut your eyes and do not dare to open them until you hear an owl hoot twice. If you don't do as I say, I shan't come tomorrow night.' Then the figure slipped silently to the other man, and, after repeating the same threat, proceeded to loosen his bonds.

Only the King knew what his most trusted and favourite sister had done with his consent!

No sooner had the King dealt with one problem created by whites than he was faced with yet another, and this time of a very much more serious nature; that of trading firearms to the King's vassals, the Mashona, in return for pack oxen. The King felt particularly hurt and disillusioned, because the perpetrator of the crime was none other than Thomas Baines, whom he held in high regard and to whom he had granted a concession to mine. Even more so, Baines had entered the King's territory with an impressive letter of introduction from the British governor of Natal.

The King tackled Baines about the firearms deal with the Mashonas and was relieved to find that his judgement of the white man's character was not at fault. Without hesitation, Baines admitted what he had done, and expressed sincere regret on hearing that a Matabele warrior had been killed by the very gun he had traded to the Mashona.

'Mr Baines,' the King confided, 'you know how fond I am of the white man, but really, some of you are driving me to desperation and are making things difficult for me with some of my councillors.'

'Why, Inkosi? What else has happened?' asked Baines. 'You forget I have been away in the veld for two months and so I am out of touch with what has been going on.'

'All right, listen to what I have to say, and then tell me what you think. First, you know how I have followed my father's policy of insisting that all people who wish to enter Matabeleland must report at the official post of entry, and that they are to camp there until I have considered their application.'

'Yes,' replied Baines, 'I know that, and so does everyone else.'

'Well,' said the King, 'my post commander has been having a lot of trouble with the whites. Some of them don't want to pay entry dues; others try to force their way through. Only last week three English army officers were annoyed at being kept waiting at the post, and when I gave orders for them to be admitted, do you think that they came to see me? Not at all; they headed straight for Tati looking for gold; they were not interested in hunting game as they had made out in their application. They did not even do me the courtesy of calling on me.

'Then there is the matter of Levert. Verbally, and in the presence of my indunas, I granted him a concession in the Tati district, on exactly the same conditions that my father before me had done, and which I have now accorded to traders and hunters. That meant that Levert and the other white men employed by him could come, work his claim, take the gold and then leave the country. In other words, they could have the gold but certainly not the country. I say again, certainly not the country!

'Now,' he continued, 'Levert is not satisfied with that arrangement. He trots out an agreement which, most certainly, I signed in the presence of my indunas after it had been read out and interpreted for me into the Matabele language. Levert now claims that according to this document, the whole of the Tati district is covered by the concession, that it is his and that it is for him and not for me to decide who may or may not enter Tati, and that he can give permission to mine in the area to anyone he chooses. This, I tell you, is wrong. I am not concerned with the intricate wording of the document. I am only concerned with my own laws and I know, and my indunas know, what I meant him to have. I gave him a cow to milk and he could have milked her dry if he so wished; but no, he wants not only the milk, but claims the cow as though he had won her by conquest.'

Not long after that conversation there was an ironic twist to that particular problem. A party of thirty Australians had been admitted to Tati by Levert. After a while they began to wonder whether Levert's authority was sufficient, and so they obtained an audience with the King to enquire the exact terms on which they might hold their ground, and whether Levert's authority was sufficient, or did it require to be confirmed by the King. That, of course, provided Lobengula with an excellent opportunity to exercise his power, and he did so straight away, by sending two senior indunas to take note of the boundaries of each and every individual claim in the area.

By such action the King had made it clear to his councillors and to everyone else that he denied the right of Levert, or any other person, to concede permission on mining rights anywhere in the country. The authority to do so remained with the King alone.

The lure for gold was making white men appeal to a black king to settle grievances between themselves!

Chapter VII

Ling En's kind deed to the two guides who had been tied with green *rimips* to trees had not gone unnoticed. Some of the indunas had become suspicious and started suspecting each other. One of them approached Mahondi, the Mashona witchdoctor, to see whether he knew, or could find out, who had dared to interfere with the punishment meted out by the King himself.

On receiving an adequate fee, Mahondi threw the bones and they pointed to Ling En's hut. The induna was surprised and scared for he knew, just as everyone else did, that Ling En was the King's confidante and favourite. He made haste for his own home and decided to keep his lips tightly closed.

Mahondi smiled to himself. He knew that he had thrown the bones in just such a way that they would point in that particular direction. Idiots! If only they would use their brains and stop to reason! Who would be so stupid as to thwart the King's edict over so minor a matter as the infraction of orders by two guides? No one but the King himself! And who would the King use as his instrument but the person whom he trusted most – his sister Ling En!

Mahondi was delighted with the train of events. The seed of doubt had been sown in the induna's mind. For how long would he remain silent? Not very long. Soon he would be whispering the secrets to other members of the council to show how clever he was. He would take all the credit and not mention the sorcerer's name.

As for Ling En, he would bide his time and test his suspicions at an opportune moment. If he was right, and he was sure he was, he could greatly increase his power by blackmailing not only Ling En but that detestable Matabele king himself, that man who was bleeding the Mashonas of their cattle, corn and ivory.

Some two weeks later Ling En slipped quietly into her hut but she was much too worried to sleep. It was only when dawn was approaching that slumber overcame her. When she awoke, all that had transpired seemed like a dreaded nightmare, but she knew only too well that it had been no dream. Even now the smell of that dreadful witch doctor was fresh in her nostrils. She felt sure he had anointed himself with juices from the stink gland of a polecat.

As soon as she had washed, she approached the King, and quietly sought a private audience with no one else within sight or hearing. The King was intrigued by her caution and gave orders for everyone to leave the royal hut. As soon as they were alone, she explained, how, in the dark, she had been walking across the courtyard, when from behind a corn store someone had hissed her name and bade her stand still. She had turned abruptly in the direction of the voice.

Standing in the shadow was the wizened figure of Mahondi, the witch doctor. With a wide grin he had sidled up to her and had had the temerity to clutch her by the arm. He had cackled at her astonishment and anger and had hissed, 'So, the King's sister thinks it is right to interfere with the King's justice. She plays with fire!'

'Shut your filthy mouth,' she had exclaimed, 'you will die for this. You despicable spawn of a Mashona toad!' She had snatched her arm away from his claw-like clutch and had made to strike him, but the little creature made no move save to spurt with contempt a jet of spittle right at her feet.

As she stood over him he had said, 'Woman, friend of the white men, friend of the missionaries, I shall not die tonight, nor tomorrow night, nor for many moons, but from now on you will do as I tell you or it will be you and your royal brother who will die disgraced in the eyes of your own people.'

With another rasping cackle the little man had disappeared into the shadows leaving her standing there dumbfounded and nauseated.

The King was worried and angered by all she had said. He knew what trouble witch doctors could incite even against royalty. A king's verdict given at a trial was irreversible, even by himself, unless the complete council of the upper house approved unanimously for him to do so. In this case they hadn't even been approached. It was to be a secret between brother and sister. If some of the less trustworthy indunas got to hear about it they could make a lot of trouble for him, and even demand the execution of Ling En, for it was absolutely forbidden by tribal law for anyone to thwart the King's judgement once it had been announced.

Lobengula decided no time must be lost. Mahondi's mouth must be closed by death, but not before it was found out whether he had divulged his knowledge of the incident to anyone else; if he had, they too must be got rid of. In the meantime, it was essential for Ling En to put a good distance between herself and the royal kraal by visiting her half-brother Mpoto at Inyati. That was not a happy choice for Ling En, as Mpoto was rather uncouth and was completely lacking in dignity. The real reason for the King selecting Mpoto was that the missionaries were living in his area and he felt he could count on them providing her with protection from the machinations of a witch doctor. She was fond of them and they of her.

Mpoto was delighted to see her but his womenfolk were less enthusiastic in their welcome. He ordered his head wife to have water brought for her to wash in and then for food and beer to be set before her. Naturally they were full of questions about what was happening in the capital. While she was outwardly relaying the news and gossip, her mind was really busy planning an excuse to be with the missionaries as soon as possible.

As soon as she had finished her meal, she informed them that she was going to pay a visit to the mission. To her surprise and relief they never questioned the reason for so sudden a decision, but Mpoto and two of his wives immediately said they would accompany her. This would never do, for what she had to say to the missionaries had to be said in complete secrecy. Glibly she lied that Lobengula had sent her on a very secret mission and so, regretfully, she would have to go on her own.

Normally, the thought of a woman acting as a secret envoy for the King would have been considered preposterous, but not so in Ling En's case, for it was common knowledge that no secrets of state were hidden from her. At first she thought Mpoto was going to be a little difficult, but with a ready joke or two she helped him save face in front of his women, and off she went on her own.

She was always a welcome visitor at the mission and once again she was regaled with food, but this time not with beer. She was served precious tea which had travelled thousands of miles by ox-wagon and which was now sweetened with sugar, from the missionaries' small store, until it was almost syrupy. That was how the Matabele like it. In their eyes, tea with only a teaspoon or two of sugar in it, was showing scant hospitality.

All the way during the long trudge from Bulawayo, Ling En had been planning how she would introduce the subject, and now that she was actually sitting in front of the missionaries she was finding it even more difficult than she had imagined.

While she was still pondering how to do it, she heard Mrs Thomas talking of how her family was being pestered continuously by the townsfolk entering their house, unannounced, and even walking into the bedrooms. One particular *matjaha* was especially troublesome. He even came at night when the family had gone to bed, and took particular delight in frightening the children. Remonstrating with him had been of no avail, so one night they stayed alert looking out for his arrival and as he was about to enter, Mr Thomas grabbed him by the scruff of the neck and flung him out. The lesson had been driven home; they had had no further trouble from him.

'That was the right thing to do,' commented Ling En. 'You can't be gentle and considerate with *matjaha*. They are expected to be tough and overbearing. Your form of teaching is lost on them. Whenever you meet with serious trouble you should report the culprit to Mpoto; he will know how to deal with them.'

'I'm afraid not,' replied Mrs Thomas. 'To tell you the truth, we sometimes think he is the one who puts the others up to worrying us.'

At this outburst Mr Thomas thought it best to change the subject, and related how some of the Matabele visitors to the mission had become partial to European food, invariably asking for a meal. On one such occasion Mr Thomas went into their kitchen to see what he could serve. There was some cooked fish left over from a previous meal, and this he mashed up with potatoes and took it through. The visitor thoroughly enjoyed it and asked for more. There were no potatoes left, only some fish, which he took through to the guest. When the man saw it, he threw his hands up in horror, and gave his host a most reproachful look.

'What is the matter with you?' asked Thomas in surprise. 'You have just eaten some and enjoyed it so much that you asked for another helping.'

'That wasn't fish I ate!' exclaimed the man in horror.

'Yes it was,' replied Thomas. 'There is nothing wrong with it; it is perfectly fresh.'

That brought on a terrible outburst of rage. The plate was flung against the wall and the man bolted towards the river screaming that the white man had insulted him; had killed him; and poisoned him; had ruined his reputation as a warrior.

Ling En laughed heartily, 'I must tell that story to Lobengula Kumalo, he will enjoy it. But surely Mr Thomas, you must know by now that fish is taboo to Matabele warriors – only their women eat it.'

The mention of her brother's name brought her thoughts back to her own problem and the purpose of her visit. From being bright and cheerful, she suddenly seemed to recoil within herself. Mrs Thomas was quick to notice the change and exclaimed, '"What has happened, Ling En? Are you ill?'

'No,' replied the girl, 'I am not ill, only worried. I need your help; Lobengula Kumalo agreed that I should come to you.'

Then it all came out in an incoherent torrent. There was no doubting that the matter was a serious one, for the girl had suddenly become transformed from an intelligent and somewhat imperious young woman into a bundle of nerves with tears pouring down her cheeks.

Thomas got up and closed the doors in case there were any intruders about. Seating himself again, he said, 'Now, Ling En, just try to be calm and tell us the whole story again, starting from the very beginning. You can trust us not to tell another soul. We will give you whatever help we can.'

When Ling En had finished describing in detail all that had happened, the missionaries just sat silent for a moment, looking from one to the other. Then Thomas leant towards the girl, and with one hand resting gently on her shoulders, said in his strong Welsh accent: 'Ling En, what you did for those two men was a good and kindly act. Indeed it was a brave act. You don't really have to worry. Lobengula Kumalo is a very powerful king; he loves you, he will protect you from any silly witch doctor, he will —'

Before he could go any further the girl cried out hysterically, 'Mr Thomas you are a fool; you are a fool! Don't you realise that if the witch doctor talks, my brother will also be in trouble – that he will lose the confidence of his councillors and of his people. That if he tries to protect me he will be destroying himself. I am finished. I am already dead unless you help me. My brother intends sending trusted men secretly to kill Mahondi, but obviously the toad will be expecting just such a move and will shout out what he knows before they can kill him. The only way I can be saved, the only way my brother and I can be saved, is for you to put a spell on Mahondi which will kill him silently and before he talks. Do this for me. Please do it.'

Thomas tried to explain to her that Christians don't cast spells; they rely on God to help them and guide them, but before he could go much further, she interrupted. 'Listen. If you do for my brother and me as I have asked, we will help you. You want permission to open another mission near to Bulawayo; my brother will give you permission to do this. Only you must kill Mahondi quickly, now'.

Thomas tried to reason with her and to get her to understand that it is absolutely against the tenets of the Christian faith to take life or to place spells and curses on people. Inwardly, they realised the girl had spoken the truth. Once it became known that it was she who had loosened the victims' bonds, regardless of whether or not she had done it with Lobengula's consent, she would be punished. There was only one punishment for such a crime and that was death.

The missionaries knelt on the floor and prayed for guidance. They prayed in English. The girl, a quiet onlooker, believed it was the beginning of a spell. Surely the spell of a white man would overcome a despicable Mashona! These very thoughts restored a sense of security in Ling En.

Strangely enough, within a matter of hours, news reached the mission that Mahondi had 'ceased to walk' – he had died of a heart attack. It is surprising how quickly a slender bamboo spike poked up the rectum can penetrate vital organs without leaving any readily visible tell-tale sign!

Later that night when they were in bed, Mrs Thomas called across to her husband 'Darling, isn't it strange how we have been here all this time and can only number three converts? Yet every time the natives are in trouble or in want, they come running to us.'

'Yes, my dear, progress is slow,' he replied, 'but it is both comforting and encouraging to know that instinctively they trust us. That is the first big step in the right direction.'

Little did poor Thomas fully realise when he was making that optimistic statement, that his fellow whites were progressively and rapidly killing that trust. The early-comers had been tough and rough but inherently honest in their dealings. The more-recent comers were a mixture of rough and of sophisticated, of uneducated and educated, but they had two things in common: greed accompanied by deceit and a contempt for all black people. The majority failed to distinguish between the dirty, wild and disorganised natives they had encountered on their trek north, and the well-organised clean-living Matabele.

The missionaries experienced a particularly tough time in those early days. Their fellow whites viewed them with suspicion and considered them a stumbling block when it came to seeking extra privileges from the King. The Matabele in turn, particularly in the days of Mziligazi, regarded them as the servants of the King and every attempt was made to reduce them to that condition. They were forbidden to shoot a wild animal either for food or in defence; they were not to fish in the rivers without special permission; they were not to buy maize from the people; and they were deprived of privacy in their own little rude homes.

Although Mziligazi held the Reverend Dr Moffat in very high regard and as a close friend, he was nowhere near so friendly and courteous to the other missionaries who came later. Often he delighted in keeping them waiting for days on end outside the gates of the royal kraal, and would bait them by offering them girls to compensate for the absence of wives. The girls, of course, would never dream of disobeying the order of their King, so they would go along to the missionary camp or wagons light-heartedly, and then be greatly surprised and offended at finding their comeliness rejected.

In general, the traders and hunters, tough as they were, kept the Sabbath and agreed not to buy on Sundays. Mziligazi delighted in putting them to the test by inviting them in one at a time, on a Sunday, and offering them an elephant tusk, or a rhino horn or a hippo tooth. Most of them declined to buy, but whenever one fell for the bait and began to bargain, the King would order it to be taken away and with a wide grin would say, 'I do not sell on a Sunday.'

Lobengula was much more considerate towards the missionaries than his father had been, but he just could not overcome the amazement and suspicion at the celibacy practised by the Roman Catholic priests who followed in the footsteps of the Protestant missionaries.

On one occasion, when he was discussing the Jesuits with a white friend, he exclaimed: 'What sort of people are these new teachers who hate women? I do not understand them. The old teachers [the Protestant missionaries] bring their own women with them and you and other white men make love to our girls and that is all right, but a man who doesn't make love to any women at all, haw! By heaven! I don't understand it. He is not a man but a witch!'

The King's subjects shared that outlook. The Matabele were brave people. Zulu blood flowed in their veins. They did not fear anyone or anything they could see and could understand, but they were awed by the unnatural, and to them, celibacy was unnatural and therefore savoured of witches. Small wonder that the poor Jesuits found themselves fighting a losing battle and in grave danger of their lives. They retired from the scene until black supremacy surrendered to white in the years to come.

The missionaries were the least of Lobengula's problems. They were not avaricious and they did not seek land; they did not seek gold; they did not seek wealth in the form of animal trophies; and, above all, they were honest, and their word was their bond – just as he boasted that his was. Christianity held little or no attraction for him. It preached brotherhood, whereas he was proud, and considered he had to remain proud and autocratic if he were to rule a warring tribe. It preached that a man should have only one wife; he could see nothing wrong in a man having as many wives as he wanted. He himself was responsible for his father's 300 wives and concubines as well as his own large harem. Yet, despite these views, the influence of the missionaries must have played some part in his life. He was out on horseback one day hunting a rhinoceros, when it suddenly occurred to him that it was Sunday. Immediately he turned his horse round and ordered the hunting party to return home.

On another occasion, when it was brought to his notice that some young warriors in the Imbesu Regiment had skinned a young bull alive, he had them brought before him, had them flogged and then bound and fed to the crocodiles in the Umgusa river. Before the influence of the missionaries, he would merely have reprimanded them and warned them not to repeat the offence.

His worry was with the avaricious whites who were seeking entry, demanding entry, or were just forcibly entering his territory. A tiny rivulet had grown into a steam and was now fast becoming a river in full spate. Not only his councillors, but his subjects at large, were becoming perturbed by the influx, and were continually pressing him to take stronger and more restrictive measures. His soldiers were becoming restless and demanding action, and it took all his power and authority to hold them in check. He kept reminding them of his treaty of friendship with the Great White Queen; he was determined to honour that in the face of all the pressure being brought to bear on him.

Many of the foreigners coming in now didn't even show him the courtesy of calling on him, being not the slightest bit interested in the protocol of his court. Many insulted his people and had taken to referring to them as 'kaffirs' and regarded them, not as a warrior nation, but as the equivalent of the rabble tribes with whom they had come in contact in the south.

No meeting could be held now without the indunas voicing old

Zulu proverbs appropriate to the situation; proverbs such as: 'A stick is straightened while it is still green', meaning, of course, that reforms need to be taken in hand early. 'They are treading on the lions tale', meaning the whites are offending the King. Or, 'The elephant must drink while the other animals are all standing', inferring that the King must maintain his own dignity and standing. 'The mouth crosses a wide river' which can be interpreted as actions speak louder than words. 'The polecat cannot smell himself', meaning that a man cannot see his own faults, and, perhaps the most telling of all, 'The eagle which seizes is the one that hovers above'.

Anger flared to an even greater height when it was found that several girls were suffering from a new and loathsome disease, syphilis, and were transmitting it to their menfolk. They traced the disease back to a white man. The king sent for the culprit and told him his heart was very sore and sorrowful that a white man should have brought such a terrible disease into his country; that if the culprit were a Matabele he would have ordered him to be put to death, but since he was white, and since the King did not wish to breach his friendship with whites, he was merely ordering him to leave the country forthwith.

Many of the uninvited guests and gate-crashers were not even honouring their undertakings. When, for purposes of peace and quiet, the King would reluctantly grant them permission to hunt or prospect in a particular locality, they would soon abuse that privilege and wander even further afield. Such intrusions, particularly those into the heart of Mashonaland, were specially disturbing to the Matabele.

The Matabele were not by nature hunters of wild game, and when they did, it was only for food in seasons when their herds of cattle and goats had suffered because of sickness or drought. The white hunters shot everything in sight. Before long the wide open plains of Matabeleland were becoming devoid of all wild life, so the hunters moved towards Mashonaland, whither the surviving game were retreating.

Mashonaland had greater appeal for the white man. Unlike Matabeleland, with its extensive grassy plains and comparatively high temperatures in the summer months, Mashonaland was timbered, the soil was better and the climate was almost ideal. Furthermore, the Mashona were a more subservient lot than the arrogant Matabele and were more willing to work for their Matabele overlords. The cry among the whites was going up: 'What a pity such a beautiful country should be wasted on blacks.'

If Lobengula was bemoaning his present problems, it was a good thing he couldn't see what the future held in store!

Chapter VIII

It was a great pity that the whites who were entering Lobengula's kingdom were so motivated by greed for gold and ivory that they didn't take time to realise that there was a properly organised and constituted government in power, backed up by not a horde of spear-throwing savages, but by a well-disciplined army composed of highly trained regiments. That the King was an embodiment of the tribe and, although in European eyes he could be regarded as a despot, the fact was that he was guided, and had to listen, to the opinions of the Izikulu or House of Commons comprising all headmen and the wisest men of the tribe and also to the Umpakati or the equivalent of the British House of Lords.

Two other great errors of judgement on their part were, firstly, not appreciating that while the Mashona clans had their own chiefs, every one of them had acknowledged vassalage to the Matabele king and were required to pay tribute in payment for protection. It was the equivalent of a Pax Britannica. The second great error was in not realising that the King was the guardian of the tribe's entire stock of cattle, sheep and goats. There was individual ownership of livestock, including the King's own private herd, but he was the guardian of the lot. When the chief of another tribe became the vassal of a Matabele king, the latter would often place in his care a herd of cattle as a mark of trust. This was the king-pin to the trouble that lay ahead.

Lobengula's great mistake was in not realising that the subjects of the Great White Queen, particularly those who lived in distant Africa, were not so obedient to her commands, and not as well disciplined, as were his own subjects. He was not to know that while the government in Westminster gave directives to their governors in Africa, the subjects in Africa were adept at mis-construing those orders, or even disregarding them, on the grounds that 'What do penpushers in London know about conditions in Africa? The man on the spot is the only one who knows how to deal with the situation.'

When the King granted a mining concession, he and his councillors were under the impression that all that was entailed was giving permission to dig up a few stones and take them out of the country, and that was all there was to it. They hadn't realised that the miner and his employees and partners would need to build houses. That it was not a question of digging up a few stones and then departing, but of going on digging year after year and so becoming permanent residents. Above all, they never for a moment thought that when they gave a concession-hunter permission to prospect in a certain area that they had given him the authority to refuse access to the whole of that area to others, even to the Matabele themselves! What it had boiled down to was that the issue of a mere licence had become the granting of a title to the land. That, most certainly, was not what the King and his council had intended.

Among the new intruders were more missionaries, but missionaries of a type totally different to their forerunners like Moffat, Thomas and Sykes, in whom the King had put implicit trust. Presumably, from his experiences with them, he had come to regard all missionaries as being equally trustworthy, and so on a day in October 1888, he signed the Rudd Concession – a document which signed the death knell of his kingdom of Matabeleland, Mashonaland and Manicaland. That document was interpreted to him by missionary Helm whose certificate as interpreter read: 'The accompanying document has been fully interpreted and explained by me to the Chief Lobengula and his full council of indunas and that all the constitutional usage's of the Matabele nation have been complied with prior to his executing the same.'

The concession provided for the payment to Lobengula and his heirs and successors a sum of £100 a month for an unspecified period, 1,000 breech-loading rifles and an armed steamboat on the Zambezi river, in consideration for which:

> I Lobengula, King of the Matabeleland and Mashonaland and other adjoining territories, in the exercise of my sovereign powers and in the

> presence and with the consent of my Council of Indunas, do hereby grant and assign . . . complete and exclusive charge over all metals and minerals situated and contained in my kingdom, principalities and dominions, together with full power to do all things they may deem necessary to win and procure the same . . . and whereas I have been much molested of late by diverse persons . . . seeking to obtain grants and concessions of mining rights I do hereby authorise the said grantees – to take all necessary and lawful steps to exclude from my kingdom all persons seeking land, metals and minerals . . . and I undertake to grant no concessions of land or mining rights without their concurrence.

It is left to history to puzzle how Helm, a missionary, could reconcile his conscience as a teacher of the Christian faith with a document of that nature. Did he understand the full significance and implications of the words used? Did he interpret correctly the wording? Did he explain the implications? Was he just an unwilling tool of seekers of power and wealth?

One wonders, too, how Lobengula and his councillors who had shown such wisdom in the past, were forced or tricked into becoming party to a document which was to deprive them of ownership and of power. They were now conceding ownership and power to complete strangers!

In view of what happened later, it is interesting to note that the concessionaires were C.D. Rudd who was a partner of the great Cecil John Rhodes in the Kimberly Diamond Mines and in Consolidated Goldfields of South Africa; Rockfot Maguire, a fellow of All Souls, a barrister and at one time Secretary to the Governor of Hong Kong, and F.R. (Matabele) Thompson who was well-versed in Matabele language and customs. Thompson would have known whether Helm was interpreting and explaining correctly.

That was the document which gave Rhodes and his close associate and second-in-command Jamieson (to be better known later for his part in the fateful Jamieson Raid into South Africa) a foothold in the door to Lobengula's domains.

No time was to be wasted. As soon as the document was signed,

Rudd started to bring in large numbers of white miners of both British and Afrikaner (Boer) descent from South Africa.

The commander of Lobengula's army informed the King of the difficulty he was encountering in holding his soldiers in check. The young *matjaha* (unblooded spears) in particular were pressing for permission to kill all the whites. The witch doctors and rainmakers were complaining that all the flags the whites were flying would affect the rain clouds and induce either drought or flood.

Then, to top all these problems, came the news which the King and his councillors had been dreading, that a white impi was approaching the southern border. Lobengula sent out a reconnaissance patrol to bring back authentic news about the strength of this impi. Back came the report that it was only a small force of sixteen mounted white troopers belonging to the white Bechuanaland Border Police, under the command of a man called Shipperd. However, Matabele intelligence revealed that a much larger white force was encamped, in reserve, further back.

Shipperd informed the guard at the entry post that he intended to proceed into Mashonaland. The guard commander sent a runner post-haste seeking the King's instructions. The King forbade entry, which was exactly what Shipperd and his superiors were expecting and hoping for as it provided Jamieson himself the excuse to enter, which he did hotfoot.

His attitude to the King was patronising as he explained that the duty of Shipperd's small force of troopers was purely to protect Rudd's miners. The King replied that the protection of the miners in his country was his responsibility; he would guarantee their safety; there was no need for the while police.

'Well, King,' replied Jamieson, 'since you have broken your word and refuse to grant me the road I shall bring my white army and we shall fight.'

Lobengula replied, 'What is this you say? I have not refused you the road, I have only said that I don't want foreign soldiers in my country. I have not refused the road to you but only to your impi.'

'Very well,' said Jamieson, 'then you acknowledge that you have promised me the road and unless you refuse now your promise holds good.'

The King was confused and dismayed by this extraordinary line of argument, but he remained diplomatically silent, despite the murmurings and growls of his councillors.

Jamieson broke the silence. 'Goodbye, Chief, you have given your promise about the road and on the strength of that promise I am bringing my impi into Mashonaland.'

The King and his councillors were flabbergasted by this subterfuge and deceit; it just did not make sense. The interpreter was questioned as to whether he had interpreted correctly; he assured them he had. The moment which Lobengula had been dreading most, a breach with the British, had arrived. As a last desperate measure he dispatched a letter to the Queen's representative at Cape Town. Unfortunately, in those days of poor communication, it took a long time for a letter to travel 1,000 miles or more. He also appealed to his friend the Reverend Doctor Moffat for guidance and assistance.

From his mission station in Bechuanaland (Botswana), Moffat wrote to Shipperd:

> I know very well that nothing is further from the thoughts of either chief or people that the introduction into any part of their country is of a colonising population. However desirable such a result might appear to us, to the natives it means only one thing which they have seen over and over further South; it means that the white men having once got one foot firmly planted on their land will soon have both feet on it till he becomes the owner of the land and the native has become a squatter on sufferance in his own country.

While Lobengula was anxiously awaiting a reply to his letter to Cape Town, a pioneer column of whites began to assemble on the Macloustie river. The King immediately sent another message to the Governor in Cape Town addressed to the Queen:

> When we joined together, why do you send an impi? Rhodes paid me money through Rudd, for which I have given him a piece of ground. If you have heard that I have given my whole country to Rhodes, it is not my words. I have not done so. Rhodes wants to take my country

> by strength. Your words were "I was to send for you when I was troubled by white men". I am now in trouble!'

Sir Henry Lock, the High Commissioner at Cape Town replied:

> Queen assures Lobengula that the men assembled by the British South Africa Company were not assembled for the purpose of attacking him, but on the contrary were assembled for a peaceful object, namely searching for gold. They were ordered to travel at a distance from the Matabele kraals and always to recall that Lobengula is the friend of the Queen and that the Queen wishes to maintain peace and friendship with Lobengula.

Poor Queen Victoria could not possibly have received Lobengula's letter nor known the contents of it.

Britain's High Commissioner was either displaying monumental hypocrisy or he had been hoodwinked by C.J. Rhodes. When one considers how Rhodes behaved towards the Afrikaners in South Africa and how he later on acted in the country which was to bear his name, the latter is probably the more correct assumption.

Be that as it may, at the time of the letter, Rhodes was voicing his advice which was later to become historic: 'Go North young man, go North'. And they were doing just that, 'for they were being promised as much land as a man could ride over in a day!

The whites were now exploring further and further into Mashonaland. Many of them were busy stirring up trouble by fermenting discontent among Lobengula's Mashona vassals and selling rifles and ammunition to them.

On 27 June 1890 a 'pioneer column' led by Jamieson crossed the Macloustie river. It was met by a party of Matabele with a letter from Lobengula: 'Has the king killed any white men that an impi is collecting on his borders, or, have the white men lost anything they are looking for?'

To this Jamieson replied that this was a working party, protected by soldiers who were going to Mashonaland, along the road already arranged with the King.

On 12 September 1890, the Union Jack was hoisted at 'Fort

Salisbury' and possession of Mashonaland was taken in the name of Queen Victoria and jurisdiction over the white population was entrusted to the British South Africa Company (BSA).

Poor Queen Victoria – a horrible travesty of justice had been perpetrated in her name. Poor Lobengula – he had lost a kingdom by honouring an agreement and abiding by his word.

Worse was to come.

The Matabele were warriors and adventurers. Brave, well-organised and clean in their persons and habits. The Mashonas were agriculturists, poorly organised and had become accustomed to being marauded by other tribes. The men had their hair twisted into spikes or teased out into a mop which was then larded with a mixture of charcoal and animal fat – a concoction much relished by flies. The women of higher rank let their hair grow and decorated it with coloured beads. Those of lower rank shaved all or part of the head. The women wore a short wraparound apron of animal skin, or two separate flaps of skin or of grass fore and aft. The men wore a leather flap dangling from the waist to protect their bottoms when sitting on the ground – and they did quite a lot of that as the women did most of the work.

They had no army as such but fought, when they had to, in individual groups armed with throwing spears or assegais, bows and arrows and knobkerries made of hard wood or of rhino horn. They knew how to extract iron ore and were skilled in making spear heads, which formed part of the tribute they were required to pay to their Matabele overlords.

A strange feature was that young Mashona boys, taken as slaves by the Matabele, were keen to learn the Zulu language and Matabele customs so that they could be enlisted into one of the slave regiments. Most of them turned into good soldiers and were quite willing to participate in the vicious raids on their own people.

Like most subjugated people the Mashona were crafty, cunning and devious, as Europeans were soon to learn when they took them into service.

A factor of vital importance was the difference in outlook between white man and black to the very meaning of land. The white man sees land as a medium to be used as he sees fit, be it for growing crops or digging it to extract minerals. He has no real ingrained love for it. To the Mashona that was far from being the case. To him it was something much more vital: it belonged not only to him but also to his ancestors going back generation before generation, for each man in each generation was the embodiment of his father's spirit. So when the Mashona witnessed the influx of white settlers taking up large blocks of land, it meant that they were condoning theft, not only from themselves which was bad enough, but also from their fathers and grandfathers and their fathers before them.

Large ox-wagons and scotchcarts were bringing in more whites from South Africa every day. Not only single men now, but whole families attracted by the offer of free agricultural land and the prospect of starting a new life. Rhodes and Jamieson were busy proclaiming that the poor persecuted Mashonas were just longing to be freed from their Matabele shackles and were welcoming, with relief and delight, the arrival of British protectors 'under whom they would cheerfully labour'.

The early settlers soon found that to be a gross exaggeration. The Mashonas were economically self-sufficient with each family growing sufficient food for its own use, plus a small surplus as tribute to the Matabele king for his protection. Also, they had no use for money at that early stage. To them, as to the Matabele, it was an unknown and unneeded commodity.

To overcome the impasse of a shortage of labour, the white administration imposed a hut tax on the Mashonas which was to be paid solely in cash, so as to compel them to go out to work in order to earn the money to pay the tax. The Colonial Office in London opposed the tax, but the local white authority argued that it was only fair that the Mashonas should pay towards 'being relieved of the constant liability to raids by the impis of Lobengula . . . and being able to gather in their crops with reasonable safety'.

To that line of reasoning, the Reverend Moffat commented dryly that 'the giraffe would rather risk the lions than live in a cage and there is evidence that the Mashonas at any rate prefer the risk of an occasional raid by the Matabele to peace and the continued presence of Europeans.'

The next few months witnessed a steady influx of white settlers and of mistrust and frustration between all these groups: Matabele, European and Mashona. The devious and crafty Mashona soon realised the deep antipathy between their Matabele overlords and the newly arriving whites, and took every opportunity to create further trouble between them. Mashona chief would fight Mashona chief and instead of appealing to the King as their overlord to settle the dispute, they would appeal to the white authority and so infuriate Lobengula and his council. On another occasion they caused a rift of major importance by stealing the copper wire used to connect white settlements by telegraph, and then accused the Matabele of doing so. Then when the white authority punished the Matabele by confiscating their cattle, they infuriated Lobengula and his council, for all Matabele cattle, be they owned tribally or individually, were entrusted to the King.

Some seven months after first flying the Union Jack on the kopje (hill) at Salisbury, the British High Commissioner in South Africa proclaimed: 'The country north and west of the South African Republic, west of the Portuguese dominion and east of the German sphere of influence falls within the British sphere of influence . . . and that anyone entering this territory with a view to the occupation of land must observe the rules and regulations established by the British South Africa Company.'

Ten days later, on 23 April 1891, the Colonial Office informed the Foreign Office in London that it had informed Lobengula of its intention to govern and punish the whites in his (Lobengula's) country and that there was 'ground for assuming the existence of "sufferance" on the part of the king, thus giving her Majesty jurisdiction in his country within the meaning of the Foreign Jurisdiction Act of 1890'.

The only 'sufferance' poor besieged Lobengula had shown was his faith in the Queen and the power he had imagined she exercised over her subjects. In the face of strong opposition from his councillors and the commanders of his regiments, he had restrained the army from fighting the Queen's subjects.

Poor Queen Victoria – a horrible travesty of justice had been perpetrated in her name. Poor Lobengula – he had reaped a grim reward by honouring an agreement and abiding by his word.

One is left to wonder what the Foreign Jurisdiction Act of 1890 meant to an African who could neither read nor write and of how an interpreter of poor educational standard could possibly interpret or explain it.

The newly arrived white women expected to have domestic servants just as they had become used to having in South Africa – and particularly women servants. But Mashona girls and women were even dirtier and more backward than their menfolk. Also, Mashona men resented their wives and daughters working in the house of the *mzungu* (white persons) so, in the end, it had to be 'boys' (regardless of whether they were youths or adults) who had to be encouraged and trained.

The first task was to provide them with soap, preferably Monkey brand, and order them to wash themselves from head to toe and, above all, to cut their hair and get rid of the nauseous fly-tempting concoction of fat and ash. Then to provide them with shirts and shorts to cover their nakedness and do away with the smelly leather pad dangling over the buttocks. All this sounds easy, but it took time and patience to teach savages the very basics of hygiene.

Even when they got their servants clean and dressed, the ladies would complain of how the boys smelt – that they exuded a strange and unpleasant body odour. Curiously enough, Africans thought the same of Europeans.

It took time to teach the boys not to blow their noses in their fingers and then with those same slimy fingers handle food and dishes. And not to throw kitchen and other refuse out of the front or back door, and, above all, not to squat just outside the house to answer the call of nature.

It is easy to imagine the consternation of the Mashona, and of the Matabele for that matter, when white farmers selected a large block of land, and then proceeded not just to lop the trees at a convenient height as they were accustomed to doing, but to stump or uproot them completely and then to plough the land with strange-looking implements hauled by a team of oxen. Naturally, to do that work, they counted on black labour. The Matabele wouldn't do it for they were cattlemen and warriors who employed slaves to do all menial work. The Mashonas were unwilling, for they were self-sufficient and only wished to be left to their own devices.

The view of blacks and whites on what constituted a desirable standard of living were at complete variance. The Matabele did not assess wealth in terms of coinage, but in cattle. The more head of cattle a man had the more important he became; they had no desire to labour for the white man. The Mashonas were not used to hard and prolonged work; men lopped the trees where the women would sow and care for the crops, and they would trap wild game when the need arose. Their women did whatever else was needed to be done.

Any Mashona who had at first thought white overlords would be preferable to Matabele kings was soon having second thoughts. Men who had never been used to doing much in the way of work were being called upon by white farmers and miners to work steadily from sunrise to sunset, so they were left with very little time to themselves or their families. Why, they thought, even the slaves of the Matabele are better off and better treated! The slaves were at least regarded as part of the Matabele family and lived in their masters' houses, but the Europeans fed and treated their dogs better than their servants.

There were many Bantu practices misunderstood by the whites even though many of them had come from South Africa. One of those practices was 'lobolo', which the whites considered to be deplorable – the practice of 'buying' a wife. In fact, lobolo consisted of cattle and goats being presented by the prospective husband to the father of his betrothed as guarantee for her protection during her marriage, and as assurance that he intended the marriage to last provided she bore children. Should the woman not bear children, or should she commit adultery, or should she leave her husband, then her father was required to return the dowry.

The missionaries preached that a man should have only one wife and keep faithful to her alone, but the African male saw no sense in this, nor did the women. They favoured polygamy, The first wife was always regarded as the senior and enjoyed certain recognised privileges and, of course, she did not have to work so hard while there were other women to assist, particularly with the more onerous tasks.

There was also a difference of opinion between the two races regarding chastity. In African society, at least in those days, a Matabele lover was expected to pursue the object of his desire with fervour, and the girl was expected to simulate fear and flight. It was improper for her to yield to his overtures without at least the semblance of a struggle.

Illegitimacy was frowned on and an illegitimate child ranked little better than a slave. Rape was almost unknown, because the act itself was considered a natural rather than a criminal one, unless it was carried out by a slave on a woman of superior class.

Pressure was never brought on a Matabele girl to marry a man not of her choice. Once a couple had decided to marry with the permission of the girl's parents, they would exchange presents, she giving him beads or other ornaments she had made, and he would give her a blanket of soft skin or a cape made out of the skin of some animal he had killed, or some other useful present.

Unknown to the groom, the bride would fix the day of her wedding, a day on which she knew he would be at home. Then she and her women and men friends would call at his kraal and wait outside the gate to it. When asked what they had come for, one of her group would reply, 'We have come to offer allegiance.' To this, the formal answer coming from a person inside the kraal was, 'We have no means; we have no cattle, we are but poor people; we have only dogs which bark whoo, whoo, whoo, and mice which squeak nsi, nsi, nsi.'

A spokesman for the girl's party then delivered the traditional message from her father, stipulating that she must be well treated by the husband-to-be and by his whole family. A spokesman for the husband then reiterated that he was poor and needy, a statement that implied modesty on his part.

Payment of the lobolo was made by the bride's father, and the bridegroom, in turn, gave presents to the girl and to her family. The bride's party was then invited to enter the kraal which they did with simulated reluctance and a mock show of violence. Eventually, they were persuaded to be seated, and eating and drinking commenced, continuing well into the night. The next day an ox or a goat was slaughtered for food which was usually eaten at a picnic on the bank of a river in some favourite glade. At dusk the bride pretended to run away, but she was soon found and taken to her husband's hut where they were both locked away in the hearing of much ribald laughter and bawdy jokes – the signal for the young male guests to grab the girls of their fancy and carry them off into the veld.

The following day the bride's hair was cut to leave only a topknot or *isicolo* as the badge of rank of a married woman.

Another misunderstanding between whites and blacks were the rules of politeness; a European would expect his servant to stand while he was addressing him and would regard it as a mark of disrespect if he were to sit down. The African code of conduct was exactly the opposite – the man of inferior status had always to sit down when being addressed by his superior. In those early days of white settlement this was often the cause of much irritation and misunderstanding.

Another cause of misunderstanding which led the African to think he was being deliberately insulted by the white man, was when the latter walked into a kraal or hut carrying his rifle or revolver, and immediately broached the subject in his mind. African etiquette required the visitor to leave his weapons outside the gate of the kraal, then enter quietly and slowly, and sit down silently. The inmates of the hut then, one by one, addressed him politely. In the case of the Matabele, the traditional opening was 'Sakubona' ('I see you') to which the visitor replied to each in turn 'En ngi ya ni bona' ('I see you. How do you do'). Only when those formalities were completed was it correct for general conversation to begin.

If only Jamieson had exercised good sense in recognising that the Matabele were far superior to other Bantu tribes by having a very efficient administration, taking pride in themselves and their traditions, and having a much higher standard of living; and, if only both parties could have talked to each directly, instead of through interpreters, who, without exception, were not knowledgeable in legal and commercial jargon, much of the bloodshed and misery which was to ensue could have been avoided.

Chapter IX

Rhodes lost no time in establishing small settlements of Europeans at strategic points, spread over Matabeleland and Mashonaland, and connected them to each other by telegraph line, but the Mashona took a fancy to the copper wire and stole several hundred yards of it to convert into jewellery. A white police officer ordered the local chief, a Mashona, either to hand over the culprit or face a fine of several head of cattle. He elected to pay the fine and did so at once. Cunningly, and unbeknown to the Europeans, those particular cattle belonged to the King and had been entrusted into the care of the Mashona chief by Lobengula, as evidence of the trust he placed in him as a vassal.

The chief informed the King that the whites had confiscated his cattle; Lobengula was furious and asked Jamieson why the Europeans had done this. Did Jamieson think that he, a king, would stoop to stealing wire? Jamieson realised he had been tricked by the Mashona and returned the cattle.

The Mashona chiefs were delighted with the ruse and the discord it had caused between the whites and the Matabele. They thought that if they continued with that line of action, soon, very soon, their two detested enemies would be at each other's throats and then, with both parties weakened, the Mashonas would be free once more.

Some time later, another Mashona chief in the vicinity of the newly created town of Fort Victoria, took similar liberties with the King's cattle, but this time Lobengula took direct action. He sent a message to the white community that he would be sending an impi to punish the offenders, but the Europeans need have no fear whatsoever for their safety. His men would merely round up for punishment, and for example, all the Mashonas in the area.

Disregarding the promise of safety, the white population hurried to take refuge in the fort and took their Mashona servants with them.

The order to the commander of the impi was that he was to punish all Mashonas in the area, so he did not regard those sheltering in the fort as being exempt and demanded they be handed over to him. The white officer in command refused.

The impi commander could not understand why anybody should wish to shelter smelly Mashonas, and thought it could only be that the whites didn't want corpses lying around polluting the atmosphere. So he assured the Europeans that his men would not pollute the water supply by killing any Mashonas near the river on which the town relied for its supply. Instead they would execute them in the bush where their bodies would give no offence. Again, the demand was refused.

By that time Matabele tempers were running high; the warriors had smelt blood. They rampaged through the town and even entered those European houses which they found vacated; they smashed furniture, took whatever they fancied, drove off the cattle from the European farms in the vicinity, and seized mules to carry the plunder. Not a single European suffered bodily harm. Only their houses had been ransacked in anger at them not handing over their Mashona servants.

The impi was still in the area five days later when Jamieson arrived. He was appalled by the holocaust. All business had been brought to a standstill; Mashona villages were burning for miles around but not a single European had been attacked.

Jamieson sent for the commanders of the impi and told them that under no circumstances would the refugees be handed over. He gave them an hour in which to leave the area and return to their base. If they were not gone in that time he would drive them out with his big guns.

One and three quarter hours later he sent Captain Lendy after them with a unit of mounted troops. His instructions to Lendy were: 'You have heard what I told them; I want you to carry that out. I don't want them to think it is only a threat; they have had a week of threats with very bad results. Ride out in the direction they have gone. If you find that they are not moving off, drive them, and if they resist and attack you, shoot them.'

Spearmen on foot were no match for cavalry and artillery. Matabele losses were high.

On hearing what had happened, Sir Henry Lock, High Commissioner at Cape Town, sent a message to Lobengula:

> My friend, the impi in the neighbourhood of Fort Victoria has transgressed your orders and has entered the streets of the settlement, killing the black and native servants of the white people before the doors of their houses . . . The whole community is smelling of blood shed by your people . . . These acts cannot be permitted. They will bring on you the punishment that befell Cetewayo . . . I wish to control the anger of the white people . . . but I shall not say stop to them unless you at once withdraw your impis and punish the indunas.

He followed this with a cable to the Colonial Office in London saying that he felt Lobengula's patience was running out; that it was impossible to say what he would do when he heard of Lendy's attack on his men when they were returning home.

The King replied to Lock's letter:

> I shall return no cattle nor compensate anybody, unless Rhodes returns to me all the captives, wives, children, cattle, goats, and sheep, which were given protection by the Victoria people, and had I known at the time when I sent my impis what I know now, I would have ordered them to capture and loot all they could lay their hands on belonging to the whites to compensate myself for the people and their property which were withheld from me . . . You did not tell me that you had a lot of Amaholi [a Matabele clan] cattle hiding with you together with their owners, and that when my indunas claimed them from Captain Lendy he refused, and told my indunas that the Amaholis and their cattle did not belong to me any longer and then turned his cannon on my people. Are the Amaholis then yours? I thought you came to dig gold but it seems that you have come to rob me of my people and country as well. You are like a child playing with edged tools. Captain Lendy is like some of my young men; he has no holes in his ears and cannot hear; he is young and all he thinks of is a row; but you had better caution him carefully or he will cause serious trouble between us . . .

The Colonial Office sent strict instructions to Lock that the British

South Africa Company must be made to understand that their duty must be limited to defending only the areas they had occupied, and that Her Majesty's Government would not support them in any aggressive action.

Lobengula saw that matters were coming to a head fast, so he recalled an impi, some 6,000 strong, on its way across the Zambezi to Barotseland. He would hold it in reserve in case of emergency. Also, he declined to accept the British South Africa Company's monthly payment for mining concessions, calling it blood money.

Rhodes bought horses in South Africa and sent them north to Jamieson. He boasted that within a month he would have one thousand mounted men posted in strategic positions. He and Jamieson exchanged laconic telegrams: 'What king,' asked Rhodes, 'going to war against another king, sitteth not down first and considereth . . . ?'

Lobengula sent a message to Moffat asking him to intercede for peace: 'Why do you keep quiet? What wrong have I done?' he enquired.

Jamieson, in considering the Colonial Office instructions that the company was to limit its action to defending the territory it had occupied, regarded the Shashi river as forming the boundary between the occupied and non-occupied areas. This, of course, was by no means correct, and Lobengula immediately queried how the Shashi had suddenly been declared a boundary, and how, in fact, zones of responsibility had been created, because at no time had he been party to any such arrangement, nor indeed had the subject been discussed. He refused point blank to regard the Shashi as a boundary and decided to appeal directly to the Queen while there was still an opportunity to avoid war. Umshete, a very senior induna, was selected to be his emissary and was to present the Queen with a present from the King and to request her to restrain Rhodes from inflicting a bloody war on the country.

Unfortunately, Umshete got no further than Cape Town. Lock would only agree to arrange his passage to London if he would agree to the Shashi river as the dividing line between the two zones. Obviously Umshete had not the authority to deviate from the directive given him by his king, so there the matter ended, and he headed north again – a journey of 2,000 miles each way by slow ox-wagon, and all for nothing!

The atmosphere got more and more tense. The whites were pressing the company to ignore London, take the law into its own hands, and settle what had now come to be known as the 'Matabele Question'. The Matabele, in turn, were pressing Lobengula to take the initiative and wipe out the whites before they received reinforcements from the south. He explained to his people that there was a 'hedge' around a king's word; that he had given his word to the Great White Queen and he would not fight until he was attacked. It was a very courageous and difficult decision to make at a time when he was fully aware that Rhodes was sending mounted men into his kingdom as well as a thousand warriors promised him by Khama, the King of Bechuanaland.

On hearing of the agreement between Khama and Rhodes and wishing to pre-empt an attack by Khama's forces, Lobengula put his patrols on the Bechuana border on full alert. When they found a Bechuana Border Police patrol in Matabele territory, they fired on them, inflicting some losses. About the same time another party of Matabele fired on some BSA Company police on what the police considered to be their side of the Shashi river – a boundary which Lobengula did not recognise as such.

Jamieson regarded these two separate incidents as indicative that the King's impis had got out of control and meant to force a war and notified the British High Commissioner in Cape Town accordingly. Lock, in turn, told Goold-Adams, commander of the Bechuana Police, and Jamieson, to take whatever measures they considered necessary.

This was exactly what Jamieson had been hoping for, and he wasted no time in forming two columns comprising 200 hastily enrolled white horsemen, 200 Bechuana Police and 1,000 of Khama's warriors. One column was to advance on the King's royal kraal at Bulawayo from Salisbury, and the other from Fort Victoria. Each enrolled man was promised 6,000 acres of good farmland, twenty gold claims and a share of half the livestock which would be taken as booty.

While this was being arranged, Lobengula was in touch with Lock. Lock cabled London: 'Lobengula sends messages denying he had impis on borders. Offers to send anyone I may appoint to verify. Says he hears whites advancing and suspects they want to fight. Asks why they do not say so.'

Simultaneously, Lock asked Lobengula to send a deputation of chief indunas entrusted with wide powers, to talk matters over with him, a message which reached Lobengula only after Jamieson had begun to move against him.

Lobengula wasted no time in sending his half-brother Ingubugobo and two other indunas, with trader Dawson to act as interpreter and to ensure the delegates were not delayed on the way by whites. When they reached Tati they were astounded to find Goold-Adams's force of Bechuana Police already in the town and on their way to attack the King. Naturally the three Matabele suspected a trap and were all for disappearing, but Dawson assured them their safety was inviolate as members of a delegation to the British High Commissioner.

Dawson met an old friend and went off with him to have a drink, calling to a mine foreman to look after his 'three natives' and not bothering to explain their rank or who they were. When Goold-Adams heard that three Matabele were in the town, he immediately suspected them of being spies and ordered their arrest. One Matabele snatched his captor's bayonet and stabbed him with it, but was himself shot dead; so also was a second delegate as he tried to escape. The third, Ingubugobo was clubbed with a rifle butt and feigned death, managing to escape later and returned to the King.

Lobengula was not only furious at the news but bitter, convinced his envoys had been murdered treacherously, and beginning to wonder whether there was any white man he could trust. Even Moffat seemed to be disinterested; he had not heard from him for some considerable time.

Meanwhile a white military column advanced steadily towards the King's capital Bulawayo. In addition to each man being armed with a rifle, the column also had as supporting weapons, two seven-pounder guns, five Maxims and an assortment of other types of machine-guns.

They were going to be opposed by an impi armed with assegais, shields, knobkerries and a sprinkling of rifles, which had been traded to individuals, by settlers and traders.

The column was confronted by a Matabele force at the Shangani river, where the Matabele adopted their usual battle formation – a massed attack by warriors charging shoulder to shoulder and shield to shield – and as soon as they were near the enemy the units on both flanks would veer outwards in an encircling movement – an ideal formation for defenders armed with rifles and artillery! Despite their heavy losses at each salvo the Matabele would withdraw, reform and again charge. They knew so little about shellfire that those with rifles were actually firing at the shell-bursts.

Another battle took place at the Imbambezi river, again with the same result. In both encounters, Jamieson's force suffered only five whites killed, one Cape-coloured (mixed race) driver killed and thirteen whites wounded. The Matabele losses were very heavy, with three whole regiments decimated and several others very badly mauled.

While the battle was raging, Lobengula was kept posted with news by a series of runners. From time to time the King would rise facing the scene of battle, stand erect and motionless, clutching a spear in his right hand and concentrating his thoughts in prayer.

When he heard that all was lost and his impis had surrendered, he decided to flee rather than stay and be humiliated by Jamieson. He gave orders for his European-style house to be destroyed and for the Matabele area of the town to be reduced to ashes, but the white settlement outside the palisade was not to be harmed in any way. He loaded his wives and personal possessions on to a number of wagons, mounted his horse and, accompanied by his bodyguards and some senior indunas, he headed north. All his subjects in the town prepared to leave with him but he forbade them to do so. Before leaving, he summoned some of the indunas who had been ordered to stay behind, and gave them instructions to see that no harm came to any Europeans nor to their possessions. Then he called a very prominent and powerful induna, Schuluhula, to him and entrusted him with the safety of the two white traders and friends who had stayed with the King all through the turmoil – Fairbairn and Usher.

One of those left at Bulawayo under the protection of the indunas wrote:

> Major Maxwell and I were the only ones left . . . who had any connection with the BSA Company. . . We of us who are alive today can never forget the kindness and care the king had shown us. Whilst he was holding back, with a few of his old induns, his people were demanding to be sent to fight the whites . . . Where have we seen such an act on record as that of a black king ordering an induna, as Lobengula did – it was Schuluhula, one of the big chiefs of Bulawayo, to watch over and defend from his own beaten people, two helpless white men who were at his mercy. . . and found alive and well on the entry of the Columns into Bulawayo in 1893 when the king and his people were fugitives, the king flying to his death beyond the Shangani!

Lobengula had kept his word; Jamieson had gained his objective. So what was to be the next move?

It is sad to account that any Matabele warrior who was too wounded to leave the battlefields at the Shangani and Imbambezi rivers was left to be dealt with by the Basuto and Mashona members of the column, and were massacred to a man, although it can be argued that, most likely, had the situation been reversed, the Matabele would have done the same.

On arriving in Bulawayo, Jamieson was disappointed at finding that Lobengula had disappeared. He felt that no settlement could be reached so long as the King was free and alive. The King was the very embodiment of the spirit of the tribe; the arbiter of every man's destiny. They would flock to his service whenever he called and from wherever he called. So Jamieson sent him a letter: 'To stop this useless slaughter, you must come at once to see me at Bulawayo, where I will guarantee that your life will be safe and you will be kindly treated.'

To this Lobengula replied by a letter written on his behalf by a semi-literate coloured (half-caste) John Jacobs: 'I . . . have heard all what you have said so I will come. But allow me to ask where all my men who I have sent to the Cape? [referring to the delegation accompanied by Dawson] And if I do come were will I get a house for me as all my houses is burn down.'

Later, two white troopers were ambushed by Lobengula's party and were sent back to Jamieson with a thousand pounds in cash and a letter requesting that all members of the royal family who had been left behind should be treated kindly and not be persecuted. The money never reached Jamieson, and no satisfactory explanation has ever been received of how it disappeared.

When Lobengula failed to arrive, Jamieson sent a force under the command of Lieutenant Colonel Forbes, with Major Wilson as second-in-command, to capture the King. On crossing the Shangani river, Forbes decided to pitch camp and sent Wilson forward with a troop to try and locate Lobengula's whereabouts; he was to be back before nightfall.

When dusk came and Wilson was not back, Forbes sent a detachment to look for him, but without luck. The following morning he sent out another mounted party with Burnham as scout. They came across several burnt wagons belonging to Lobengula and abandoned for want of oxen. A few miles on they met up with Wilson and the two parties proceeded to go forward together, and soon were attacked by a group of about forty Matabele, but Burnham got them out of danger by sheer coolness and pluck. From the prisoners they took, they learned that the King's original bodyguard had now been reinforced by at least three more regiments and that each day more warriors were flocking to his assistance.

It is best to quote from Burnham's own report:

> On crossing the Changani River we came upon a large number of armed natives. We told one of them to show us the king . . . It was now getting dark . . . As we went forward we saw camp fires and halted. I went forward to examine and found a large number of natives. Major Wilson ordered us to advance at a gallop across an open valley and we totally surprised them. They had women and children with them but also a large number of armed men. We asked for the king and they pointed up the valley. We rode through the bush for two miles up this valley lined with natives. Owing to darkness and rapidity

of our movements, we surprised skerm after skerm. At first the natives hardly believed it possible that fifteen white men would be so audacious as to ride among thousands of them in their own camp and demand the surrender of the king . . . At last we came to the king's wagon standing in a circle of poles . . . and rode up to this. Captain Napier shouted Major Wilson's command for the surrender of the king. All was silent! . . . By the flashes of lightning, for a storm was brewing, Napier saw armed natives filing out of the skerm with guns in hand and at the same moment I saw others rising up to surround us . . . Wilson said we had better retire at once . . . and we slipped away individually into the forest where the natives seemed not yet to have gathered . . . We struck the open valley and a deep donga and hid in the forest opposite the king's wagons . . . All of us were tired, some had been in the saddle for forty hours . . . The storm was now very heavy. . . We decided to retreat towards the main column, get into thick bush and rest the horses and men . . . We hid about two hundred yards from the first skerm we had charged . . . The men flung themselves down in the mud, holding the horses by their reins . . . We could hear natives shouting all through their camp . . . We decided to send for the column and Maxims at once so as to attack at daybreak as the natives intended evidently to fight . . . A party was sent back to Forbes with the request. Wilson turned to me and said 'Do you know we have lost three men in the darkness. You must find them.' He went with me. We shouted to them and roused the whole camp and heard the answering shout of the three. Wilson called them to us and we returned to where the others were. Wilson sent me to scout around. I could hear the rustle of wet branches. It seemed to be large bodies of men moving between us and the column. At day-break I heard the tramp of horses and rushed to our men and we all gladly went out to the spoor to meet the column! But, alas! It was only poor Captain Barrow and twenty men!

We decided that to retreat direct to the column would mean meeting all the regiments, therefore it would be better to turn north and hit the king hard and draw off his men until Forbes came up with the column. This we did and at light we were again in front of the king's wagons; we were then attacked by about one hundred men at once; we fought them; they had cover and we retired and dismounted behind a large ant heap, but the natives were reinforced and came out

> into the open with a rush; we reserved our fire and at two hundred yards we opened up and many men fell. Wilson stood on the top watching and directing in his usual cool way. . . We fought very hard. Suddenly we were cross-fired at from heavy bush on our left flank; so we rode slowly away as most of the horses were done up and some men wounded and dismounted. The fire on us then ceased and we retreated towards the column weak and dismounted . . . After retreating a short distance Major Wilson rode up to me and said: 'Do you think it is possible for you to get through to Forbes and tell him to come up at once as we are nearly finished? I asked for a man and he gave me Gooding and I told him I wanted my fellow scout Ingram as I expected to be ambushed.
>
> We three rode away and were opened on by a horn of the enemy and in a few moments they rushed into us with the assegai and in the heavy bush came very close. For the next two hours we rode and doubled and hid to give our horses breathing time and to throw the natives off our spoor which a number, however, persistently followed. At last we reached the banks of the river and found it a torrent; so we swam it and on crossing saw bodies of natives firing on Forbes' Column. We rode slowly until natives opened up on us and then, with a last effort of our jaded horses we cantered into the column and delivered Wilson's last words to me. But Forbes was himself retreating towards the old lager of the previous night. Finally, we took shelter in bush close to the river. Ingram and Lynch left that night in the height of a terrible gale of hail, wind, and rain, which enabled them to pass through the lines of natives and carry the news to Inyate where the relief expedition met us with Selous as chief scout, Jamieson and Rhodes.

Meanwhile Wilson, realising the position was becoming hopeless, tried to cut his way through to the river, but a Matabele force intercepted his approach and he was forced to stand and fight, surrounded and greatly outnumbered. He and all his men died fighting gallantly.

Rhodes felt that with the rainy season having set in, the wisest course was to let the King remain a fugitive in the hope that hunger or illness would force him to surrender.

The whole attention of the BSA Company was then riveted on disbanding its military force and settling a score of vexatious problems with the British High Commissioner and also with the Imperial Government in London. In the British House of Commons the Government was facing stiff criticism from the Aborigines Protection Society as well as from the opposition benches.

Chapter X

Rumour followed rumour as to what had happened to the King. Was he alive? Would he be returning to free his subjects from white domination? Was he dead and, if so, was it by the hands of white men? Finally, the truth was revealed. Two very senior indunas who had chosen to go into exile with the King had now returned. They revealed that as time had gone by, Lobengula had become more and more depressed and had lost the will to live. One day, as they sat side by side, the King had turned to Magwegwe, his mouthpiece (the King never addressed his subjects personally, but always through his mouthpiece), and said, 'Magwegwe, do you remember your words?'

'Yes,' replied Magwegwe.

'Then,' said the King, 'what were they?'

The answer came promptly: 'When the great bull elephant dies, so shall I.'

The King took a small bottle and drank from it. Magwegwe picked up the bottle and drank too. In minutes both were dead.

All the people who were with them cried out 'Our fire has gone out.' They slaughtered a black ox and wrapped the King's body in the freshly skinned hide. After a few days of lying in state and when the smell became too overpowering for the mourners, the body was buried in a standing position in a cave.

Now that the death of the King was confirmed, Rhodes was recognised as an empire-builder. The whole venture had been financed by him with the proceeds from his gold and diamond mining interests in South Africa. The vast areas already shaded red in atlases were now extended by another large track, bearing the name Rhodesia.

Unfortunately, the birth of the new nation was heralded by a whole series of unforeseen and unpropitious misfortunes. It was the second successive year for a severe drought to damage the grazing in Matabeleland – a calamity indeed for cattlemen such as the Matabele – and that was followed by a particularly devastating plague of locusts. The swarms were so dense and so heavy that they broke even thick branches of trees with their weight and numbers; this time it was the Mashonas and the white farmers who suffered most. Next came an epidemic of that most dreaded of all contagious cattle diseases – rinderpest. Again, it was the Matabele, and again it was the whites, who suffered the greatest losses.

White farmers were up in arms demanding that greater restrictions be placed on the movement of cattle owned by natives. The BSA Company responded by shooting infected beasts wherever found. As the Matabele owned far more cattle than did the whites, it followed that more were slaughtered in native areas than on white-owned farms, so the Matabele claimed victimisation. It was hard to make them understand that the disparity in numbers shot was because their herds were so much larger and were more concentrated, but it remained a seed of discontent.

Each disaster on its own would have been bad enough, but a combination of three was near catastrophic. There couldn't have been a more damaging start for a new administration which had to deal with people immersed in superstition, and with newly arrived settlers who hadn't had time to find their feet and were struggling to get established.

It was abundantly clear that neither Rhodes nor his principal lieutenant Jamieson had had much experience of African culture. All their dealings had been as employers of labourers in mines, on farms and as factory and domestic workers. Their only knowledge of African villages were the collection of poorly constructed huts amid absolute squalor. If only they had taken the trouble to learn and realise that Kings Mziligazi and Lobengula had established a very sound and effective form of government, on which the new administration could build rather than destroy.

There were two advisory councils. One was made up of representatives of the people – the lower house. The other was made up of the most senior indunas – the upper house. Their duties were to act as advisers to the King. He was not bound to take their advice, but if he ignored it, he did so, accepting full responsibility for his action.

Matabeleland had been divided by Mziligazi into two provinces, each under the control of a military division. The regiments comprising each division were stationed at strategic points, and each was responsible for building and maintaining a garrison town. The royal town, or capital, was where the King resided and was regarded as neutral territory – it was outside the jurisdiction of the army, and was presided over by the King himself.

The principal royal wife lived in the capital, but most of the other queens resided in the different garrison towns, and had to be treated with the full respect deserving to their station. The chief indunas and garrison commanders had to consult them on all affairs, other than those of purely a military nature. That was an astute move, because it enabled the King to keep his finger on the pulse of the nation. Nothing could take place in the towns without the queens being aware of it and they, of course, kept the King fully informed.

In addition to commanding the regiment and governing the town, the garrison commander also served as magistrate in settling minor offences. More serious matters were referred to the King, and he, alone, could impose the death penalty.

Then there were the *amankusa*, the policemen, whose duty it was to maintain law and order and also to serve as the King's executioners. Each town had four categories of doctors. They were the medical doctors to treat the ailments of the body, who were experienced herbalists and blood letters. The second category were the war doctors, whose duty was to 'doctor' the army before battle so as to make the warriors courageous and invulnerable. One of the 'mutis' they used was a concoction of the droppings of the Bataleur eagle, kneaded into a paste with bull's urine, and sprinkled on the soldiers. The theory behind this was that the eagle was known for its swiftness and the bull for its ferocity and bravery. Those characteristics were being transferred to the warriors to make them into fierce and bloodthirsty men.

The third category were the rain doctors. Each man had his own recipe. One used the woodpecker, the bird which searches out the heart of the tree. Its flesh, mixed with secret ingredients, was pounded into a paste, which, on the first three days of the new moon, he would imbibe while gazing steadfastly at the moon. His hair had to be bleached white because the power of divination was entrusted only to the aged. If it failed to rain, some dreadful offence must have been committed on earth for it to have been withheld.

It was not unknown in periods of exceptionally severe drought, when people were dying of starvation through failure of the crops, for live children to be sacrificed on bonfires and for the smoke to rise up to heaven. An alternative sacrifice to appease the spirits were very black virgins being thrown into a river to feed a specially pampered crocodile. The blackness of the girl was fairly sound proof she was not a full-blooded Matabele.

Witch doctors were the fourth category. To many Europeans the term witch doctor conjures up the impression that they are the creators of the witchcraft. That is completely wrong. The duty of the witch doctor was not to indulge in witchcraft, but to 'smell out' the witch – the individual responsible for creating the problem. Their dirty appearance, enhanced by a weird regalia of necklaces made out of the claws of leopards and lions, the talons of eagles, the beaks of vultures and earthen figurines, were intended for psychological effect.

The secret of their power was derived from the information they and their acolytes collected and used to their advantage. No rumour went unheeded and no act went unobserved. They kept themselves fully informed of all that went on in their neighbourhood. All that information was stored away in their minds and memories and came in useful when called upon to 'smell out' a 'witch'. It was also very valuable material for blackmail and from the King's point of view they were his intelligence service.

A shock for the new administration was finding that Mashona slaves, on being freed from their Matabele owners, had no desire to rush back to their homeland. That, of course, was a disappointment to white farmers who were finding difficulty in getting local Mashonas to work for them, and had been led to believe, by the Company, that the freed slaves would be only too pleased to find employment. The slaves preferred to go on living with their masters who treated them as members of the family and permitted them to share their houses with them.

There was rather a similar reaction when Mashona chiefs were told they no longer needed to pay tribute to the Matabele, nor fear the violence of Matabele raids. Their first reaction had been one of relief, but on second thoughts they realised they were to become a source of labour for the white farmer and miner, and they couldn't see that as being a change for the better.

Colenbrander, a newly appointed commissioner for native affairs, asked Selous – a famous white hunter who had spent the greater part of his life among Africans and was well versed in their traditions and outlook – to explain their strange reaction. He replied:

> We Europeans make the mistake of thinking that when we free a tribe of savages from what we consider a most oppressive and tyrannical form of Government . . . we ought to earn their gratitude. We invariably fail to do so . . . Give me the good old time of superstition and bloodshed; then, even if I did not know the hour when I might be smelt out as a witch and forthwith knocked on the head, I could have basked in the sun till my time came; and then too, I revelled in blood and loot. That is how the Matabele feel! [I wonder in 2000 whether Tony Blair and Robin Cook have ever considered such a viewpoint when meddling in the affairs of Sierra Leone, Nigeria and other African countries.]

Unnoticed by the native commissioners, Matabele men were gathering in small groups lamenting the death of their king and blaming all the evils they were suffering on the white man: it was he who had introduced syphilis and gonorrhoea; before the advent of the white man no drought had lasted more than a year, but now, because of him, the spirits had extended the drought into the third year. They had lost over 9,000 head of cattle confiscated by the white administration as booty for the war, and because of the European's lack of understanding of the Matabele laws concerning cattle ownership, many an owner of only a small herd had been completely impoverished. White men were buying Matabele women and ignoring the rules of lobolo. Despicable, cowardly, Mashona policemen were being given authority over Matabele warriors and were molesting their women. The Matabele, people of proud Zulu stock, who served no man but had others working for them, were now being called upon to labour for detested intruders who did not even treat them as the Matabele had treated their slaves. They were having to pay a tax for living on their own land, the very land which they themselves had gained by conquest.

Feelings reached fever pitch. Some of the leaders asked, is it not better to die fighting than to live like dogs? Others, with more sense, preached patience; wait, they pleaded, for an opportune moment. But the seed of discontent had been sown.

Nearly every action of a white man or woman, no matter how innocent, had come to be regarded as an insult. One day an Afrikaner, Fourie, was making bricks and building a house for a Mr and Mrs Ross and their adopted daughter on an isolated farm. Fourie noticed that his Matabele labourers were suddenly becoming more and more inept and truculent. He shouted at one of them in exasperation for making deliberate mistakes; the 'boy' cheeked him, Fourie threatened to strike him, whereupon the whole gang turned on Fourie and clubbed him to death with their picks and shovels. Then they made for Fourie's pole and daga huts and slaughtered his wife and six children. Maddened with the smell of blood they broke into a hut in which Mrs and Miss Ross had hidden; both women were killed. Amazingly they didn't sexually molest either of them, something they invariably did when attacking women of their own colour. Mr Ross, who had been supervising work in a field some distance from the house, came running to investigate when he heard shouting and raving and he too was slain.

The Ross's Hottentot servant whom they had brought with them from South Africa escaped and broke the news to the nearest white neighbour, who immediately summoned all the other white farmers in the area by a prearranged code of signals. A small force of white men, mounted on horses, scoured the countryside shooting down all the Matabele they could find. No quarter was given nor asked.

A few days later, three white miners were murdered, although it was never known why, because they seemed to get on well with their labour force. Their mine was only 3 or 4 miles from Selous's farm, yet neither he nor his wife were harmed. Ironically, only the day before, some distant relatives of Lobengula had borrowed and sharpened axes at Selous's place. It was not known whether they were the murderers.

In another incident, seven white men, two coloured (mixed race) and an Indian cook were murdered. One 'Colonial native' (presumably a Hottentot or Bechuana) was left for dead with many body wounds and his mouth slit from ear to ear.

Every week more and more murders on isolated farms and mines were reported. In one incident, a whole family was wiped out! Eight bodies were found lying on the ground some twenty yards from the homestead. They had been chopped to death with axes and their brains bashed with knobkerries. The grandmother had been murdered reclining on a couch, reading a newspaper.

At about the same time a native policeman was murdered by a Matabele gang; the murderers fled into the Matopos hills taking their women, children and cattle with them. The authorities sent a detachment of native police to bring them to justice.

According to Selous who appeared well informed on the subject, the police had camped for the night outside the kraal from which they suspected the murderers had come. After their evening meal, they were gossiping by the fire, when a group of Matabele approached and ranged themselves around the police and began to dance in a provocative manner, made all the more obvious by each man being armed with a stout knobkerry. Soon they commenced to 'Jia' or point with the handles of the knobkerries, and then one of them ran out of the line and, coming close to the police, stooped forward and drew his left hand rapidly backwards and forwards across his own throat and said, 'You are killing us. Why don't you cut our throats and be done with it?' Then another ran forward and repeated 'You are killing us', pressed a finger against his temple and said, 'Why don't you shoot us? Why don't you put a bullet in just here?' The expression 'you are killing us' meant you are making life intolerant for us by enforcing the white man's laws.

The sergeant in command of the police unit urged the dancers to go home and go to sleep because his men had no wish to fight with them. But his words had no effect and the dancing and provocation continued. Then suddenly one of the policemen saw a man, armed with an assegai, creeping up stealthily behind them and called out a warning. Before the man could use his assegai, two policemen seized him and were handcuffing him, when a shot was fired from a nearby cattle kraal. It had been aimed at the police but had killed the prisoner. The police rushed into the kraal but the gunman had escaped.

In the meantime, the dancers too had left the scene. The police were standing in the light of the camp fire debating what action to take when they came under a volley of rifle fire – two policemen and a civilian blanket carrier were killed.

After the police had returned to their base to report on what had happened, one of the dancers, a man called Gonyona, went alone to the kraal of Umfondisi, son of Lo Magzi, a nephew of Lobengula, to tell him what had happened: 'Come Umfondisi, why are you sleeping? Don't you know we are fighting? We have killed some policemen, come! Blood is running and men are lying dead! Come with us and let us do some more killing!'

Both men went off to a neighbouring kraal to spread the news. A native policeman came out of a hut to enquire what all the noise was about.

'Who are you?' asked Gonyona.

'I am so and so, one of the native commissioner's policeman.'

'What!' exclaimed Gonyona. 'Do you tell my you are one of the witches who are always troubling us?' and shot him. As he fell, Umfondisi plunged his assegai into him.

Hardly a week passed without a murder of a white person being reported somewhere in Matabeleland. In all, 147 were killed including 6 women and 16 children. Another 58 could not be accounted for and so were presumed to have been killed.

To add fuel to the fire, an oracle or a seer, either a Mashona or a Ma-kalanga, named Mgwali, who had received the patronage of Lobengula himself, was prophesying the downfall of the whites. An old trader, Clarkson, had tried to persuade the King that the seer was a charlatan and had offered to go to the cave in the Matopos hills where Mgwali lived and expose the man, but Lobengula was too afraid to consent. When Mgwali had heard of Clarkson's offer, he had threatened him, publicly, with sudden death as punishment. Strangely, very strangely, Clarkson was struck by lightning shortly afterwards – truly an alarming coincidence.

What had inspired Mgwali to forecast doom for the whites was a total eclipse of the moon. He had interpreted it as heralding the spilling of white man's blood in the very near future. Prophesies such as that, coupled with all the other problems the Matabele were suffering, and which they attributed to the European, encouraged them into planning a concerted rebellion. Secretly they were reforming their regiments.

A few heads of clans, but only a few, decided not to take part and they soon found themselves being regarded as traitors. One of them, Marzwe, was camped with a fairly large party of his people at the foot of a hill on which a fort had been built by the whites on the Bulawayo to Figtree road. He had expressed his fear to the native commissioners at the fort, that the rest of his clan at their kraal some 8 miles away might be attacked by other Matabele, so he was granted permission to bring all his people to the immediate vicinity of the fort but although they could not be allowed into it, they were assured of protection outside it.

Marzwe accepted the offer and sent a messenger to bring in the women and children. Instead of coming straight away they decided to wait till next morning which proved to be too late. That night the kraal was attacked and many of the residents killed. Marzwe's own personal kraal had been surrounded and every man, woman and child murdered, except for a little girl who had managed to escape despite an assegai wound. It was she who brought the sad news to the fort.

Marzwe accepted the news stoically, only remarking: 'They wanted me. They wanted my skin. So be it.'

The Native Commissioner was reluctant to take punitive action for he had only ten serviceable horses at his disposal and the country around the fort was a mass of small hills and rocky ridges covered in dense scrubby bush, an ideal situation for ambushing men on horseback. However, amongst Marzwe's men who had escaped the onslaught was one, Obas, who at once hurried round to the outlying villages and assembled a small force of his chief's retainers. They followed up the raiders and not only rescued all the women and children who had been taken captive, but also killed eleven of the enemy and retook all the sheep, cattle and goats.

The Native Commissioner described Obas as a well-built, active-looking kaffir of middle height, light in colour and with good features; altogether a good specimen of the best type of Matabele. He had been armed with a Martini-Henry rifle as were some of his small band, whilst the others carried assegais.

When Jamieson realised that the Matabele were actually rebelling, he was shocked and dismayed, for he had considered the murders of whites in isolated places as being the work of odd malcontents. He had not regarded the horrible acts as evidence of mass discontent by the Matabele and so had depleted his armed forces to a dangerous level in massing them on the Transvaal border in preparation for his disastrous raid into South Africa. With the exception of the native police, there was practically no organised force left in Matabeleland. Of the native police, half went over to the enemy and the remainder had to be disarmed for lack of trust. Of the white mounted police there remained only forty-eight officers, NCOs and men, and twenty-six of these were on duty in outlying towns and posts many miles away.

However, he managed to muster a mixed force of white volunteers, colonial natives (South African) and 800 regulars from Mafeking. A strong patrol under Colonel Napier suddenly came upon a small force of 200-300 Matabele who had taken up a position on the crest of a stony ridge covered with bush. When the white force was about 400 yards distant, the Matabele foolishly opened fire with their few rifles and charged. Captain Grey immediately ordered his cavalry to charge. A man who took part described the action as follows:

> The sight of the long line of cavalry thundering down upon them in extended order seemed to have turned the hearts of the savages to water... for after having fired a few more shots they turned and ran, trusting to evade their enemies in the bush. The chase was continued for a mile and half and when it was at last abandoned a long line of corpses marked the track where the whirlwind of the white men's vengeance had swept along. Vae victis! Woe to the conquered! Woe indeed; for amongst the men who took part in the pursuit of the Kaffirs on this, to them, most fatal day, were many who, maddened by the loss of old chums, foully slain in cold blood by the natives, were determined to use their opportunity to the utmost and to inflict a heavy punishment for the crimes committed, while all were bent on exacting vengeance for the murders of the European women and children who had been hurried out of existence during the first days of the rebellion. Once broken the Kaffirs never made any attempt to rally, but ran as hard as they could, accepting death whenever overtaken, without offering the slightest resistance; some indeed, when too tired to run any further, walked doggedly forward with arms in their hands which they never attempted to use, and did not even turn their heads to look at the white men who were about to shoot them down. No quarter was either given or asked for, nor was any mercy shown than had been lately granted by the Kaffirs to the white women and children who had fallen into their power. This realistic picture may seem very horrible and all those who believe themselves to being superior beings to the cruel colonists of Rhodesia but let them not forget the terrible provocation!

Napier's column surprised many kraals, but at the first sign of the approach of the white soldiers, the occupants vanished into the bush leaving behind pots still cooking on fires, and corn bins full of maize, sorghum and ground nuts. After removing all the grain they could carry, the troops destroyed the rest and burnt down the huts. In every village they found goods of some kind which had belonged to the whites murdered in the district. There were many articles of women's clothing and especially a hat which was recognised as having belonged to a young girl, Agnes Kirk. The sight of this made the troopers determined to exact vengeance as every opportunity presented itself.

It seems appropriate, once again, to quote from the report of another soldier who took part in the battle on the Umgusa river:

> A large impi took up its quarters on the Umgusa river. Here, previously large impis had already tried conclusions and had failed. This action naturally took us by surprise.
>
> A man professing himself to be the prophet and mouthpiece of Umlimo [God] and possessing the power of throwing himself into an ecstatic condition, under the influence of which he swallows stones, rolls on the ground, dances on hot ashes, puts burning coals into his mouth and goes through many other strange performances and is known by the name of Si Ginya Amachi (He who swallows stones) is implicitly believed by the people; so much so that when he called for an impi to go and destroy all the white men in Bulawayo he had no difficulty in getting a number of picked men from several different regiments to obey his behests.
>
> His orders were that men composing this impi should take up their quarters where he found them on the Salisbury Road and there wait for the white men to attack them. They were on no account to endeavour to prevent their enemies from crossing the Umgusa river, but were to offer encouragement to do so, for he told them: 'Once they had crossed to the east of the river the Umlimo will strike them all blind, and you will then be able to kill them without trouble and then go on and murder all the women and children in Bulawayo!'
>
> Naturally their casualties were tremendous – it was not a fight but only a pursuit – and the pursuit was only abandoned when the fleetest footed gained the shelter of the thick bush which runs down from the western side of Thaka Induna towards the Umgusa. The natives were killed as fast as they were overtaken! The Matabele lost more heavily on this occasion than on any other occasion during the campaign. The panic-stricken savages accepted death when the horsemen came up to them, without making any attempt at resistance, except in a few instances.

The number of settlers who had lost their lives during these troubled times was 250, to which must be added 89 military personnel, making a total of 339 or approximately 10 per cent of the entire white population.

The settlers' reaction was one of anger. They blamed the British South Africa Company for not having dealt severely enough with the Matabele during Lobengula's time and they blamed the British Government for interfering in matters 6,000 miles away. They only wished pen pushers in London would leave it to the men on the spot to make the decisions!

What were Rhodes and Jamieson going to do now? they wondered.

Chapter XI

Jamieson called an *indaba*, or conference, of all Matabele chiefs to be held at a site on the Matopos Hills. Before the conference proper commenced, Rhodes insisted on meeting the chiefs, alone, except, of course for an interpreter. Jamieson and the chief Native Commissioner tried to deter him from being so brash, for undoubtedly the indunas would be feeling humiliated and disgruntled at such an ignominious defeat. Rhodes argued that for him to go alone would have two useful effects: firstly, it would show that a white man, unarmed and alone, was not afraid to go among them, and they understood and appreciated bravery; and secondly, it would make them realise that from now on he himself was replacing their autocratic ruler and so his word would have to be obeyed.

Rhodes asked them why they had rebelled. The most senior induna answered without a moment's hesitation: 'Is it not better to die than to live like dogs? Your Native Commissioners don't treat us as well as they do their own dogs. They want us to influence our people, but they seize every opportunity to insult us and belittle us among our own followers.'

He then called on another senior induna to relate what had happened to him recently: 'Yes, Inkosi, I will tell you how I was treated a few days ago. I had gone with my Councillors and young men, as befits a chief, to pay my respects to the chief magistrate in Bulawayo. My arrival was announced. I was told by an orderly to wait outside as the magistrate was busy; he would see me when he had the time. We waited and waited. Eventually the magistrate came out, not to see me, but to go to his house. I told him I did not wish to hurry the great man, but my followers had not eaten all day; that when a white man came to visit me, I killed a beast and gave him a meal. The answer came: "There are stray dogs in the town, you can kill them and eat!".'

Rhodes made a mental note to deal with the chief magistrate later.

Others recounted instances, not as bad, but bad enough. It became obvious from all that was being said, that with few exceptions, the Native Commissioners had been chosen badly. Many of them did not speak the Matabele language and made no attempt to learn it. The result was that neither party knew whether the interpreter was putting the point properly or was saying what he himself wanted to be said, which created a grave element of doubt and led to a loss of confidence. Not only did they not speak the language, but most were completely ignorant of Matabele customs and traditions, and were apt to take umbrage where no offence was meant.

Another source for serious complaint, and voiced as one of the main reasons for the rebellion, was the complete unsuitability of the Gwai and Shangani Reserves. The grazing was poor; water was almost non-existent in areas away from the banks of the rivers, and the whole area was infested with tsetse fly, the conveyor of sleeping sickness.

Many a chief had suffered badly in loss of social status by the way in which cattle had been seized by the Company as booty. The owners of small herds had suffered the worst, and many had been rendered destitute. Then had come the vets who shot animals indiscriminately on the pretext of protecting the white man's cattle from disease. The upshot of all this was that many Matabele were now starving.

Rhodes assured them he would bear in mind all he had heard and would see what improvements could be made in the future. They must understand that, just as they had conquered the Mashona and required the latter to serve them, so now the British had conquered the Matabele and would dictate the rules by which the country was to be governed. He would now leave them, and would ask Doctor Jamieson, his Chief Administrator, to come and address them.

Jamieson ordered all firearms to be handed in without delay, and declared the carrying of assegais and knobkerries as absolutely forbidden. Anyone disobeying this order was liable to be shot. They were to return to their kraals and continue with their agricultural pursuits. As a gesture of kindness, the Company would give back a proportion of the cattle which had been confiscated as booty. All chiefs would be required to ensure a supply of labour to European farmers and miners, for which, of course, they would be paid wages. Payment of the hut tax would continue to be compulsory. Those who refused to pay it would be made to work on the roads at a wage of eight shillings and sixpence a month until the tax was paid. The chiefs and headmen would be appointed by the Company and must regard themselves as employees of the Company. Finally, a commission would be set up to enquire into the reason for the rebellion. The leaders of it and those who had perpetrated murder and other crimes would be brought to justice.

In reply the chiefs said they acknowledged defeat and realised they would now have to live under the rule of the Company. It was foolish of them to have believed in the prophesies of the oracle, for how could any reliance be placed on the words of a Mashona or Ma-kalanga toad! However, there was one important matter which would affect the rest of their lives, and also the lives of their children, and of their children's children. 'How can the Company expect Matabele men to work as labourers? Our women have cared for our homes, our children have herded our livestock, our slaves have taken care of all the menial tasks, our men have been warriors, so how can you expect us to toil from sunrise to sunset with only an hour at mid-day in which to cook and eat a meal? You insist on imposing a hut tax and demand that we earn the money to pay it by working on your farms and in your mines. We think it is unfair to call upon us to pay a tax for having a hut on ground which belongs to us, and which was won for us by our fathers with assegais. If you insist that the tax must be paid, we would rather earn it by trading sheep or goats or the trophies of wild animals.'

The Chief Native Commissioner replied briefly and curtly: 'You must understand this is now a white man's country. We don't expect every one to turn out to work all the time. You will please the government very much if you would work for only three months and have nine months to rest in. I will have all indunas realise that they are government officials; we will look to them to assist in supplying labour. It becomes your duty to see that your boys turn out to work. It is only through work you will progress.'

No sooner had the company settled one revolt then they were faced with another. For no apparent reason a white family of four were brutally killed on an isolated farm in Mashonaland. They had retired for the night when a gang of natives attacked the front door. The husband went to investigate and was immediately hacked from left shoulder to right ribs almost severing the body in two. His wife, while attempting to get out of bed, was ripped open and left to die with her innards trailing on the floor. The little girl was bludgeoned to death and the young boy assegaied.

The police could find no reason for the attack, for these were people who had been particularly good to their labour force. They had paid wages higher than the prevailing rate, and had supplemented them with extra food rations. In fact, their white neighbours accused them of creating a precedence and looked upon them as Negro-lovers.

Soon the administration was made aware of a rumour spreading among the Mashona that the Matabele had rebelled. That they were victorious everywhere; had slaughtered many whites with their accustomed ferocity, and were driving the rest over the border into Bechuanaland. Kagubi, the oracle of the Mlimo, who was much revered and feared by the Mashona, and who was probably the instigator of the rumour, was openly calling on all Mashona chiefs to arrange attacks on European farms and mines, to slay their owners, to destroy their homesteads and property and to drive off the livestock. He threatened that before long the Matabele, having got rid of the settlers in their part of the country, would then be on their way back to Mashonaland to resume their sway and would know how to treat those who had not helped them in ridding the country of all whites.

The authorities had learned their lesson in the Matabele rebellion, so without delay rounded up all ringleaders and attacked Kagubi's fastness in the hills. When he surrendered unconditionally, the Mashona realised he had lost his powers of divination, and the uprising was over. In all, 99 settlers were murdered, including 4 women and 3 children; 7 men were killed in action or died later from wounds received in action; 18 others were wounded in action but not fatally. The total white casualties amounted to 124.

Both the BSA Company and the settlers were at a loss to understand why the Mashona should have risen. It was easy to understand the swashbuckling, arrogant Matabele doing so, but not the subservient, obsequious Mashona. The missionaries had been saying how pleased they believed the Mashona were at being relieved from Matabele forays and atrocities, and were gradually getting reconciled to the idea of working. But Colonel Harding, a police officer, held exactly the opposite view. He maintained that they far and away preferred the periodic raid by the Matabele who plundered, killed, purloined women and cattle and then went away, to the occupation by their white masters who simply remained as irksome governors.

A more puzzling question was why so many of those who had been murdered were people who had been particularly kind to their servants, while others with a reputation for being unjust and cruel had gone unscathed. For instance, there was the farmer who used to boast that when any of his farmhands declined to work, he had only to say '25 of the best' and the kaffir would give a sickly grin and get back to work. Nor did they molest the man who copied Lobengula's punishment of having the two guides tied to a tree with *rimpis* (rawhide thongs). This particular individual had one of his employees, who had deliberately killed a cow, tied to a tree overnight; the heavy dew had caused the *rimpi* to shrink so that by morning the poor wretch was nearly dead and had to be resuscitated. Yet, neither he nor his family were hurt in any way.

Perhaps an even more outstanding example of a white man going unpunished by the natives, was the case of a senior government official who had blackmailed a Mashona chief into giving him his own daughter as a concubine, without paying lobolo, or any other remuneration. A missionary had reported the case and the officer had been dismissed from the service and had left the country. Later on he returned, and at the time of the uprising he was actually living close to the chief's kraal yet was not affected in any way.

Such strange reaction was to be seen some sixty years later in another far-off African country – Kenya. There, during the Mau Mau rebellion, several Europeans who had been on very good terms with the Kikuyu were brutally murdered, while others with bad records of behaviour to Africans, were not harmed in any way.

For instance, there was the savage killing of a veterinary officer and his wife. He had done far more than duty demanded in treating Kikuyu-owned cattle under particularly difficult and dangerous conditions, and his wife, a retired qualified nurse, who often accompanied him on safari, treated sick women and children in Kikuyu villages. Despite all that kindness, both were murdered in a truly vicious fashion.

Then there was the proprietor of a country pub only a few miles out of the capital, Nairobi. He was proclaiming to American tourists at the bar that Europeans who were kind and friendly to the Kikuyu had no cause to fear. 'Look at me,' he had boasted, showing scars on his wrists, 'I have been made a blood brother of the Kuiks and admitted into the tribe. I never lock a door or a window at night. I have nothing to fear.' The very next day, headlines in the *East African Standard*, revealed that during the night he had been buried alive, head downwards with only his feet showing above ground.

An even more explicit example was the case, again during the Mau Mau rebellion, of two lifelong friends, a Briton born in Kenya and a Kikuyu. Both had been born on the estate owned by the father of the white boy. They had played together as children, gone shooting and fishing together as boys, and when the white lad went into business, he left the farm he had inherited from his father in the managership of his black companion. One weekend, when he was inspecting the property, and was rummaging among a pile of trash stacked in the corner of a shed where it shouldn't have been, he felt the barrel of a gun being pressed into his back. On turning his head he was shocked to find it was his friend. He heard the click as the trigger was pulled and was amazed to find he was still alive. The gun was a home-made one and the hammer had jammed. There had been no animosity between them; in fact they had enjoyed a drink and a meal together just before the incident.

So why do Africans vent their pent-up feelings, if that is what you can call it, on the very people who have shown them kindness and friendship? Is it that they regard kindness as weakness and therefore employ a bully-boy's technique, like the thug at school who delights in harassing the weak and the timid? Or is it that they resent patronage and regard kindness as being just that?

In those early days in Rhodesia, when the white population numbered only a few thousand, many Europeans were inclined to regard their native servants as having the mentality and outlook of children, and would joke and laugh about the silly things their employees did. They liked to be thought of as strict but kindly parents. Few knew anything about the history and the background and the culture of the people they were now living among. They felt the Mashonas should like them and be pleased to have them living among them, for had they not freed them from the tyranny of the Matabele? Similarly, they thought the Matabele should be grateful for having freed them from the autocratic rule of Lobengula.

The two races were poles apart, not only in culture, social organisation, and belief, but in what each expected in life, and in their attitude to leisure, work and money. The British Government, the British South Africa Company, and the settlers felt obliged by public opinion to bring progress to the savages; but what did progress really mean, and did the natives want it? Putting it crudely, in so far as the Mashona were concerned, the European attitude was to pull them off the trees and cut off their tails in order to turn them into human beings! With the Matabele it was different, because they were already well organised. So in real terms progress meant teaching cleanliness, the rudiments of hygiene, the wearing of clothes and, above all, a desire to work.

The last-named objective was to be the most difficult to achieve, for the Mashona felt himself alien from his employers and from his employer's objectives. All he wanted was freedom to live his life in what was, in the European view, idleness. The outlook of the Matabele, shortly after the collapse of their rebellion, can be summed up in the words of an induna: 'Are we not humbled every day by our masters? There is nothing worth living for; better by far to have perished like men, than to grow fat like dogs on the white man's crumbs and offal.'

Many years before, poor Lobengula, while talking to the missionaries when he was allocating them land for the Hopetown Mission Station, said he thought God had made each nation as He wished it to be and as He intended it to remain – the white man skilled in all work; the black man possessed of cattle and well accustomed to the hunt and war. If he had intended the blacks to follow the same role as the whites, it was unfair that they had been left for so long in ignorance. Blacks should continue to live as God had intended them to do, and the whites, the way He had intended them to live. They should not interfere with each other's lifestyles.

Part II

White Overlords

Chapter XII

It was 1934, just fifty-four years since the Union Jack had first been flown in Rhodesia, that Gordon Maclaine, having graduated in agricultural science at Edinburgh University, arrived in the country.

Britain was still suffering the aftermath of world recession and jobs were hard to come by. Immediately after the graduation ceremony, he had addressed application after application to the departments of agriculture in all the British territories in south, central and east Africa, as well as to the large companies with estates and agricultural trading interests in those territories. Most didn't bother to reply, and the few that did were sorry they had no vacancies and none was likely to turn up in the near future.

So he decided that to be on the spot would probably be the best way to get a job. He limited his choice to Kenya and Southern Rhodesia; he had boyhood knowledge of Kenya, but of Southern Rhodesia, only what he had read in the brochures designed to attract settlers. It was a difficult choice to make, but in the end it was decided on the throw of a coin; he offered a silent prayer that in three throws the coin would be directed to the right destination – heads for Kenya and tails for Southern Rhodesia it would be. Then a few moments later he began to wonder whether, sub-consciously, he had influenced the toss of the coin; another and more fervent prayer for guidance, and yet again all three tosses said Southern Rhodesia. Six tails in a row couldn't possibly be wrong! He booked a passage on a Union Castle ship and disembarked at Beira in Mozambique, Portuguese East Africa.

Beira in those days was small, dusty and uninteresting. He spent the hot day seeing the few sights on offer, lunched at the one and only good hotel and caught the evening train to Salisbury. Unfortunately darkness prevented any view of the countryside. The train service was good and the bedding clean and adequate. At

Umtali, the first town on the Rhodesian side of the border, a customs officer and an immigration officer boarded the train. Both men were young, very polite and most helpful. Gordon explained to the immigration officer that he had only £50 on him and so could not afford expensive hotels. No problem; he was given the address of a boarding house which was clean and reasonable.

In his mind's eye, Gordon had pictured the country to be fairly heavily forested with wide grassy glades intervening, but now he was to see it was nothing like that. The trees in the wooded areas were not massive and dense but light, with spreading tops, and bore exotic-sounding names such as msasa, mfuti, mnondo. There were wide stretches of grassy plains spreading as far as the eye could see, with trees scattered here and there, to create a park-like effect. The vista was pleasant and far from monotonous, for the flattish landscape was broken by hilly outcrops or kopjes. The countryside bore no similarity to the vast grassy expanses which the train passed through on its way from Mombasa to Nairobi, with herds of wild animals grazing within sight of the railway line. Here there was not a wild animal to be seen. A fellow traveller explained the absence of game as being due to intensive and indiscriminate shooting by early settlers of practically everything with four legs. What a difference the sight of an odd lion or giraffe or zebra or of even a common or garden buck would have made!

The first stop of any duration was Inyazura. The railway station was an unpretentious brick building comprising a ticket office, a rest room, another room or two, and two separate blocks of toilets, one for each race. The area around the station was a scene of activity with white men dressed in open-necked shirts and shorts and with socks rolled round the ankles; their womenfolk were in colourful cotton dresses or in blouse and skirt. They all seemed busy directing their black staff in loading or unloading produce. Great 16-foot wagons were standing by with a *piccanin* squatting patiently at the head of the leading span of sixteen oxen. The driver armed with his very long-lash whip stood by chatting to onlookers. There were more half-ton pick-up trucks than cars parked in the yard. The African men were in shirt and shorts or in vest and shorts and barefooted, some of the upper garments being so full of holes that they must have had difficulty in getting head and arms through the right ones. The women, and there were not so many of them, wore long ankle-length dresses and seemed to have nothing to do but sit and gossip, or just gaze at the train in idle curiosity. The thing that struck Gordon most was that not a single African, neither adult nor *piccanin*, was to be seen begging or pestering the passengers – so unlike what he recalled on railway stations in Kenya. One other point: all seemed cheerful and healthy.

The next main stop was Rusape. The station buildings and the scene of activity were a replica of Inyazura, and so also was every other station on the line. Salisbury was different, with a more dignified building, no ox wagons or scotch carts but many more cars. Gordon took a taxi, driven by an African, to the address in Fife Avenue given him by the immigration officer at Umtali. It was a large colonial-style bungalow with five or six bedrooms. The proprietress, very obviously a Yorkshire woman, was sorry there was only a small back room available. It was small and had no outlook, but Gordon felt it would do until he could find something better. Lunch and dinner were his first two meals, and both made him decide to make his stay a short one.

The following morning he walked down to the Standard Bank of South Africa in Manica Road, to see whether the draft he had sent from Edinburgh had arrived, and whether there were any letters for him, as he had given the bank as a temporary address of convenience.

The receptionist at the enquiry desk was friendly and helpful and gave him the address of the guest house at which she was staying and directions on how to get there. These took him through one of the nicest parks he had ever seen. It stretched over several acres and the person who designed it must have had a wonderful eye for art and planning. Beautifully kept lawns, graceful colourful trees and frangipanis, oleanders, hibiscus and a myriad of other colourful shrubs were all there. The splendidly kept roads and pathways leading to the centrepiece, a raised and covered bandstand, were bordered by masses of annuals and biennials. No cycling, and no cars, made it a tranquil haven.

As he got to know Salisbury, the more Gordon realised how beautifully it had been planned. The planners had used to full advantage the fairly level site and had laid out the roads in the residential area on a grid system, with avenues running east to west and streets north to south. Each was bordered by a double row of trees, either mauve jacarandas, or scarlet flamboyantes, or deep red spathodeas, or leafy green tunas. The roads were wide, and behind each row of houses a sanitary lane was provided for the removal of dustbins, and for the clearance at night of the toilet buckets from the servants' quarters.

The guest house was in Rhodes Avenue, which fronted the park. Once again it was a colonial-style bungalow with verandas and corrugated-iron roof. This one was owned and run by a lady from Dundee and, on seeing a fellow Scot at the door, she was more than usually helpful. Certainly he could have a room in the annexe, a single line of five bedrooms fronted by a veranda, with a toilet and bathroom running at right angles at one end. Cold water was laid on in the bathroom, but when hot water was needed the bedroom boy would bring it in the ubiquitous four-gallon kerosene tin. What a host of uses was found for this tin right across the length and breadth of Africa!

Gordon's next place of call was the Department of Agriculture to let them know he was on the spot and eager for a job. To his surprise and relief he was taken straight through to see the Director himself, and not some junior official. Doctor Charles K. Brain was of medium build with keen bright eyes and a warm and friendly manner; there was nothing pompous about him. Unfortunately, there were no vacancies in his department at the moment, but there were plans in hand to establish a research station for tobacco in a few months hence. He was sure the board, which would be responsible for administering it, would show interest in a young man who had travelled at his own expense from Scotland, to a country about which he knew nothing and where he knew no one.

Gordon explained he would have to find a job, any kind of job, because his funds were very limited. Doctor Brain undertook to find out from farmers who called at the office whether any of them wanted an assistant or a manager, and he warned Gordon not to expect much in the way of wages, for Rhodesia, like Britain, was suffering from the world recession. Then came the most friendly and hospitable gesture of all – an invitation to sundowners and pot-luck that evening. 'I'll call for you at six.'

Mrs Brain was a particularly attractive and charming lady who made Gordon feel at home instantly. Both she and her husband had come to Rhodesia from South Africa only a couple of years earlier and were already very taken with the country. Gordon thoroughly enjoyed his evening in the friendly family atmosphere with the two children playing on the lounge floor. He bade them goodnight feeling braced and optimistic with Mrs Brain's parting words: 'If Charles says he will help you, you may count on it that he will.'

A couple of days later there was a message at the guest house for him to call at the Agriculture Department at 2 p.m.; he was there promptly. Dr Brain informed him that a William Dewksbury-Brown (not his real name) was in need of an assistant, as he himself was on so many boards and committees that he was unable to devote as much time as he should to the farm. The snag was that he was not in a position to pay much. However, Gordon could discuss this with him as he was due to call at the office at 2.15 p.m.

Dewksbury-Brown was a very hail-fellow-well-met with never-a-care-in-the-world type of man in his late thirties. Gordon was to learn later on that he was a remittance man of whom there were quite a few in the Colony, having been the black sheep in a highly respected and influential family in Scotland. In order to get him out of the way, his father had offered to set him up in farming in Southern Rhodesia and to pay him a generous allowance each year, provided he undertook to stay well away from Britain. The idea suited son William down to the ground and came just in time to avoid the problem, which would have arisen, of a girlfriend with an expanding waistline! Within a week he was packed and was boarding a ship at Tilbury Docks for Rhodesia via Cape Town.

Unfortunately he knew very little about farming and still less about cattle. He did know that Friesians were a good dairy breed and that they were black and white. The wide-awake cattle dealer whom he approached had no difficulty in summing him up as a rooinek. Afrikaans for red neck, a term used somewhat disparagingly to describe inexperienced Englishmen. He supplied poor William with ordinary black and white native cows at prices prevailing for top-grade Friesians! It did not take long for the story to get around and for poor William Dewksbury-Brown to become the butt of many a joke. Mistake followed mistake, until he met and married a South African girl who had been born and brought up on a farm. By the time he met Gordon, he had learned a lot from her about farming, and was now an active member on sundry boards and committees where his natural flair for debate, and the art of persuasion, were useful assets.

Gordon's first impression of him was of a man you could not help but like, even while harbouring doubts in the back of your mind about his dependability and trustworthiness. There was no doubting the excellence of his salesmanship; he kept stressing what a wide range of experience Gordon would gain of local conditions, and what a pleasant life he would lead in Inyazura with a regular round of invitations from neighbouring farmers and tobacco growers to tennis, sundowners and the occasional dance. The only snag was that owing to a bad season or two 'Mark you, through no fault of mine, but of Mother Nature, I can only offer you £10 a month and, of course, your keep and good accommodation, excellent meals, old boy, for my old lady is first class at housekeeping. Be nice to her and she'll darn your socks and stitch on your buttons!'

To the holder of a BSc degree in Agriculture from the best of Scottish Universities, £10 a month was a shock indeed, but he felt the practical experience he would gain would stand him in good stead. So he accepted, on the understanding that he would not be bound by any contract and would be free to leave any time he wished. 'A deal it is,' said William Dewkesbury-Brown. 'I'll collect you from your digs at 4.00, and just call me DB, everyone does.'

He was right on time and accompanied by a very attractive redhead with green eyes, full bosom and lovely legs who he introduced as the secretary of the board meeting he had just attended. They headed straight for Meikles Hotel where DB delighted in playing host and would not hear of Gordon standing a round. It soon became obvious that DB and Stella were seeing quite a bit of each other, and that the next committee meeting he was due to attend was really an assignation with her. So that's why he can't afford more than £10 a month, thought Gordon. But, in all fairness, he couldn't blame him, for she was really a lovely piece, and he began to wonder what Mrs DB was like.

On leaving the wide streets of town they came onto tarmacadam strips – two strips set apart the distance of car wheels by an intervening metalled area, not ideal by any manner of means but an excellent way of curtailing costs of road construction. After a few miles, the strips came to an end, and then Gordon was to find out what corrugations and potholes were really like. He was to learn that the only way to deal with corrugations was to drive as fast as the potholes permitted, so that the wheels skimmed from crest of ridge to crest and avoided the hollows in between.

For most of the way the road and railway line ran parallel to each other, so the countryside was the same as he had seen from the train on the way up from Beira. But between Salisbury and the township of Marandellas, they drove close to some extraordinary rock formations. It was just as though giants had been at play piling enormous boulder on boulder at angles defying all laws of gravity. What was even more extraordinary was to see an occasional fully-grown tree, generally a wild fig, having grown, in some miraculous fashion, through the narrow cracks and crannies between the rocks. There was not a wild animal to be seen apart from lizards and very occasionally rock rabbit.

Suddenly the car was brought to a stop. 'See that very large boulder?' enquired DB, 'Well, a week or so ago I was giving a hospital nurse a lift. When we got here she asked me to stop as she was bursting to spend a penny. I went along with her to make sure there were no *skellums* [insects] or snakes. When we got back to the car she suddenly realised she had left her panty girdle behind. What do you think of that for a novel invitation? After that the rest of the journey became a lot more interesting, I can tell you!'

It took Gordon quite a time to puzzle out the conundrum, so long that he became sure his employer's opinion of him had slumped badly, while DB found it hard to believe that a young university graduate could be so ignorant about women's underwear, putting it down to Scottish prudery.

Marandellas, the first township they came to, was only a small place with a railway station, a hotel, a store, a post office, and a few houses. They went into the small and rather unpretentious-looking hotel where DB was immediately waylaid by a couple of farmers and their wives, with a problem connected with one of the boards on which he was a member. Gordon was interested to see the able way in which he dealt with the matter; it helped to reassure him that there was more to DB than met the eye. It also caused him some amusement to note with what pride he introduced Gordon as 'my manager; just out from Scotland – a professional man waiting for an opening in the Department'.

While the men talked business to DB, the ladies chatted to Gordon. One of them gave him a carefully guarded hint not to take DB at face value, for while he was a very sociable and likeable character, he had been linked, rightly or wrongly, she didn't know, with a shady deal or two in land. The other said how sorry she was for his wife. 'He can't resist a bit of skirt.'

'It's not the bit of skirt he can't resist,' her friend commented, 'it's the bit underneath it!'

Both assured him he would be very welcome at their homes any time he was passing through.

Rusape was the next town and also the next stop. From the train it had reminded him of a film version of a Wild West town. Now, standing in the main street, he felt he should see a rider coming in leading a second horse with a body draped over the saddle. There was no sign of life around the one and only hotel except for a light on the veranda and one in the lounge. The silence however was no deterrent to DB who strode through the passage to the back of the building, hailing the proprietor. An elderly man with distinctly Jewish features appeared and was none too pleased at being disturbed. 'I just wanted you to meet my new manager, as you will probably be seeing quite a lot of him.'

The proprietor was not taken in by this lame excuse. 'Come on into the lounge. I suppose you want a drink.' He led them to a table and then went off to return with a newly opened bottle of Black and White whisky. He slammed it on the table with a couple of glasses and a note pad and pencil. 'Sign for what you drink and make sure you close the door when you leave.'

'He was not very pleased at being disturbed,' remarked Gordon.

'Oh, don't be worried about that,' replied DB. 'He is a taciturn old blighter at the best of times. You must get him to tell you about his experiences in the old days. He made a mint trading with the natives. When he likes, he can be the most interesting man going; he knew all the old-timers, both black and white. Now, his main interest is his very young and attractive wife.'

'A young wife?' exclaimed Gordon.

'Yes, rumour has it that he traded her in for her father's bad debts, but I don't believe that story. The fact is he is married to her and is very jealous of her, so watch your step.'

'With a shape like his,' remarked Gordon, 'I don't suppose he poses any risk to her virginity. What is wrong with him?'

'It is supposed to be a very bad, and very neglected hernia, from the old days when there were no doctors around.'

At Inyazura, the next and last township on their journey, DB made straight for the bungalow behind the one and only store, for he wanted Gordon to buy a pair of tackies (gym shoes) as he felt sure they would get a game of tennis at the weekend. Gordon protested at the late hour for it was past nine.

'You don't need to worry about that. They are dagoes, Greeks. They don't mind being disturbed so long as money reaches their greasy little paws. Incidentally, another branch of the family farms next to me and they have two lovely young daughters. The younger one is an absolute peach. I bet you'll fall for her, but you'll have a hell of a job getting her on her own, for the grandparents watch like hawks. They are a couple of real old peasants who speak not a word of English; the old girl looks like a witch in the long black dresses she wears, just as she did in her Greek village.'

DB was right about them not becoming annoyed at being

disturbed at so late an hour. A young member of the family was sent to open up the store, and they were invited to return to the house for drinks after they had bought what they wanted. Gordon couldn't get over such hospitality. Where in Britain would you come across anything like this?

Once more, back on the road, Gordon asked DB whether his wife didn't mind being left so much on her own on an isolated farm of 2,500 acres. 'No,' DB explained, 'on farms, when any man is to be away for a night or more, he arranges for one of the bachelors in the district to move in and keep guard. I always call on our local policeman. Una likes him, she has a strange opinion about him: although he is always smartly dressed, she accuses him of not being too fond of water, so willy nilly she drags him off to the bathroom and scrubs his back. At first he used to be upset, but now he takes it like a man!'

Gordon wondered whether there was a double meaning to the last sentence, but he thought better not to ask. 'Lucky young bachelors,' was all he said.

'No, no. We have an unwritten code which must be observed. No hanky panky, even if the woman asks for it.'

Gordon wondered who was to know whether or not hanky panky took place, for only the man and the woman would really be in the know.

As the distance between the township and farm was reduced, so DB seemed to become more and more on edge. He started to talk about his wife in short staccato sentences: 'She is very tall – and big, but a good-looker. Very outspoken, but with a heart of gold. Plays a jolly good game of tennis. Stands for no nonsense. Will be in a hell of a temper at my being so late, but don't pay any attention to what she will have to say – she won't mean any of it.'

She must have seen the lights of the car approaching down the long driveway, for she was standing on the front veranda as they pulled up. DB had not exaggerated when he had said she was tall. Her height was accentuated by the black pyjamas she was wearing with not a spot of colour to brighten them. He had barely got his car door open when the tirade started: 'What time is this to be getting home? It's not fair; I slog from early morning looking after a child, looking after a farm, looking after a house, while you go enjoying yourself!'

'Hush my love, hush! I have someone with me, a big surprise for you. This is Gordon Maclaine; Gordon my wife Una. Gordon is going to be our new manager – so that will save you a lot of work.'

'Manager! Did you say manager? You must be out of your mind!'

'Leave it for now, love. Leave it for now. I will explain later.'

'It's just not fair, Mr Maclaine. I am worried sick when he is late getting back, for he can never say no to a drink. One day he will kill himself, or worse still, someone else.' Then the inherent trait of colonial hospitality overcame anger and anxiety: 'What are we doing standing our here! Come on in. I'm sure you haven't had anything to eat. I'll get you something while you help William get a bed for you.'

It was a very tiny room – just the end of the veranda partitioned off to make a room, which was cluttered with a writing desk, two saddles and bridles and an assortment of odds and ends. A space was cleared in the centre for a camp bed – presumably the one kept for George the policeman when he came to spend the night on guard. An upturned box was to serve as bedside table. Gordon began to wonder whether this was to be a sample of the 'excellent keep' he was promised as part of his remuneration.

Had William been on his own, Una would have warmed up the food she had set aside for him all evening, but now, with Gordon there, she decided on a mixed grill and strong black coffee. After the meal, and when bidding Gordon goodnight and checking to see he knew how to turn off the pressure lamp, William explained apologetically that they would have to make an early start the following morning: 'Roll call at 6.00 so don't bother to wash and shave till after breakfast at around about 7.30 or 8.00.'

Gordon was roused at 5.30 by the houseboy bringing in a pot of tea and buttered toast. Gordon noted he gave no form of greeting, so unlike servants in Kenya with their friendly 'Jambo, bwana'.

He quickly slipped on shirt and shorts, with socks rolled down to the ankles, and was just lacing his shoes, when there was a knock on the door and William's head poked through the opening. Gordon was somewhat surprised to see how bright and cheerful he was so early in the morning and after a day of fairly heavy drinking.

It was a glorious morning with a bright blue cloudless sky and just a slight nip in the air to make it pleasant. The two men strolled down towards the outbuildings, where a gang of about thirty natives were squatting on the ground, absorbing the morning sunshine. There was a murmur of interest at the sight of the new white face and speculation as to whether he was just a visitor or someone who had come to stay, and if so, in what capacity. As William and Gordon approached them, they all rose to their feet and those who had been wearing caps or hats removed them and held them in their hands. A well-built man came forward carrying a board to which tickets were pinned. William introduced him as Zebedee, the *capitao* or foreman, and told him to tell the men that this was Mr Gordon who was to be the new manager. Most took the news with a friendly grin, but to the others it appeared to be of no interest at all.

Gordon noticed that the *capitao* didn't look very pleased and actually asked, 'Is the inkosikaas going away then?'

'No,' came the reply, 'She will be here but Mr Gordon will manage the farm whenever I am away.'

For each boy there was a ticket marked off into thirty squares. As the roll was called and he answered to his name, the day's date was entered in a square. When thirty squares were completed, he became eligible to draw his month's wages. It was quite a good scheme, because if the employee didn't wish to work on a particular day, he didn't turn up for roll call and had the day off without pay; and from the employer's point of view it was also useful, for he could see at a glance who was a reliable worker and who took ages to complete a ticket through frequent absenteeism.

When the roll call was completed, those with fixed jobs like the ox-team driver and his *piccanin* who led the leading span, the dairyman, the cattle herd and the five boys working in the tobacco nursery, strolled off to their respective tasks. The *capitao* took the remainder off to stumping or land clearing. William and Gordon wended their way to the tobacco seedbeds, sited on open level ground, near to the borehole which had been drilled to a depth of some 70 feet. It was essential for the beds to be adjacent to a permanent water supply, because in the early stages the seedlings had to be kept moist all the time, which meant watering them anywhere between three and five times a day.

As they strolled along, Gordon asked, 'Have you any Matabele?'

'No, not one. The *capitao* and about seventeen of his cronies are Mashonas and the remainder of the gang is divided fairly equally between Nyasas from Nyasaland and natives from Mozambique in Portuguese East Africa. The Nyasas and the Portuguese boys are good; the Mashonas are pretty hopeless, not because they are any less intelligent, but because they live too close to home – there are too many attractions and interests close to hand for them to work regularly; they are also more light-fingered, lazy and cute. Una thinks a lot of Zebedee, largely because he plays up to her. I don't care for him much, but he has his uses; he carries some influence in his reserve and always manages to recruit temporary labour when I most need it for planting out tobacco and at reaping time.'

'As a matter of interest' enquired Gordon, 'Why did they all stand up when we approached? All the books I've read on African customs say that politeness demands that the lesser fry remain seated before their superiors; that it is a gross breach of etiquette for a junior to stand while being addressed by a senior.'

'True, fellow-me-lad' (Gordon winced at the horrible expression) replied William, 'that was the custom in native times, but now they have to observe European custom. We regard it as cheeky for a labourer to remain seated while we speak to him, unless of course, he is sick or disabled.'

The seedbed site was enclosed by a tall grass screen on all four sides to protect it from the breeze and from stray animals. At the entrance stood a pail containing a solution of potassium permanganate, in which everyone entering the site had to wash his hands, as protection against introducing the virus carrying the disease known as mosaic. The boys working on the site were specially selected, not only for being conscientious workers, but also as non-smokers and non-takers of snuff, because the virus was carried in both cigarettes and snuff. Each bed was 30 yards long by 1 yard wide, and was protected from the weather by cheese cloth stretched tent-fashion over it. As the seedlings grew, so they were subjected to an increasing amount of sunlight each day, until they were completely exposed for hardening off a few days before being transplanted in the field.

After breakfast, William took Gordon on a tour of the farm outbuildings. These comprised a block of five tobacco curing barns each 20 feet x 20 feet x 20 feet high; a large tobacco bulking shed; a large tobacco grading and packing shed with clear glass or perspex let into the corrugated-iron roof for lighting; a large shed open in front and partitioned off into stalls to serve as a milking shed; a grain and general farm store, an implement shed and a 'kaffir store' which did a good trade in cheap cotton blankets, sugar, tea, cigarettes, mealie meal and the odd bicycle. An employee could buy on tick against his wages – a useful way of keeping one's staff.

The homestead was an unpretentious bungalow, comprising a large living room, two bedrooms leading directly off it, a kitchen with a wood-burning stove, and a bathroom with both hot and cold running water. The cold came from two large corrugated-iron reservoirs which collected rain water from the roof, while the hot came from a 44-gallon petrol drum heated over an open-hearth furnace. The front veranda was the main feature of the building, with one end partitioned off to make a small third bedroom or storeroom, the one being used by Gordon.

In the back yard was the dry lavatory or *piccanin kaia* (literally small house normally referred to as the PK) – a deep hole in the ground on top of which was mounted the thunderbox! Sand or ashes took the place of water. Many a tale was told, sometimes true, of the snake which popped out from between the persons thighs!

With the exception of the PK, all the buildings were of brick which had actually been made and fired on the farm out of a mixture of clay, sand and antheap. How truly proud the British settlers should be of the amazing progress made in a short span of some forty years!

It was now 1934, only forty-four years since the Union Jack was first flown on the kopje at Salisbury. In that short time land had been cleared for farms and settlements across the length and breadth of the colony. No longer did the Mashona go around naked or semi-naked, covered in flies and dirt. Gordon wondered how the African mind really reacted to such rapid transformation. People who had not known what a wheel even looked like, were now seeing, and even travelling, in cars, lorries, and trains. Bush paths were giving way to metalled roads. In towns the mere touch of a finger on a switch changed darkness into light. People whose greatest achievement had been the building of pole and dagga huts, were now seeing and helping to construct large dwellings made of brick. Where there had not been a sight of water, boreholes and wells were now pumping it out. The more sensitive might dislike the wording, but there was much truth in the often-heard maxim 'We pulled them down from the trees, cut off their tails and made them into human beings'.

From the nursery site William and Gordon made their way to the area being stumped (cleared). Each boy had been allocated a tree by the *capitao*, but there would be two boys to a very large one. All the earth was dug out with *badzas* (mattocks) from around the base of the tree to expose its roots, and these were then severed a good two feet or more below ground level. 'What you have to watch out for,' explained William, 'is that no roots are left near the surface to snag a plough share and twist or break it; not only are shares expensive, but they are also hard to get in a hurry. So don't let them fill up the holes until you have inspected each one. Don't take the *capitao*'s word that all is well.'

In most cases the weight of the treetop caused it to crash, but if that failed, then, of course, it would have to be hauled down with ropes. Once felled to the ground its branches would be lopped off and dragged away from the site being cleared. The trunk was chopped into lengths of four feet to be stacked in 'cords' which were later transported by ox-wagon to the tobacco barns to serve as fuel during the tobacco curing process.

Gordon wondered what the Africans made of this work, the very basis of a permanent form of agriculture. All that they had ever done for themselves was to select a piece of land, chop off the tops of the trees at a convenient height and set fire to the lot. When the embers had cooled down, the site would be dug over by hand, ready for planting whatever crop they intended to sow – maize or sorgum. When that particular piece of land lost its fertility, they would move to another plot and repeat the process – a very wasteful form of land usage.

On his first Saturday on the farm, Gordon was included in an invitation to tennis on a neighbour's farm a few miles away. This was a well-established property as one could easily detect as they drove up the long tree-lined avenue leading to the house – a fine colonial-style building with deep veranda and lovely Dutch gables. The grounds around the house were closed off from the rest of the farm by a hibiscus hedge. The clay tennis court, with an attractive summer-house, formed the main feature on a well-tended lawn, on which widely spaced clumps of shrubs were planted to lend colour to the whole scene. Added colour and shade were provided by jacarandas and a beautifully spreading flamboyant and silver-grey eucalyptus. All this had been achieved by the Thompson family in less than twenty years. Gordon vowed that one day he would have a place like this. How different from the Dewksbury-Browns', where the only pretence at a garden was a narrow bed of marigolds edging the length of the veranda, and a few eucalyptus trees planted at random in the yard.

Two houseboys in well-starched white jackets buttoning at the neck, and wearing long white trousers brought afternoon tea to the summerhouse, so different from poor Tom in his shabby shirt and patched shorts. These two boys were grinning broadly and took pride in their own persons. Strange, thought Gordon, how servants whether they are white, brown or black, reflect the status of their employer. A colonel's bearer considers himself, and acts superior to a captain's; and both look down on an NCO's servant. Snobbery prevails at all levels.

While sitting out a set, Mrs Thompson asked Gordon how he was liking the country and expressed the hope that he would stay with the Dewksbury-Browns longer than had his predecessor.

'My predecessor?' he asked in surprise. 'I thought I was the first white person they had employed.'

'Oh no,' came the reply. 'They had a very capable young Dutchman called van Rensburg, but he left after a couple of months; he couldn't get on with Mrs Brown. Apparently they fell out over the *capitao* – incidentally that is someone you want to watch. My husband has warned him off our property, and so have some of the other neighbours – we've caught him black-birding right in the middle of the busy season!'

'Two questions, Mrs Thompson. By Dutchman I take it you mean an Afrikaner?'

'Yes. We British always refer to them as Dutchmen. After all, most of them are of Dutch descent – the progeny of the old Boers who were the first whites to settle in South Africa.'

'My other question is, what is black-birding?'

Mrs Thompson laughed, 'Oh that means pinching your black labour – a most heinous offence, as you can well imagine. That *capitao* of theirs is a thorough rogue in many other ways too. Just you watch him!'

Later on, Gordon was again sitting out a set, this time with the local Native Commissioner for the district – a golden opportunity to find the answers to some of the questions he was asking himself. 'Aren't there enough Mashonas and Matabele to supply all the labour that is needed on white farms, without bringing in Nyasa and Portuguese?' he enquired.

'Yes, I suppose there are, but firstly the Matabele are cattlemen and don't make good *badza* [hoe] boys, and prefer to remain in their own homeland. Also, as they were the previous and rather ruthless overlords, they wouldn't be very welcome among the Mashona who now enjoy British protection. Secondly, government policy is to encourage the Mashonas – and the Matabele for that matter – to farm their own reserves in a form of stable agriculture, putting into practice the methods they see the white farmers employing. Thirdly, the Mashonas are more attracted by city lights and the less arduous work of houseboys, to labouring on farms.'

'Another thing that puzzles me,' remarked Gordon, 'is that the settlers don't bother to learn the local languages. In Kenya all white settlers speak Swahili, and a few speak even Ki-Swahili.

'Ordinary Swahili is quite a good lingua franca in which one can express themselves fairly well, but the kitchen-Kaffir being used in Rhodesia is very limited in scope. Surely the main purpose of language is to express, in depth, one's thoughts and intentions and so get to know and understand each other's viewpoint. But that is impossible with kitchen-Kaffir; as far as I can see it is only suitable for conveying orders: *Buisa lapa*, bring it here; *faga lapa*, put it there.'

'Yes,' laughed the Native Commissioner. 'You are perfectly right, it is just a *lapa lapa* language with very limited scope. The lack of free expression between the Matabele and ourselves was the cause of much misunderstanding and bitterness – and bloodshed. That is why, after the rebellion, native commissioners were required to pass examinations in the local tongue.'

As soon as the run of conversation permitted, Gordon managed to veer it back to local custom. 'Why is it,' he asked 'that only men are employed for housework, when in their own homes, the native women do all the work, both in and out of doors, while the men sit around drinking and telling tales?'

Mary Thompson thought it was because the women were less intelligent than the men and were more smelly. 'You want to be present at my morning clinic, when not only our own boys turn up for treatment, but the women and children too. Sometimes the smell from the women is almost overpowering. Also it is difficult to get sensible answers out of them.'

DB thought it was because the men resented their womenfolk working in white households in case they got led astray by their bosses. 'Don't forget, they know from the Mozambique boys who come over how the Portuguese have black mistresses sleeping on their back verandas in case the wife develops a headache! Besides, if the women worked in our houses, who would do the work in their own houses?'

Another guest intervened. 'We don't stand for our women fraternising with blacks, and I suppose they don't want their women doing the same with whites and browns.'

The Native Commissioner joined in. 'All three of you have made valid points, but already I am noticing a change in the outlook of native women. They are seeing how white women enjoy equality with white men, and so, now, they too are beginning to exert themselves. My guess is that in a very short time they will be going out in large numbers to work and earn money for new clothes. Mary, you made the point that the women are dirty and smelly, but don't forget that Mashona males, only a few years back, were described by the early pioneers as being incredibly filthy and covered in flies. Close contact with whites has worked wonders for their menfolk and I am sure it will do the same for the women.'

As the party broke up and the farewells were being said, Mary Thompson pressed Gordon's hand, and whispered, 'Don't forget what I told you; be on your guard. We would like you to stay among us.'

The law required every employer of native labour to provide each employee with 2lb of mealie meal (maize meal) per day, 2lb of protein in the form of fresh meat or beans or ground nuts per week and with salt ad lib. This, of course, was in addition to wages. Alternatively, they could give a cash equivalent. All farmers opted to provide the ration rather than the money, because experience had shown that the African worker would spend most of the cash in buying items other than food and so, by mid-week, would be too hungry to work and be pleading for food.

On the Dewkesbury-Brown farm Friday was ration day – much looked forward to by the labour force – particularly the meat ration. The drill was for the *capitao* to lay the meat out in heaps, one for each boy, and as meat was the most coveted part of the ration, he was to ensure that the division was made absolutely fairly so that each would receive the same proportion of flesh to bone. Obviously the *capitao* was expected to favour himself a little, but otherwise there was to be complete impartiality.

On the Friday following the tennis party, Gordon went along to supervise the rationing. He wasn't altogether surprised to find some lots of meat with more flesh than others and some which were practically bone alone. Equally not surprising was that the number of favoured heaps neatly coincided with the number of Mashonas employed. He ordered Zebedee to make a redistribution and this time fairly. Zebedee was furious, but said nothing other than that the inkos left it to him to do the apportioning as he saw fit. 'Well, from now on,' said Gordon, 'you will do it under my supervision.'

That night at dinner Una informed Gordon that she had heard that he had interfered with the rationing and had upset Zebedee. 'Please don't do it again as I don't want trouble while DB is away. We don't want to lose Zebedee. He is most valuable in recruiting labour when we most need it.'

'Yes. I have heard that he black-birds for you, to the annoyance of your neighbours.'

'I know where you got that from,' she snapped and remained quiet for the rest of the evening, not even condescending to say goodnight when she went off to bed.

A week or so later there was more trouble, this time over an order given by Gordon being countermanded by Una at Zebedee's request and without Gordon's knowledge. More words passed between Gordon and Una and she sulked for a couple of days.

It became increasingly obvious that each time DB was away on one of his innumerable committee or girlfriend meetings, that Zebedee played up, and that Una always swallowed his plausible lies. Seeing that he couldn't count on any support from her and that his authority was being undermined, Gordon reminded her that his terms of employment did not require him to serve notice, so he would pack his case and catch the train to Salisbury the following morning.

Back in Salisbury, Gordon called on Dr and Mrs Brain. They were pleased to see him. 'This is quite extraordinary,' said the Doctor, 'I have heard of a job that is going, and which I think would suit you down to the ground. I have been debating with myself how to get in touch with you without giving Dewkesbury-Brown cause to complain, about first introducing you to him and then attracting you away. However, now that you have left him of your own accord the road is clear. A Mr Charles Holland [not his real name], one of our bigger landowners, is looking for someone to run the cattle side of his business. I thought of you and spoke to him about you, but, of course, neither of us could take any action.'

'That sounds just my cup of tea. Animal husbandry is my forte, or was, at Edinburgh. How do I get in touch with Mr Holland?'

'I'll take you to his place tomorrow afternoon. It is only a few miles out of town.'

Charles Holland was in his seventies, of slender and erect build with very fair complexion, silver hair and most courteous Old World manners. He was proud of having held a senior position in government service before retiring, and was now the owner of three adjoining farms totalling just over 8,000 acres. There were buildings only on the home farm, the other two being left undeveloped and were kept as grazing land for his herd of several hundred cattle. Mrs Holland was an invalid, confined most of the time to an easy chair in an attractive chalet, built especially for her in the garden. He had three daughters but no sons.

Gordon's eye was immediately caught by the youngest girl Lorna, with her father's clear rosy complexion and large blue eyes set wide apart; but it was the eldest girl Dora who set her eyes and mind on him. She was married to Peter Richards, Mr Holland's general manager. He was a quiet unassuming man who looked more like a studious intellectual than a farmer. He is too good for his wife, thought Dr Brain, as he watched the flirtatious looks Dora was giving Gordon. He had to admit to himself, though, that she was a real beauty with her unruly mass of shiny auburn hair, bright green eyes and a mouth just bordering on the full. The middle girl, Creena, was quite unlike her sister, rather delicate looking with pale complexion and gentle brown eyes. She was sent off to arrange afternoon tea.

Peter had been running the entire property: several hundred head of cattle, a small dairy herd, a few pigs, 50 acres of maize and 25 acres of flue-cured Virginia tobacco. Mr Holland explained that with the future of tobacco now looking so much more promising, he was intending to increase the acreage to 50 or 60, which would keep Peter fully occupied. Hence the need to find some one to manage the livestock and maize side of the business.

After tea, Charles Holland invited Gordon into his office where they could discuss matters in private. It resulted in Gordon accepting the job at £20 per month, plus board and lodging, and the services of a personal servant. The salary was double what DB had paid him, but it still fell short of what he thought the holder of a science degree in Agriculture could expect. However, the thought of seeing Lorna's blue eyes every day could be regarded as a bonus; also, his cash supply was reaching a low level.

He wanted a couple of days free to look for a second-hand car within his financial limits, and so agreed to start work on the ensuing Monday. 'Come now and I will show you and the Doctor round the homestead, and I am sure you would like to see your quarters.' As they were going out, he was called away by Creena to attend to something, so Peter and Dora conducted them on the tour.

Gordon was more than pleased with his quarters-to-be, a rondaval normally used as a guest house; a large circular building of brick under thatch, set on its own in a coppice of trees, with the usual outdoor PK. His servant's duties would be to make his early morning tea, make his bed, do his washing and ironing, polish his boots and shoes. The washing facilities were a galvanised bathtub, and china jug and basin. There was a nice carpet on the floor, a couple of easy chairs and a writing desk and chair. 'Have you got a houseboy?' Dora enquired.

When he said he hadn't, she offered to pick a clean and intelligent boy from the work force and to train him in his duties. She was then leading the two visitors to her house when her father rejoined them, and insisted they return to the homestead for sundowners. Gordon felt he was going to be happy here; the whole atmosphere was so different from that at the Dewksbury-Browns.

As they were taking their departure, Dora suggested that as he would be on his own for a few days, why not come out Sunday afternoon in time for tennis at 2.30? She said, if he hadn't got a car by then, she would call for him; they usually had a few friends and neighbours over on Saturday and Sunday afternoons. She also invited the Brains but the Doctor declined.

A very nice tea was laid out by Creena for the tennis. Justin, the senior houseboy, in spotless white uniform and wearing white cotton gloves, stood by to hand round finely cut sandwiches, cakes and freshly baked scones. One could sense his feeling of pride at being in the service of the biggest landowner in the area.

Peter, with his thick lenses and apparently poor physique, played a far better game than Gordon had expected him to do. Obviously he was more tough and wiry than he looked. Dora was a very good player with a strong, accurate serve and a fairly powerful forehand drive. Lorna played a fair, steady game, but Creena was the biggest surprise. She looked so pale and slender and rather tired when off the court, but on it, she seemed to come to life, moved well, and was most sprightly at the net.

Tennis was followed by sundowners on the front stoep (veranda). Conversation centred mainly on what promise the sale of the tobacco crop held in store for them, and severe criticism of the grossly unwise statements, and behaviour, of a left-wing politician from Britain, who was visiting Rhodesia at the time.

It was felt that he was stirring up trouble by preaching greater opportunity of advancement for Africans, while completely losing sight that only forty years or so earlier, they wore smelly leather flaps and were covered in flies. Surely few colonists anywhere else in the world could have achieved so much in so short a time! Why, it had taken a lot longer for the Romans to civilise woaded Anglo-Saxons!

A few days later Gordon reported for duty, complete with a secondhand Chev 20cwt pick-up. Creena was the first to greet him and said, 'I'll come along with you to the rondaval to see that the boy has done all I told him to do. I am lending you our second houseboy, Sixpence, until you find and train someone yourself. He doesn't know a lot yet, but he is keen to learn, clean and honest.'

'Oh, Creena, I should have told you, Dora has offered to choose a boy for me and to train him.' She gave a little gurgle of laughter and said, 'Gordon, you can forget that. My sister means well, but she is hopeless at teaching servants. She is too happy-go-lucky and is not fussy enough. Halfway through she gives up. Some day when you are in her house you will see what I mean.' Gordon left it to her to do as she thought best.

Peter took over and showed him round the homestead farm with all the buildings for the tobacco crop, the dairy, the piggery and the poultry runs. Three horses were looking enquiringly over the half doors of their stables. Peter ordered Shillingy, the stable boy, to harness two, and they then rode out to have a cursory look at the other two farms. They had no buildings on them and were being used purely for grazing cattle. Each was under the management, if it could be called such, of a Mashona, who, in addition to his wages, was given a plot of land on which to grow his own food crops.

Gordon expressed surprise that Mashonas were being employed for that job, rather than Matabele, who were recognised as good cattlemen. 'I wish we did have Matabeles, but the boss insisted on Mashonas, for purely diplomatic reasons,' was the reply.

On the ride back, Peter explained one or two of the house rules. The 'old man' had some odd idiosyncrasies; one was strict punctuality, another was that he always changed into a dinner jacket for dinner and expected the ladies to wear long dresses or cocktail frocks, and the men to wear lounge suits or, preferably dinner jackets. Gordon said that in his case it would have to be a lounge suit for he didn't possess a dinner jacket and, on £20 a month, he couldn't afford to buy one. Grace was always said before dinner and a loyal toast to the Royal Family was always drunk after dinner.

Apparently, on Sunday nights a full dinner was not served – just a cold buffet, so that Moses, the old cook, who had been with the family for seventeen years, could go off duty from midday till Monday morning. The other house servants were given time off during the week.

Another routine was sundowners on the stoep every evening at about six. Whiskies and soda – Old Grouse and only Old Grouse – for the men, and brandies and ginger ale, or whatever other drink they fancied, for the ladies. That was the time set aside for Mr

Holland to receive reports on all the activities of the day and to discuss the projects for the morrow. After sundowners, Peter and Dora usually returned to their own house, while the others bathed and changed for dinner.

That first evening after dinner Mr Holland headed straight to his easy chair armed with a book. Creena went off to see to her invalid mother, and Lorna said she had to go up to a shed where the incubator was housed to turn the eggs. Gordon seized the opportunity to accompany her and took her arm as they stepped into the dark night. He was hoping she would show some sign of interest in him, but when he gave her arm a gentle squeeze, she didn't draw away but neither did she respond.

When she had finished with the incubator, they stayed on for a while chatting. By the light of the pressure lamp he thought her eyes looked bluer and larger. He was tempted to kiss her, but some second sense warned him not to go too fast with her.

He went to bed with her very much in his thoughts. Little did he know that she was thinking of him too, and was comparing him in her mind's eye with David, a young man of similar age and with a promising job in town.

Gordon was roused at sunrise by Sixpence bringing in a pot of tea and a couple of hot-buttered toasts. How nice to see a servant in clean uniform, and how nice to drink out of a bone china cup, instead of a heavy, thick, railway-type one like those at the Dewkesbury-Browns. But once again, as at DB's, there was no morning greeting from the boy. He just came into the rondaval, dumped the tray on the bedside table and went out to bring in a jug of hot water for shaving and washing.

Hastily, Gordon pulled on shirt and shorts, but when it came to rolled-down socks, he wondered whether that would be approved of by a man who dressed for dinner right out in the bundu (countryside), so he decided to test the water with stockings.

His first duty was to supervise the work being done in the milking shed, the creamery, the piggery and the poultry runs and then to go along to the main house for breakfast. The instructions were 'If

Creena isn't there, just tell old Moses what you fancy and he will prepare it for you.'

After breakfast he went to the office to ask Mr Holland which horse he could take as he wanted to take a good look at the cattle on all three farms. Dora was with her father and promptly said she would accompany him. Her father argued against her going, saying he was sure Gordon would prefer to be on his own. 'And how do you expect him to find out where the boundaries are without someone to show him?' she had asked and had got her way. She next sought out Creena. 'Be a dear and rustle up a packed lunch for two.' Poor Creena, thought Gordon, she seems to be at everyone's beck and call.

It was rather monotonous country the pair rode over, and yet, in its very stillness, there seemed to be a sense of majesty, triggered by its very loneliness. It was flat, open, grass-covered veld with only the occasional tree, but with a fairly generous distribution of anthills (termite-built mounds) some of them reaching 8 feet in height. They would be regarded as a dreadful nuisance by persons seeking land for cultivation, but they were not a problem for pastoralists.

The grass was bone dry and sadly lacking in nourishment for livestock. Two years earlier, when it had been green and lush, a dense swarm of locusts had left a swathe of devastation many miles wide. Then, the following year, when everyone was living in the hope of better times, the rains failed to such an extent that it turned into the worst drought ever experienced, even by African standards. It was only in the vleis (meadows) and along the banks of rivers that the grazing amounted to anything worthwhile.

In the 1990s, colonialism came to be regarded as a bad word in Britain. Children were even being taught to be ashamed of our past. Even in the mid-1900s, armchair critics sat in the comfort of their homes, invariably picturing colonial settlers as living in luxury in a beautiful climate. Few chose to consider the heart-breaking problems colonists were required to overcome; of how many families were made destitute by inclement weather, or by pest, or by the diseases which inflicted both man and his beasts. It was easy to envy settlers their servants, but, apart from India, those servants had to be taught the very rudimentary hygiene, and how to carry out the most elementary tasks.

Charles Holland had divided his beef herd into three groups, with one group per farm, each under the care of a Mashona *capitao*. The first one that Dora and Gordon visited was in the care of Ntizima. He was a tall lean figure, well past middle age, with grizzly grey hair and much-lined face; he was wearing khaki shorts with tears and patches and, although it was a hot day, a greasy old tweed jacket. Despite the bedraggled attire, there was a certain air of quiet dignity and of authority about him.

Ntizima took them to see the herd dispersed over a wide area of veld. Gordon was shocked by what he saw for there was not a plump beast among them. Many were just skin and bone, with ribs showing, and hide stretched tight over hipbones. At one place, a group of five men and boys were struggling to get a poor cow onto her feet from where she was lying, too weak to do it on her own. One man had her tail wrapped round his fist and was heaving upwards to raise her hindquarters; at the other end a man was pulling on her horns, while the other three had managed to get a rope under her and were pulling and tugging on that. The intention was good, but the method was sheer brutality. How many vertebrae in the poor emaciated tail would be completely disjointed, leaving nerves jangling horribly for the rest of her life – however long or short that life may be? He made the man release his hold on the tail and heave on her haunches instead.

Some distance further on, three men were trying to raise an emaciated steer to its feet, but this time the man at the fore end was dragging on its ears, for its horns had been polled. At the rear end the tail was once again wrapped around a fist, but, worse still, the third man was lighting a small fire under the belly of the poor creature. Once again, Gordon had to intervene.

They found the same sort of performance being repeated at the other two groups. It is strange, Gordon thought, how little regard men have for the pain they inflict on the very animals on which they rely for their livelihood.

At midday, Dora suggested they should ride to a kopje nearby and picnic in the shade of a tree growing successfully through the cracks between the boulders. Unfortunately they were beaten to the spot by a horde of red ants feasting on the carcass of some small animal, however, they soon found another site not quite so shady but reasonably comfortable. After the meal they relaxed. Gordon leaned back against a boulder while Dora stretched out with her head pillowed in his lap. He felt a great sense of pleasure in the natural way she did this; there was nothing coquettish. It was just as though they had been close friends for ages instead of for just a few hours.

She looked really lovely lying there fully relaxed with eyes closed against the glare. He was tempted to lean forward and kiss those full tender lips, but held back knowing it would break the magic spell of peace and togetherness. Instead, his fingers trailed caressingly through her mop of auburn hair, now shining like gold in the bright sunlight.

As though she was ashamed by the state of the cattle and the brutal methods being used, she broke the silence by explaining that although she rode all over the estate, she had never until now taken a real interest in the cattle. This had been one of the few occasions she had ever been in the midst of a herd.

Gordon took the opportunity to glean some information about her family. 'How did your father come to own such a big acreage – was it as a grant in the old days from the British South Africa Company?'

'No, nothing like that. He was a civil servant on the admin side. Land was going very cheap years ago, between £1 and £10 an acre. Sandy soils were going a lot cheaper than loams, and, as you can see, this is pretty poor stuff, so he got it really cheap. Then he bought the two neighbouring farms from their owners when the poor fellows were busted by the locusts and the drought. You have probably gathered he knows very little about farming; just what he has picked up from books and from the visits by advisory officers of the Department of Agriculture.'

'What about Peter? I take it he has a farming background.'

'Good heavens, no! He read history at Oxford, but as he wasn't very strong, particularly about the lungs, so his family sent him to Rhodesia. There was no demand here for historians, so he was cooling his heels in Dad's department as a clerk. I met him at a dance. He was so different from all the other men I was meeting in those days, that I was attracted to him and married him. We couldn't live on his salary as a clerk, so Daddy took him on to help with the estate. You will see he is not very experienced, but he makes up for it by being so hard working and conscientious. Dad thinks quite highly of him now.'

'Forgive me asking this, but doesn't he mind you going out riding for a full day in the bush with someone he doesn't really know?'

'Why should he?' she exclaimed in surprise. 'He trusts me,' and then as an afterthought added, 'I suppose he knows that no other man would want to take on a woman with three children!'

'I thought I saw four children at your house!'

'Heavens above, you don't think that little cafe au lait is mine! Her parents, Cape coloureds, worked for my bachelor uncle. Both were killed in a car accident, and as no other relatives could be traced, Peter and I took her in. We are very fond of her but haven't taken out adoption papers in case some member of her family turns up eventually. She is a dear little thing. In fact, there are times when I prefer her to our own – I suppose you think that's terrible!'

'To have three children, you must have been very young when you got married.'

'Yes, eighteen, and a darned idiot not to have played the field first.' All of a sudden she sprang to her feet saying, 'I must do a wee. Don't look; women's plumbing is so much more difficult than men's and it becomes worse when wearing jodhpurs.'

As she strolled back towards him from the bush behind which she had taken cover, he thought what a real beauty she was with her green eyes and thick auburn tresses. Strangely enough, instead of her rather wide hips and general untidiness detracting from her appearance, they seemed to emphasise a voluptuous sexiness. He felt he could fall for her most readily, if only he hadn't set eyes on Lorna, with her large blue eyes and blonde hair and dainty figure.

At sundowners that evening, Gordon reported his reactions on what he had seen. As an immediate measure, he suggested cutting their losses by putting the most emaciated animals out of their misery with a bullet through the head. Raising beasts that had fallen through starvation and weakness was a waste of time unless they could be put on a strengthening diet – and of such, none was available. Then to segregate the remainder into two herds: into one, those which were weak but not so far gone that they would not respond to supplementary feeding and careful attention; and into the second group, those in sound condition and let them graze the best areas without the excessive competition.

After that first day, Dora often accompanied Gordon on his daily rounds, but would stay for only an hour or two before returning to be with her children. If she didn't go with him in the morning, she would either take his lunch to him at midday or go out later in the afternoon. She was beginning to take a real interest in the cattle and he was teaching her all he could, for he knew the day must come for him to leave to take up a more promising job. Dora would then be in a position to take over from him without disrupting the progress he was initiating.

They were also becoming close friends. One day she was leaning against him as they sat at a favourite spot on the kopje, and his hands wandered from her hair to her cheeks. He brushed them with a kiss and then as his hand wandered further to cup a breast framed prominently in her thin cotton shirt, she looked up at him with eyes full of love and passion and whispered breathlessly, 'No, my darling, no, it isn't that I don't want you, because I do, but it would spoil everything. Our conscience would get to work.'

'Yes, dear, dear Dora, you are right.' They lay back silently, holding hands and deep in thought. The only sounds were the cooing of Namaqua doves and the chirring noise of the cicadas in the trees.

It was becoming equally apparent that, in spite of familiarity breeding contempt, as it is supposed to do, it was having exactly the opposite effect where Gordon and Dora were concerned. She found herself falling in love with him; or is it love, she would ask herself, or just infatuation because he is so different from Peter? Many women would consider Peter to be an ideal husband and father and hitherto she had regarded him as such, but now she was finding his kindness towards her, and his trust in her, becoming boring. His lovemaking too was becoming stereotyped. She had begun to compare his kisses with Gordon's. With Gordon, both she and he would experience violent surges of passion when their tongues would dart in and out avidly and search each other's mouth. Perhaps, she wondered, it felt more marvellous, because both knew that that was where it must end – she, because of the children, and he for the same reason and because of a strict Presbyterian upbringing.

Gordon was very happy in his work, but as month after month passed without any definite news from the Department of Agriculture he was becoming restless. Then, just as he was on the point of accepting an appointment in South Africa, he was offered a post as Agriculture Officer in the Department of Agriculture.

He learned that his first duty was to report on the state of the agricultural industry in the Melsetter and Chipinga areas of the eastern district, bordering on the boundary with Portuguese East Africa. It was an area settled almost exclusively by descendants of the famous Moodie Trek, few of whom spoke any English.

Since he was required to give Mr Holland a month's notice, he decided to spend his leisure hours during that time studying Afrikaans. He called at the local country hotel to find out if the proprietor's wife, who was an Afrikaner, would give him lessons. She was delighted at being asked and refused absolutely to accept any payment.

The thought of being parted from Gordon deeply affected Dora, but he comforted and assured her by promising to remain in touch and always to regard the Holland estate as his Rhodesian home.

When the day came to say au revoir, everyone was surprised by the quiet and reserved Creena wrapping her arms around his neck and shedding unrestrained tears. Gordon, too, felt sad at the parting, but in his case the depression was counter-balanced by the excitement of starting a new future and of working among Afrikaners – the community of farmers who, in the years gone by, had taken on the military might of Great Britain in the Boer War, and whose style of fighting had given birth to the commando units now forming an integral part of most modern armies.

He salvaged his conscience at leaving Charles Holland by knowing he had taught Dora a great deal about animal husbandry and had put in train plans for the production of ample hay and silage to counter another year of drought, should it come.

As he walked towards his car, Dora whispered there was a present in it for him. It was a little Great Dane puppy – she bred Great Danes. As he gave her a thank-you kiss, she told him to look at his collar. As he did so, he found a bill for £10. He laughed, thinking it was another of her jokes – but it wasn't!

Two years later he turned the tables. At the Salisbury Dog show, at which she carried off the first prize year after year in the Great Dane class, Gordon's Bruno beat her entrants!

Chapter XIII

The road from Umtali to the eastern districts was absolutely appalling and was one in name only, being deeply potholed and corrugated. It twisted and turned up steep inclines, and often followed the same pattern down equally steep declines; the situation was made even worse by it being the start of the rainy season. Most of the drifts were under water, and rivers and streams which had been almost dry for many months, were now running rapidly. Even at the drifts it was not easy to judge the depth of the water from the car, so Gordon had to get out to look and judge. At one stream where he stopped, the water was running at a steady pace, and then, all of a sudden, there was a veritable wall of water pounding down. It was an awe-inspiring sight. There was nothing he could do but sit and wait and be thankful he had not been crossing just as it came into spate; there would have been no hope for him or the car.

If travelling was difficult now when there was at least a road in name, how on earth had the original settlers coped when there was not even a track? Not only would they have had to select the best gradients when traversing ridge after ridge in timbered country, with restricted visibility, but they would also have had to chop down the trees and bushes in their line of travel, cut down banks, and man-handle the huge boulders which bottomed many of the rivers. They would have been lucky to cover 5 miles in a day.

To get those heavy, cumbersome, 16-foot wagons, laden with all their household goods and stores, up the steep hills would have needed more than the usual team of sixteen oxen. Gordon could just picture the tough drivers shouting threats and encouragement, while cracking those long-lashed whips over the backs and heads of the poor beasts, straining in their yokes, till their knees almost touched the ground.

It would have been challenge enough slogging their way up the hills, but it made Gordon shudder at the risks they would have had to take in going down the steep rough slopes with only home-made brakes to grip those large wheels.

The pioneers would have been faced with other problems too. Were the natives in the area friendly or antagonistic? Were they cowards who would sneak in the dark to rob, or were they warriors who would stand up and fight? That part of the country was known to be rich in wildlife, for, as the settlers had moved into Matabeleland and Mashonaland, so the game had tried to escape northwards and eastwards to this region. Every evening, as tired as they would have been, the men would have had to throw up zarebas of bushes and branches in which to kraal their cattle and other animals against lions and leopards.

Equally dangerous would have been the small creatures, such as the tsetse fly, the carrier of trypanosomiasis or sleeping sickness; the anopheles mosquito, the carrier of the dreaded and ubiquitous, malaria; and the creepy crawly creatures like scorpions, centipedes and snakes.

What remarkable women the wives of those pioneers must have been – they went, without grumbling, wherever their men led them. They knew that that was going to be to some area isolated by a hundred miles or more from other white people, and from those amenities which white women, everywhere, take for granted.

They must have realised only too well the hardships that lay ahead. They would have to continue to live in wagons for a while until pole and dagga huts could be built and, only much later on could they hope for a decent house. They would be required to give birth to children and to bring them up miles and miles away from proper medical facilities and from schools.

Rhodes had been very wise when he agreed to Moodie and his followers settling in the isolated eastern district, for he knew he could count on the isolation-loving Boers to keep the Portuguese in Mozambique from infiltrating across the border into what he regarded as Rhodesian territory. In return for that service, the British South Africa Company gave the head of each family as much land as he could encircle in a day's ride – which meant 5,000 or 6,000 acres of virgin veld.

Rhodes and Jamieson were well aware of Portuguese designs, and must have recalled the rather pompous letter from a Portuguese dignitary addressed to the British representative in South Africa. It was dated 11 July 1870 and read:

> The governor of Quillimane, President of the Portuguese Diplomatic Deputation, Carlos Pedro Barahona e Costa Carlos of the Military Order of our Mistress of the Conception of Villa Vicora, First Lieutenant of Artillery, Governor of Quillimane and President of the Portuguese Diplomatic Commission in the South African Republic, by His Majesty the King of Portugal whom God save.
>
> Be it noted:-
>
> **FIRST** – That the territory north of the Limpopo in which the British South Africa Company is at present conducting its operations belongs to the Crown of Portugal and is an integral part of the District of Sofala in the province of Mozambique.
>
> **SECOND** – That no contracts or commission of lands or any other kind made between the said company and Kaffir or native Chief in that country can have any value without the previous sanction of His Most Faithful Majesty.
>
> **THIRD** – Before the said company or any other can legally explore or operate in the Tati Gold Fields Matabeles and others in the regions (sic) it is necessary to have the permission of the Government of His Most Faithful Majesty either directly or through the Governor of Sofala in which district, as I have said, the mines lie.
>
> **FOURTH AND LAST** – by the next mail for Europe I will forward to my Government an authenticated copy of this protest and I shall inform him (sic) of everything I know officially and extra-officially upon the subject of which I speak and equal communication I shall forward to His Excellency the Governor General of Mozambique.

On arriving at his destination, Gordon was so taken by the loveliness of the countryside that he felt the long arduous journey had been well worth the trouble. He was also glad he had taken lessons in

Afrikaans, because at the first farm he visited when he had introduced himself in English he had sensed a distinct feeling of chill and suspicion; but, as soon as he had plucked up courage and ventured into Afrikaans, his hosts at once relaxed and became less reserved.

Also, it soon became apparent that he would be more likely to make headway with the middle-aged and the younger element if he could receive the confidence of their elders, for it was the elders who held sway and, it was their word which carried weight in the community.

As the years had progressed since the arrival of the first pioneers, the original holdings of 5,000 and 6,000 acres had been reduced by gifts of 1,000 or of 1,500 acres to a son when he married.

The farmers' outlook towards their black servants was both patriarchal and paternalistic, once the employee had been in their service for any length of time. They took an interest in their welfare and in that of their families. An employer might deliver the odd slap, but then made up for it by some kind act – just as they did with their own children.

They conversed with their servants, which was more than Gordon had found English-speaking farmers doing. It was early days to form a judgement, but Gordon felt that the African was more at home and at ease with the Afrikaner than he was with the other white race.

To Gordon, as a fairly new immigrant – a 'rooinek' – that was an interesting feature, for those were the days when the Nationalist Party of Dr Malan in South Africa, was beginning to make headway against old Field Marshal Jan Smuts and his party, by originating and exploiting the use of the word apartheid.

Segregation of races, on the basis of colour, had existed from the very first days of the landing of Dutch settlers in South Africa, but it was treated and regarded as a normal attitude by both black and white. It was only when segregation began to be advertised and publicised by notices of 'whites only' that bitterness began to develop, and was brought to a pitch when it came to affect the tenure of land. Few people in Britain, Gordon thought, realised that the Bantu tribes were only just arriving in the south from their homeland in the distant north, when the Dutch Boers were already settled in the country.

In the remote eastern district of Rhodesia, there was no change of attitude and no bitterness between black and white. In fact, much of the labour force on the farms in the Melsetter and Chipinga areas were natives who had crossed the border from Portuguese East Africa. Ask any of them which they preferred to work for or to live amongst, the Portuguese or the Afrikaner, and, without exception, they preferred the latter. By and large the Portuguese were hard task masters, and the poorly paid officials in the hinterland were inclined to interpret the law to suit themselves. They were by no means averse to augmenting their salaries by accepting backhanders. It is better not to describe their country jails; one of the most common punishments meted out to natives was the *bastinado* – beating the soles of the feet till they were puffed and swollen – a most painful and not easily forgotten experience!

Prior to the arrival of white settlers in Rhodesia, the local tribes living in this remote eastern part of the country were being harassed continuously by the Matabele from one side and by the Portuguese from the other. The harassment reached such a pitch that the paramount chief in the region wrote to Queen Victoria imploring her protection. Unfortunately that request was made at an inopportune time – at a time when the British Government was finding itself to be the meat in the sandwich between Lobengula and Rhodes – and so it was side-tracked. Years later, however, Rhodes took advantage of it by encouraging Moodie and his followers to settle in the region in order to protect it from Portuguese intrusion.

From one of the older settlers, with whom Gordon had struck up a firm friendship, he learned of the exploits of Fernando Gonzalez, a Portuguese half-caste. He was a truly savage and bloodthirsty free-booter, who operated on both sides of the international boundary, with a gang of other half-castes, every one of whom had served prison sentences for crimes such as murder, rape and assault. They preyed on isolated Portuguese-owned farms, killing the menfolk, raping or absconding with wives and daughters, and rustling the livestock. They raided native villages, seizing boys and girls for sale to Arab slavers on the eastern coast.

For quite a time they had given the Afrikaner settlers a wide berth, then one night they took a risk and got away with several head of cattle. Success prompted them to try again. This time they were unsuccessful, because the lowing of the animals in the boma roused the farmer and his sons and they rushed out armed with rifles. One intruder was wounded and captured, but the others escaped getting away with only two calves – and they were retrieved in the pursuit that followed.

At a third attempt, Gonzalez set fire to the homestead with the intention that his men would be able to drive away the livestock while the occupants were busy extinguishing the flames. Unfortunately for him, he was ignorant of the strong community spirit which bound the settlers, who quickly formed a mounted commando and gave pursuit. On the second day out, the forward scouts sighted the gang holding a drunken orgy and feasting on some of the stolen cattle. As soon as the rest of the commando arrived, they surrounded Gonzalez and his men and shot the lot.

Those early settlers were faced with other problems too. Many of the horses died from an undiagnosed disease, and as the area was fairly rich in wildlife, they had to guard the stock constantly against leopards and lions. One family, at great cost, had set out from the Orange Free State with six large mules, which were their pride and joy. While still in South Africa they lost one from a snake bite, then two more in Matabeleland from a form of food poisoning, while a fourth broke a leg on the journey from Umtali by slipping down a steep embankment which gave way under it. They took great care of the remaining two, making a specially strong boma or kraal for them. Unfortunately, one night the farmer was wakened by the noise of galloping hooves outside. Lions had terrified the mules, one of which had jumped the palisade and was chased by the lioness towards her mate, and so to its end.

As he heard this story, Gordon was shocked to think that only a few decades earlier, wildlife had been abundant in this area and now there was not a wild animal to be seen. Anyone now wanting venison would have to search for the deer (and search was the operative word) in the remoter areas of Portuguese territory. The destruction which had been commenced by the early professional hunters, such as Selous and his contemporaries, had been completed by the settlers. A similar fate was fast befalling the native vegetation.

The church was the focal point of social activity. After services on Sundays, all would stay on for a buffet lunch with the women providing the eats – and in what quantity and variety! The tables literally groaned under the weight. There were games, dancing and, gossip in plenty. It was a time for boy to meet girl and for courting couples to slip away quietly out of sight. In a small and isolated community, cut off almost completely from the rest of the world, it was inevitable that there were ties of blood between family and family, some distant, some close and some uncomfortably close. There was bound to be some inbreeding.

At one farm which Gordon visited in the performance of his duties, the young housewife invited him to coffee while she sent the houseboy to call her husband from the fields. It was the usual, almost universal, design of house in that locality: simple, plain, comfortable and scrupulously clean and tidy. There was the usual round table in the centre of the living room, covered by a brown or green velveteen cloth with baubles dangling from the border.

As Gordon sat down, a young man wearing shorts drew up a chair immediately opposite him and sat down with his knees pressed against Gordon's bare knees. As Gordon took a sip of coffee he took a sip; as Gordon put his cup down, he put his cup down; as Gordon raised his again, he followed suit, and that went on until a baby in an adjoining room began to cry. He jumped up, rushed into the room, brought out the baby and plonked it on Gordon's lap. The baby was soaking wet and Gordon, who was not used to handling infants, looked plaintively across at its mother, but when she took no notice, he lifted it as gently as he could and placed it on the floor.

It was only then that the mother picked it up, and while changing its nappy, asked Gordon how old he thought the young man was. Gordon was set back by the directness of the question for he had been wondering about that answer himself. The lad had a young-looking face, but it was somewhat lined, making it look older and giving it the appearance of a slightly wizened monkey. He hazarded a guess; twenty or twenty-three? She laughed merrily: 'He's seventeen.' His father was also his grand father!

Gordon was just reaching the point of being accepted as a welcome member of the community, enjoying Mrs Baskoff's *baboote* (a kind of curry), Mrs Botha's beefsteak and kidney pudding, and a variety of Boer dishes, when he was informed that development work was due to commence on the new tobacco research station at Trelawney, some 65 miles north of Salisbury. He was to proceed there to assist the farm manager in the initial stages of development and, later, to serve as biologist.

So it was with a sad heart that he bade goodbye to the remote eastern province and its hospitable settlers.

Trelawney is only 65 miles north of the capital Salisbury, but the state of the road made the journey feel considerably longer. The first few miles of tarmacadam gave way to strips and, they in turn to corrugations, potholes, and dust when dry, muddy pools when wet. It was fairly flat countryside with extensive plains giving way to woodland.

When Gordon came to two buildings by the side of the road, he went in to seek directions to Trelawney and was told he was at Trelawney – just a long building, the country store run by Greeks, with near it their dwelling house. The research station-to-be was some 7 miles from the main road. For the first mile or two there was a reasonably good dirt road, but it soon turned into nothing more than a barely discernible track, although he knew he had reached his destination when he arrived at a pole and dagga hut in a small clearing in the woods.

The occupants, Mr and Mrs Capeling, gave him an hospitable, if somewhat reserved, welcome. Gordon's first impression was that although they had been living there for only a matter of weeks, they resented their privacy being interrupted. Mr Capeling was short and wiry and put Gordon in mind of a short length of top-quality resilient steel wire. A pipe, whether full or empty, was a permanent part of his face.

The Capelings had graduated from a grass hut to a pole and dagga one, so the grass hut was now to become Gordon's until he too decided to build a pole and dagga one.

The work schedule for the first few months covered such things as sinking a well for drinking water, while a borehole, 60 feet deep, was being drilled. There was no running water on the property, only seepage from a vlei (meadow). Trees had to be stumped and cleared for building sites and for tobacco and other crops which were to be grown. Bricks had to be made and kilns constructed in which to bake them.

Fortunately, as the days went by, Capeling found that he and Gordon could work happily together, so much so that on the first Saturday, Mrs Capeling invited Gordon to dine with them. On a wood-burning stove, housed in a detached pole and dagga kitchen, she had turned out a really delicious beefsteak and kidney pudding. She was delighted at the way Gordon tucked into it, so much so, that in future Gordon would dine with them every Saturday and they with him on Wednesdays. It was obvious to Gordon who would benefit, for he was no cook and he doubted whether the 'boy' he had taken on was capable of doing more than boiling eggs and frying meat.

A young white was engaged as handyman carpenter. Mentally he was only nineteen shillings in the pound but he was excellent at his work. One morning, Gordon heard piteous and agonising cries coming from the man's hut and went over to investigate. He was horrified to find him poking a red-hot metal knitting needle into his pup's eyes. Gordon ordered him to stop immediately. On enquiring why he was torturing dogs in that way, the reply came that blinded dogs made better hunters than those with sight, as blindness enhanced the sense of scent. On threat of being sacked, he gave an undertaking never to repeat the cruel and stupid action.

As soon as each house had been built, a professional officer arrived to occupy it. The last to arrive caused many a snicker of amusement among both white and black onlookers as he stepped out of his car. He had just arrived from England, was pink-faced and had obviously been kitted out by one of those London firms of the day who styled themselves 'colonial outfitters'. Rhodesians wore their shorts very short and fairly tight fitting; Keith wore his down to his lily-white knees, and they were ultra wide. Instead of the ubiquitous broad-brimmed felt hat, he wore a shiny pith helmet. The poor fellow took the inevitable chaffing fairly well, but at the first opportunity got himself rekitted à la Rhodesian style.

He must have been an avid reader of Ryder Haggard's books, for he expected to see assegai-carrying Africans, and an abundance of game grazing the grassy veld, but all he could see were natives who were parodies of the white man in tattered shirts and shorts, and not a buck or a zebra anywhere in sight. He was bitterly disappointed, and continued to be disappointed, until Gordon suggested they spend a long weekend on a hunting safari in the Zambezi Valley – one of the very few places where wild animals were still supposed to be plentiful.

Gordon chose as gun-boys two of the most reliable men in his field force. Misi was a tough and ugly Mozambiquan native, and Petro a light-skinned Yao from Nyasaland (now Malawi). Both had accompanied him in the past when he had been shooting guinea fowl and partridge.

Much to the disappointment of all four, they found the valley still suffering seriously from the drought which had struck the area during the previous two years. 'The game had been forced into concentrating within approachable distance of the few waterholes that still contained water. After tramping for miles in a hot humid temperature of well over 90°F, and braving hordes of flies, gnats and mosquitoes, they came to a waterhole which was little better than a puddle. The plenitude of fresh spoor around it indicated that it was still being used. Both white men agreed it would be dastardly to take advantage of any animal forced into relying on such a meagre and foul supply.

Though the valley was foreign to them, both natives were adept in tracking the spoor of a pride of lions. Where there were lions there were bound to be the lesser game on which they fed. The thoughts of both Petro and Misi were concentrated on enjoying a tasty meal of gazelle that evening, so they pressed on at a speed their bosses found hard going. Poor Keith was wishing he hadn't come. The insects showed an obvious preference for his fresh English blood; his bare arms and legs were a mass of scratches from the thorny bushes; and his temper was tested to its limits by the 'wakem biki' (wait-a-bit) tendrils which clung on to his socks.

It was amazing that so little game was to be seen miles and miles away from civilisation, but suddenly, and unexpectedly, three natives appeared out of the blue. They were an absolutely horrid sight, with heads, and faces and bodies covered in congealing blood. Had they been skinned alive they could not have looked a more bloody mess.

Gordon tried to speak to them in kitchen-kaffir, but that meant nothing to them. Petro tried in Chinyanja, the language of Nyasaland, but that too was of no avail. Misi was more successful, though he gleaned more information through sign language than from words.

It transpired they had not been involved in savage warfare, as Gordon had imagined, but were members of a large gang which had killed a cow elephant and had been feasting on her. They were early leavers, leaving most of the gang still feasting, and were happy to guide the *inkosi* to the spectacle.

It was an unbelievable sight. The poor animal had been wounded by several bullets of too small a calibre to be effective, and had then been turned into a pin cushion with dozens of spears sticking out of her at all angles. The stomach had been ripped open and naked men and women were actually moving about inside the stomach, tearing and devouring the liver, heart and other organs. Others who had feasted already on the raw meat were lying sprawled out under the shade of trees, completely comatose, some were so covered in blood and offal that it was impossible to make out their features. They had gormandised to such an extent that it was easy to imagine that meat was exuding from nostrils and ears. It was the most revolting sight anyone could ever expect to see.

One individual hacked off a large chunk of meat which he offered to the white men, but they declined the offer. Misi and Petro, however, were not so fussy and took it with them for their evening meal. Gordon would have liked to have been able to boast he had tasted elephant meat, but the gruesomeness of the sight they had witnessed had dispelled all idea of food.

Some miles further on they came to a waterhole with a fairly reasonable supply of water. A warthog with his wife and young family were enjoying life wallowing in wet mud, quite oblivious of being watched. Keith was creeping up to photograph them, when a zebra, drinking at a spot further down, spotted the onlookers and neighed a warning. Father warthog quickly assembled his family and made for the bush nearby. The cocky little animals cut an amusing sight as they sped off in more or less single file, snorting loudly as they went, each with its little tail held erect. Every now and again they would stop for a second and look back to see what all the fuss was about.

Since it was getting late in the afternoon, Gordon decided to seek out a fairly safe spot within sight of a waterhole at which to camp for the night. As lion spoor was visible, and as they hadn't brought a tent, they hurriedly built a thorn zareba for protection as they slept under the stars.

Both white men had been so disgusted by the sight of a once large and noble elephant being so desecrated, that they hadn't the heart for more destruction, so decided to content themselves with photography during the rest of the safari.

During the night Keith let out a startled shout – he had felt something crawling over his face and thought it was a snake. Gordon told him to lie still while he shone a torch. It was no snake, just a black millipede some 9 inches long. 'Don't try to brush it off in case it digs its legs in; I'll lift it off.' The boys had wakened too and were greatly amused at Keith's discomfiture. Millipedes are harmless, but if they are brushed off the wrong way, their curved legs take hold and can result in a nasty rash.

At daybreak the animals began to collect at the waterhole. It was fascinating to see herds of zebra, wildebeest, hartebeest, giraffes, monkeys and baboons all drinking side by side quite unconcernedly, while relying on lookouts to sound the alert should danger approach. It soon did, but surprisingly there was no pandemonium, just a sense of tense alertness as a pride of seven lionesses and cubs came for their morning drink. Leisurely, and with quiet majesty, the adults approached the water, disdaining to show any interest in the other animals. The cubs were too busy sparring and rolling each other over to take much interest in anything or in anyone else. Obviously the family had fed well during the night. The monkeys and baboons set up a chatter and started to move or pivot around, but the other animals stopped drinking, raised their heads and watched the lions with careful attention. Having satisfied their thirst, the lions moved off a short distance to the shelter of trees, threw themselves down and began a meticulous toilet.

After an early wash and breakfast, the little party set out again in the direction of the great river. Apart from gazelles, baboons, a herd of wild buffalo and a solitary rhino, they saw little of interest. But late in the afternoon the clean fresh air took on a sickly sweet smell of putrefaction. Gordon thought they must have disturbed a nest of stink ants, but Misi and Petro thought otherwise – it was the smell of death. They were quite right. About a mile further on they came on a sight of such wanton destruction that paled the elephant episode into insignificance; and this one had been perpetrated by so-called civilised beings, by people who were supposed to know better, and who were not killing for the pot or for trophies, but purely to satisfy a lust. A large party of businessmen from Johannesburg had camped in the vicinity of a large and isolated waterhole – the only good one for miles around – and had shot just about every animal that had been attracted there by thirst. They had killed deliberately and indiscriminately, male or female, big horns or no horns, good specimens or poor specimens, and had just left the carcasses to rot in the heat and humidity.

The perpetrators of this holocaust had broken camp and had moved on a day or so earlier, but Gordon and Keith were determined to catch up and confront them. Their tracks were easy to follow. Gordon and Keith were greeted with a show of goodwill and good humour on the lines: 'Dr Livingstone, I presume, and you, of course, must be Mr Stanley, and these are your faithful and trusty servants.'

Gordon was in no mood for friendly overtures and replied with: 'And you are bloody butchering bastards!' The rest of the meeting was too vitriolic for recording. Suffice to say that when Gordon reported the matter later on to the authorities, no action was taken, nor could be taken, because no law had been broken. In those days preservation of the environment and of wildlife did not feature on any agenda.

Sickened by the elephant episode and then doubly sickened by the later atrocity, Gordon and Keith decided to call a halt to the safari and to return home. In any case the time left at their disposal would not allow them to reach the Zambezi itself, where, no doubt, wildlife must abound.

While travelling along the dusty main road, the drought was suddenly broken by a veritable downpour. After the long dry spell, all that each man wanted to do was to strip off his sweaty shirt and shorts and just relish the rain pouring on to his body. The air was thick with the smell of dust being dampened down. Streams and rivers were responding, as only they knew how, with trickles turning into torrents. One large stream that they reached late in the evening was so swollen and impassable that they decided it would be best to turn back half a mile or so and seek shelter in a road ganger's cottage that they had passed.

The ganger had left with his men to attend to a section of road some miles away and would not be back until the following day, but his wife, a bright and buxom Afrikaans lady in her early thirties, was delighted to have visitors. Without any preamble about enquiring their business, she invited them into her humble dwelling. Once they were seated in the small, spotlessly clean living room, she bustled off to fetch them coffee, homemade biscuits and scones. When Gordon asked if they could spend the night, she was embarrassed that there was only the one bedroom and, as they could see, the living room was small and cluttered with furniture. In any case, it wouldn't do for the kaffirs to be spreading the rumour that their boss's wife had been entertaining two presentable young men – and then added with a mischievous smile – much as she would like to!

However, they would be very welcome to spend the night in the shed; she would clean it up and make them as comfortable as possible. Their boys, of course, would find accommodation in the compound with her servants. Off she went to dish them out rations and to give her houseboy instructions to look after them.

Supper was a plain and enjoyable meal of broth, made from venison and her own homegrown vegetables, followed by fried venison and eggs.

Gordon laughed when he saw the look of dismay and of horror on Keith's face when he realised he was to spend the night among a medley of road-making tools, bags of cement and of lime, sacks of mealie meal, and about twenty cocks and hens who were cackling and fluttering their annoyance at humans invading their sanctuary. Mrs Van Der Merwe cleared a space big enough to take two camp beds, apologised for not having any spare mosquito nets and bade them a good night's rest.

They were awakened at early dawn by the cocks welcoming in a new and sunny day, and the hens displaying their displeasure at having had to sleep with humans for company.

In the years to come, Gordon had more interesting and personal experiences with African elephants. One such was in Uganda, accompanied by his car attendant Okot, who was sitting on the back seat of the Morris Isis. They were travelling along a rough bush track when they came to a sudden stop. Standing right in the middle of the track was a young bull elephant who had isolated himself from the herd – one lot of cows were grazing several hundred yards away to the right, with mother among them; and another herd far to the left.

The young bull was just standing there flapping his ears and doing no more than glance at the car. The track was only wide enough to take the car, so, with much patience and hope, Gordon waited for passage to be granted. When a good half hour had elapsed in the blazing sunshine, he decided to take a risk and drive past on the very edge of the road, hoping no tree stumps or boulders were hidden in the long grass at the side to damage the oil sump, but as he got level with the animal, it swung a blow at the car with its trunk. Gordon swung wide and was steering through the grass when Okot yelled, 'The peoples is coming!' 'The peoples is coming!' (he always referred to elephants as peoples). Sure enough, out of the corner of his eye, Gordon saw, coming at full speed from the right, an enraged cow elephant, ears flapping, trunk raised in anger and trumpeting loudly.

Suddenly the back of the car went up into the air and then it rolled over to one side. Okot began to cry out 'We are dead! We are dead!' Both men lay crouched in most uncomfortable positions, expecting, any second, to feel a massive foot trampling on them as elephants usually trample on their victims as a final gesture of annoyance. Miracle of miracles, this time this one didn't.

After a very lengthy pause which seemed interminable, and when no sound of movement was heard, the two men crawled out, stared at each other in amazement and clasped each other's shoulders.

They tried to lever the car back on to its wheels, but without success – there was no alternative to having to walk back to base at the small township of Masindi, some 20 miles distant. While there was daylight, the going was not too bad, but when dark came on, nerves were at full stretch. The veld, which had been quiet in daylight, suddenly became menacing in the dark, with the hooting of owls, the cries of nightjars, the howls of hyenas and jackals and the occasional roar of a lion or of a leopard. Every anthill took on the shape of a lion or of an elephant.

African elephants are not only the largest of all land mammals, but they are also one of the most gentle and sociable of all animals, and live in peaceful family units. Their life patterns are, in many ways, similar to those of mankind. For instance, they reach sexual maturity at the age of fourteen or fifteen, they are ready to mate at any time, and they live to about seventy. Gestation, however, is quite a bit longer, usually 24 months. As soon as a young male reaches puberty he is required to leave the females and join a group of males.

Bull elephants don't live with the cows. They live apart and only visit girls when one of the latter is on heat. Several aspirants may arrive at the same time, but the prize always goes to the biggest and bravest.

A very large bull used to reside near to a ferry crossing of the Nile in Uganda. He was to be seen there, always grazing, or studying humans, or just deep in thought. One day, Gordon saw him sniffing the air with his trunk and then careering off trumpeting loudly with ears flapping. 'What's up with him?' Gordon asked the boatman who had spent all his life in that locality and was on good terms with the bull.

'Oh, he has smelt a female on heat and has gone off to try his luck.'

'I haven't seen any females around for many miles,' remarked Gordon.

'No, but you haven't got an elephant's sense of smell. A bull can smell a hot female from many many miles away!'

During a spell of leave, Gordon spent almost two months observing a large group of cow elephants and their calves. He had chosen that particular group because one of the females was, obviously, very pregnant, and he wished to observe the birth. At first, the animals resented his presence, but after a while when they were satisfied he presented no danger, they allowed him to come fairly close.

Day followed day, just tramping from one grazing area to another, covering many miles at a time. Then, early one morning, the pregnant cow left the group, accompanied by two others, presumed to be near relatives, and walked towards a large tree. There, she delivered a young male calf. To Gordon's amazement, the two attendants helped the mother clean the calf and raise him to his feet. Then, while mother was devoting more time to the baby, the other two pulled down branches from the tree to cover the afterbirth, and finally, with their trunks, they covered the pile with soil.

After a short pause and when the infant was fairly steady on his feet, they all walked off slowly to rejoin the herd. Mother helped the baby along by steadying him against her foreleg with her trunk.

What could have been the purpose of the midwives covering the afterbirth?

Chapter XIV

Rhodesia had no regular army prior to the outbreak of the Second World War, relying for its defence on a territorial force, and on the full-time British South Africa Police (BSAP). A permanent staff corps was responsible for both defence and for law and order. The BSAP derived its name from having been raised in South Africa as a para-military unit for service in the early days of the colonisation of Rhodesia. With a lifetime record of smartness and efficiency, it was classed as being on a par with that other famous force, the Royal Canadian Mounted Police. Gordon was always proud of having served in the intelligence section of the force, while at the same time holding his appointments in the Department of Agriculture.

When it had become obvious that Chamberlain was making no headway with Hitler and war was imminent, there was a rush by young white Rhodesians to enlist for service beyond the borders of Rhodesia, with British and British colonial forces. They earned for themselves a fine reputation. King George V recognised their splendid service by awarding the title of Royal, so that they were no longer the 1st and 2nd Battalions, the Rhodesia Regiment, but the 1st and 2nd Battalions The Royal Rhodesia Regiment.

It is not known, generally, that Rhodesia provided the highest percentage of serving men – in relation to the total white population of the country – then did any of the other allies. That was one of the grounds for a feeling of resentment against Great Britain, and a feeling of having been let down by her, when, in later years the whites were forced into handing the country over to African rule.

At the end of the War, the country showed its appreciation of the services that had been rendered by its servicemen, in a very practical manner. All who had been associated with agriculture in pre-war years were assisted with land for farming and with generous financial assistance through the state-owned Land and Agriculture Bank, so that men who had had little hope of ever owning their own property were given a marvellous opportunity to do so now.

Gordon, himself an ex-serviceman, was posted once again to the advisory branch of the Department of Agriculture, to assist the new farmers with advice on how to plan the layout of their farms and to advise them on crop production.

The speed at which thousands upon thousands of acres of woodland and bush were suddenly becoming developed was absolutely phenomenal, particularly so when it was realised that practically all the areas being developed lay well beyond the regions which had been settled already. The work entailed extending roads, surveying and demarcating hundreds of farms, most of which were in heavily wooded country; ensuring a permanent water supply for each farm, more often than not in the form of boreholes drilled to a depth of 60 feet or more; clearing land of timber and bush; ensuring that each new field, as it came into use, was properly contoured to prevent the soil being eroded during downpours of rain; and in making and burning bricks. Great credit must go to the white women who had to face up to a lot of hardship and loneliness. It was by no means easy for women who had been used to living in towns, or near to towns and the amenities they offered, now finding themselves 80 to 100 miles or more from even a moderately sized town, and the closest neighbour being some 3 miles or more away.

Just picture them leaving comfortable, well-founded homes, for grass huts with mud floors, and constantly having to be on their guard to protect the furniture from white ants. The legs of tables and chairs would have had to be stood in jam tins full of water to protect them from termites.

Progress from grass huts to pole and dagga huts earned a sigh of relief, but the real comforts were still missing: there was no full-length bath in which to stretch out and relax; there was only a small tin tub in which to squat, with hot water being carried to it in pails or in 4-gallon kerosene tins. No large windows with panes of glass to let light in on to the dressing table; no electric or gas oven, but only a wood-burning stove housed in a separate hut; no electric refrigerator, only one with a temperamental paraffin burner; no carpets for fear of termites or other *skellums* (harmful insects); no popping your foot into a shoe or slipper without first giving it a shake to make sure it wasn't harbouring a scorpion or a small snake; no flush toilet, but a hole and a thunderbox out of doors. Mosquito nets were almost a necessity to keep out not only mosquitoes and gnats, but also the dust and the pieces of straw which fell from the thatched roof.

It was heart-breaking, and temper-threatening, for wives to see the building of tobacco curing barns, grading sheds, bulking sheds and other farm buildings, receiving priority over a house. Many had to wait years before being able to enjoy the luxury of even a modest brick dwelling.

With few exceptions, those new farmers made good by sheer dint of hard work. The camaraderie that had been created between serving men during the war years proved invaluable when struggling, side by side, to convert virgin bush into commercial farms. Each man was always ready to help his neighbour.

At one farm which Gordon visited, he was surprised to find a man with whom he had been on friendly terms in the North African campaign. He was even more surprised to find a baby in a pram standing outside the front door to the pole and dagga hut. The man was by no means young, and had been such a tearaway that it was difficult to imagine him being the marrying type. His host introduced Gordon to his wife, poured out three pink gins and proposed a toast to the baby. Gordon raised his glass in response, but found it difficult to take even a sip, because, stretched right across the glass, was a picture of the infant lying dead. He tried hard not to show his feelings and gulped down the drink. He strove with himself to write off the phenomenon as imagination, but it continued to linger. As he was taking his departure, his hosts invited him to make up a four for a game of bridge the following evening.

Next morning, while filling up with petrol at the one and only local store, a farmer asked him whether he had heard the sad news about his hosts of the previous day. 'No, I am due to dine with them this evening.'

'I'm, afraid not, old boy. Their baby died last night. Extraordinary thing! There was nothing wrong with the wee mite. She was in excellent health!'

At another farm which was being developed by a veritable giant of a man, 6 feet 6 inches in height, broad shouldered, deep chested and with an elephantine thirst for whisky, he was invited to spend the night. His host's wife was a very dainty little woman barely 5 feet tall. At night, on going to bed, Gordon left his shoes outside the bedroom door for the houseboy to clean and polish. Barely an hour after getting into bed, he heard a scuffing noise outside the door and presumed it was the houseboy. As the noise continued, he thought he detected a woman's whisper and called out 'Come in'.

To his surprise, his petite hostess was standing in the entrance, with the light shining behind her, dressed only in a diaphanous nightgown. His heart jumped as, with a lovely naughty smile, she walked towards the bed and began to pull back the blanket. He held on to it and said, 'What about your husband?'

'Don't worry about him,' she replied. 'I doctored his last two drinks. He'll be out for a good few hours.'

Work in the advisory service was seldom boring. Always something interesting or amusing turned up. There was the case of an elderly Pole who was farming in a very remote area, where there was little opportunity of meeting any single white woman interested in establishing a relationship. So he advertised in Polish newspapers for a woman with a farming background to come to Rhodesia and marry him. In due course a lady in her mid-thirties arrived. She made up for a lack of beauty by being caring and hard working. In fact, after a month or two she was doing all the work while her husband sat back spending much of his time listening in to other peoples' conversations on the party-line telephone.

Unfortunately she had no idea that the African buffalo was, perhaps, the most dangerous and the most persistently vindictive, of all wild animals. To her they looked like ordinary domestic cattle. So, when she saw a herd of them grazing on the farm, she approached them to shoo them away, but the massive bull who lorded it over the herd thought otherwise. He walked steadily towards her snorting and bellowing and with head bent low and horns ready to toss her to kingdom come. She bolted for the refuge of a tree so he followed her at full speed, but she managed, just in the nick of time, to swing up onto a branch. Unfortunately one leg was hanging down and soon she felt it being rasped. The bull, with his very rough tongue, was licking it until it started to bleed. She managed to pull it up, but that made her sitting position a lot more uncomfortable.

All this happened just before sunset. Fortunately, one of the African farm labourers had spotted what was happening and had run to the homestead to inform the boss. To his astonishment, the boss merely nodded his head and went back into the house and sat down. The 'boy' thought that perhaps he had not made it quite clear how dangerous the situation was and so urged his employer to go out quickly armed with a rifle. Mr Powlaski once again nodded his head, and said he would go out to rescue her first thing in the morning!

It was not until nine o'clock the following morning that he ventured out to find not only the bull, but also two other buffaloes, on duty at the foot of the tree. Poor Mrs Powlaski had spent sixteen hours in a crouched position. Each time she had been forced to stretch a leg, it had been scraped by a rough tongue. The wounds took several weeks to heal, as in places the flesh had been scraped down almost to the bone. One wonders what she had to say to her husband and what excuse he had to give – but they lived happily ever after.

While lunching at another farm, this time owned by a very perky and publicity-craving man, Gordon thought the meat had a peculiarly sweet flavour and wondered if it is was 'on the turn'. However, as his bachelor host seemed to be enjoying it, he assumed it was alright and continued to eat his, though somewhat tentatively. Later, as they were walking towards the fields, his host asked whether he had enjoyed his meal.

'What was the meat?' Gordon asked.

'That, old boy, was the leopard I shot yesterday,' came the reply. Gordon felt green and disgusted – he had eaten cat!

The outbreak of an unusual disease in the tobacco crop meant Gordon having to carry out an on-the-spot investigation. On arriving at one farm he found a party of five farmers assembled to go on a baboon shoot – apparently a troop of baboons had been playing havoc with the tobacco crop. Baboons are great mimics. From their vantage point on a rocky kopje they had seen a gang of farm boys topping the tobacco plants (breaking off the flower heads, so as to induce more body into the leaves). So, when the gang had finished and departed, the baboons decided to try their paws at it – with dire results for the farmer. It meant that more than half of each plant was lost to him.

Gordon was invited to join the shooting party. He had heard about baboon shoots but had never taken part in one, so he agreed to go along, purely as a spectator, for he had vowed never to shoot again after having witnessed the massacre of game in the Zambezi Valley which had sickened him.

The tactics of a baboon shoot entail taking advantage of the animal's inherent sense of curiosity. Baboons just have to know all that is taking place in their area, even if it means taking great risks to do so. The hunters spread themselves around the foot of the kopje, and sent beaters forward, shouting and banging on tins to create as much din as possible. Out of curiosity, the baboons exposed themselves to see what all the noise was about. On seeing that they were being attacked, the big males strutted about in a most menacing manner with their big yellow fangs fully exposed, warning the females and youngsters to stay well back. A shot rang out and a big fellow fell. As the females attempted to scoot into safety, another shot rang out, and a female stopped dead in her tracks, looked at the wound, put a paw to it as if in wonderment, then, at the sight of the blood, she screamed, took a step forward and fell over dead, with her infant still clinging to her.

That scenario was repeated again and again until the survivors bolted away from the area, never to return – or so the farmer hoped.

A baboon shoot is not a pleasant sight and is far from being a sporting event. However, if you are a farmer whose tobacco crop, or worse still, your maize crop is being destroyed by cob after cob being plucked off in a wanton spree of destruction, you too would be tempted to take drastic action.

How different, Gordon thought, was that experience to a previous encounter he had had with baboons. He had pulled the car up at the remote farm he was visiting. The house was the usual type, a single-storey brick dwelling with a veranda running the full length of the building, and edged with a low wall, some 18 to 24 inches high, with a gap in the middle providing an entrance passage to the front door. Sitting on the wall, on each side of the gap, was a large baboon – a most unusual sight. As Gordon stepped out of the car, neither animal moved. He had expected them to bolt, but neither made the slightest attempt to move; they just sat there, staring at him menacingly. He got back into the car and tooted the horn, but to no avail. Neither farmer nor servant appeared.

After a pause he walked round to the back of the house to see if anyone was about. No luck. No sign of anyone. Plucking up courage he walked between the pair. They made no attempt to move, but just turned their heads as he went past, and glared and snarled. He tried the front door which was not locked, but for some unknown reason he suddenly decided it would be unwise to enter. He braved passing between them again on his way back to the car, and again with the same reaction.

He had travelled well over 80 miles of bad road to see this particular farmer, so decided to just sit and wait for him to return from the fields or wherever he had gone. It was a long wait of an hour or so. As Mr van Rensburg came in sight, both baboons ran off to meet him just as dogs would have done. His greeting to Gordon was 'I'm glad you didn't try to go into the house, my two watchdogs' (pointing to the two baboons, with a grin) 'would have attacked you. They make far better guards than dogs or geese!' He had rescued them from a baboon hunt when they were only a few days old, and had trained them in guard duties.

Chapter XV

Gordon had been enjoying his work in the Advisory Service when he received instructions to proceed to the opposite end of the country, to Matabeleland. He was to establish and take charge of the Turkish Tobacco and Plant Breeding Station in the Umgusa Valley, some 15 miles out of Bulawayo, the capital of Matabeleland, and only a few miles from the Umgusa river, the site of one of the last battles fought against the Matabele.

In addition to managing the station, he was also to run an advisory service for farmers in the area. For the duties of car attendant he engaged an intelligent young Matabele, from whose general appearance and behaviour it was obvious that Alfeyo had come from a very respectable family.

It was not long before he proved his trustworthiness. Gordon had just drawn cash for staff wages and other expenses from a bank in Bulawayo, and had given Alfeyo money to go and buy a meal, while he himself made towards a nearby restaurant for lunch. Just at that precise moment a farmer had approached him and, in course of conversation, Gordon had inadvertently left the bag of money on the front seat of the car and failed to lock the doors. In the middle of lunch he realised what he had done and and raced back to the car. There, to his immense relief, Alfeyo was standing on guard.

Apparently the boy had noticed Gordon hadn't locked the car and so, instead of going for a meal, he had stayed to protect the money! What temptation that must have been for a man earning only a few pounds a month to disappear with close on to a thousand pounds!

One evening, while driving home in the dark, Gordon saw a cyclist approaching him on the wrong side of the road. Gordon flashed his headlights to attract attention, but the other paid no heed. When

Gordon realised that the cyclist was sticking to the wrong side, he moved over to his wrong side, but at that very moment the cyclist corrected his error and veered to his left. The result was a head-on collision. To avoid running over the body Gordon veered sharply into a tree; Alfeyo feared the worst and yelled, 'We are dead! We are dead!' Gordon told him to keep quiet and to get out and help with the cyclist. The poor fellow was a bloody mess. As Gordon leant over him to sound his heart, a voice in English said, 'I'm afraid he is dead, Mr Maclaine.' Looking round in astonishment, he saw that it was the white police trooper who called regularly at the station when patrolling the area.

'No, he is not dead,' Gordon replied. 'I can feel his pulse beating, but it's very weak.' He took off his jacket to wrap round the poor boy and they lifted him carefully into the back of the station wagon. Fortunately the car, though badly dented, started up without trouble.

They made straight for the hospital, but the boy was dead by the time they got there. The next stop was the police station. After statements were taken and the police doctor had confirmed that Gordon was not under the influence of alcohol, a police sergeant drove him home because his car was to be kept for a mechanical check, and Alfeyo was to be detained for further questioning.

To Gordon's surprise there was no sign of Alfeyo during the next two days, but on the night of the third day Gordon was roused from bed by the sound of someone knocking on the back door. It was Alfeyo looking very tired for he had walked all the way.

'Oh good, it's you, Alfeyo. They've kept you a very long time.'

'Yes, inkos. The Police have worried me and worried me trying to get me to say you were driving too fast. I kept telling them no, my inkos was not driving fast. They said you were driving on the wrong side of the road. I explained to them what actually happened, they kept on and on, but I wouldn't give way.'

Gordon realised that Alfeyo was determined to let him know that he had defended his boss loyally, and that he would continue to talk in that vein for hours on end if given the opportunity. So he suggested, tactfully, Alfeyo was to go home and not bother to turn out for roll call, but sleep on as he must be tired.

Gordon had been back in bed a good ten minutes when there was more knocking on the back door. Alfeyo had returned. 'Inkos, I forgot to tell you that when I was crossing the Umgusa river I saw that a car had turned over and that a white man was in the water, hanging on to a rock, and calling out "Help me, help me, I am drowning." So I went to him and said, "Sir, I have been a witness in one car accident and the police have harassed me for three days, so I am not going to be witness to another car accident, but I'll tell my boss when I get home, and he will come and help you."'

Gordon was flabbergasted. To think it was only as an afterthought that Alfeyo was telling him a man was struggling for his life, and, more to the point, in a crocodile-infested river! A good example of how differently blacks and whites view a dilemma.

He tore off his pyjamas, pulled on shirt and shorts and drove at speed to the Umgusa, only to find that the man had been rescued by a passer-by.

One of Gordon's most interesting farmers on whom he called quite frequently was an elderly lady, an early settler who lived some miles out of Bulawayo at the site of much activity during the Matabele rebellion. She was much respected by the Matabele and it was from her that he learned a lot about their tribal customs and history. One of the stories which stuck in his mind related to more recent events. During a royal visit to Rhodesia, the Government had arranged an *indaba* to be held in the Matopos Hills at which all major Matabele chiefs were to be presented to Their Majesties. The chiefs sought permission to turn up in leopard skins as befitted them, but the government officials insisted on them wearing the long red robes and carrying the black ebony staffs with which they had been issued. The chiefs protested on the grounds that they would look like dressed-up apes but the native commissioners refused to give way.

The day came. The chiefs turned up in their scarlet robes. His Majesty, King George, moved forward to shake hands. To his amazement, the chiefs peeled off their robes to reveal themselves in leopard skins over glisteningly polished bodies and, in unison, bayed out the royal salute of 'Bhayete'! The King was delighted and so were all the onlookers!

Breakfast was interrupted one morning by the houseboy informing Gordon that the *capitao* wished to speak to him urgently. Gordon went out, and as soon as he saw the *capitao*'s face, he realised that the man was terribly worked up. Not waiting for the usual greeting, he exclaimed: 'Come quickly to the compound, sir, Njima is going to die!'

'What are you saying?' Gordon asked in astonishment. 'What is the matter with him? He is a big strong fellow and was perfectly alright last evening.'

'Yes, sir, that I know, but now he is dying. Please come quickly.' The man was in a real state of panic; even of terror.

Strange, very strange, thought Gordon. The *capitao* was a steady, stable character, not given to panicking. There was something very fishy about it. Something the *capitao* didn't want even to mention. 'What medicines should I take? Is he hurt? Is he bleeding? Is he vomiting?'

'I don't know, inkosi, truly I don't know. Just come quickly!'

The thought of witchcraft flashed through Gordon's mind, but was quickly dispelled. The Government had forbidden the practice and was strict in enforcing the law against it.

As he approached the staff compound, he heard a loud, ululating dirge coming from a large group of women and girls squatted on the ground, the kind of dirge that betokens the passing of a spirit. It had a most eerie effect – men were sitting beyond the circle of women and looked more scared than worried.

Njima's hut, like all the others, was a thatched rondaval with a single door. It was dark inside. Men were squatted shoulder to shoulder against the wall. Njima, stark naked, lay stretched out full length on the floor. One man sat at his feet, gripping both, and keeping his legs fully stretched; at each side of him sat a man, grasping a hand and keeping the arm fully stretched and close to the body. At his head sat another holding poor Njima's nose tightly closed, forcing him to breathe through his mouth.

Gordon ordered all four men to release their hold and allow the patient to relax; a deathly silence prevailed. They looked at each other enquiringly but wouldn't let go and the onlookers hissed through closed lips. Gordon ordered them out of the hut. No one moved; the atmosphere was tense. Gordon turned enquiringly to the *capitao*, but all the poor man could say was 'Forgive me, sir, but I am of a different tribe to Njima. I can't interfere. I will be cursed if I do. This is a bad case.'

Gordon realised that the situation had grown tense and that he would have to act decisively. The *capitao* had revealed, inadvertently, that a curse was involved, so Gordon announced that he would bear the consequences, and not they, if they obeyed him. 'Now get out, all of you. Let the poor fellow have some fresh air!' Very reluctantly they left the hut to squat just outside the entrance.

Njima's body was as cold as ice to Gordon's touch – even though it was a particularly hot day. Not only was his body ice cold, but it felt very dry – like that of a corpse, Gordon imagined. He sent the *capitao* scurrying back to the house for hot water bottles and blankets and, in the meantime, massaged Njima vigorously to get the circulation going. When the bottles arrived he placed them around the body and tucked the blankets around him tightly.

Njima whispered, 'Thank you, inkosi Gordon, but there is nothing you can do. The spirits have ordered me to die, so I must die,' and he turned on his side to face the wall. His eyes remained wide open and staring – staring at nothing.

Gordon decided there was not much more he could do, so he ordered the *capitao* to stay with the patient. On no account was he to allow anyone into the hut. The *capitao* remonstrated that, as he was of a different tribe to Njima, trouble would ensure if he was left alone and the patient died. Gordon appreciated the implication and so ordered a man of Njima's tribe to keep him company; they were not to allow anyone else to enter the hut. He assured them he would be back as soon as he had breakfasted.

Gordon hurried back to the hut with a hot toddy for the patient, only to find the two guards had been ousted and the four men were in position again holding on to Njima's limbs and nose. He was livid at his orders being disobeyed. Once again he ordered everyone out of the hut, then massaged Nzima briskly and wrapped him up in the blankets with the hot water bottles tucked close.

Njima looked up at him and said 'Inkosi, please leave me. There is nothing you can do, I am destined to die. I must die. Please see that my wages go to my wife in Nyasaland,' and he turned on to his side again to face the wall. Gordon decided there was nothing more he could do and left him.

An hour or so later the *capitao* reported the death so Gordon phoned the police in Bulawayo. They turned up promptly and, after questioning all the witnesses, they took the body away for an autopsy. The result: cause of death unknown. Heart, lungs and other organs were in sound condition; there was no sign of poisoning or of injury.

What then had been the cause of death? Had Njima just willed himself to death, or had there been some other influence at work?

Months later Gordon discussed the case with a Matabele police sergeant who had been involved in the enquiry. In his personal opinion, based on similar cases, he believed witchcraft to have been involved.

Gordon's next posting was as Senior Professional Officer in charge of the newly created Henderson Research Station, some 15 or so miles out of Salisbury in the lovely Mazoe Valley. The estate had been bequeathed to the Government by an old settler, Archie Henderson, on the strict understanding that it would be used as a centre for agricultural research.

A large part of the property was taken up by a steep range of hills with deep and narrow ravines and covered in boulders, trees and dense bush. Unsuitable though it was for agriculture, it became an ideal haven for the money-conscious native women of Salisbury. There, in complete seclusion, were sites a-plenty for them to conduct their trade in prostitution and *skokiaan*. Kaffir beer brewed by fermenting maize or sorghum is a healthy drink, but when it is converted into *skokiaan* by the addition of any substance which will hasten fermentation, such as carbide or rats, cats, dogs and amputated limbs and organs from hospital bins, it becomes the devil's own brew.

The women made it in large 44-gallon petrol drums, and sold it for as much as two shillings and sixpence a small cup, which was all that was needed to produce a headache and tummy trouble; two cups were liable to drive a man mad. The police from Salisbury, and from the small patrol post at Mazoe, carried out periodic raids at weekends. When they were lucky enough to come across one of the shabeens they would overturn the drums and take the women to court. The magistrates would fine them as much as £50 – a very large sum for the average native to pay, but peanuts for those women. They forked out the £50 quite happily, knowing full well that they were left with a profit of two or three times that amount. That of course, was apart from the money made by prostitution.

At weekends those shabeens were a nightmare for Gordon, for not only did they attract, in their dozens, black hooligans from the capital, but they were also a dangerous attraction for the African labourers on the station. Very frequently he would be summoned to his back door at night by drunks, or by non-drunks, seeking first aid for the injuries received.

One Saturday night he was wakened by even more noise than usual. A crowd had gathered in the backyard of his house clamouring for him to hurry to the labour-force compound, because a drunk had chopped off Mangwe's foot and he was fast bleeding to death.

His first reaction was that it was *skokiaan*-induced exaggeration, but when the clamour for assistance rose, he realised the situation was serious. Sure enough, lying in a pool of blood was poor Mangwe, his foot only just connected to the ankle by the back tendon. Gordon wondered what would be best to do – whether to completely sever it and staunch the bleeding with hot embers, or to strap it into position and rush him to hospital.

Fortunately, it was an absolutely clean cut with no ragged edges so he decided on the latter course – not easy with the blood flowing fast. However, applying a tourniquet and using an abundance of lint and strapping, he rushed the patient in his car to the Salisbury hospital. There, the doctors decided, amputation was the only remedy.

Naturally, the police were summoned and it transpired that a man, drunk on *skokiaan*, had walked into a hut, similar to his own, and, on seeing a man and woman in bed together, he had assumed the woman to be his wife, and so, with the little axe he always carried, he had slashed at the man's foot. The poor victim was in his own hut and with his own wife!

Chapter XVI

The outbreak of the Second World War became a major turning point in the development of the Colony. What Gordon noticed most was the subtle change in the relationship which was taking place between black and white, accompanied by a marked deterioration in security. In pre-war days he could, and usually did, leave his house without bothering to close doors and windows and would have returned a week or so later to find everything as he had left it, nothing stolen, nothing damaged; but not so now.

Just as war was becoming imminent, Rhodesia, that is Southern Rhodesia, the country south of the Zambezi river as distinct from Northern Rhodesia, the territory to the north of it, was selected by the British Government as a training ground for the Royal Air Force. Rhodesians were proud their country had been chosen. Sadly, the whole question of security took a change for the worse. The vast majority of the rank and file among ground staff were fine fellows, but, unfortunately, there was a minority who just did not know that in a colony the whites were expected to set a decent example to the blacks. Sadly their officers – and one of the most senior among them was a relative of Gordon's – didn't take pains to teach them.

Many of the young aircraftsmen were 'all mates together' with the African one moment and then swearing at and thumping him the next, so the African was finding it hard to know where he stood.

The social situation for those overseas servicemen in Rhodesia was very good and there was no shortage of invitations for them from the residents. Unfortunately a minority abused it, and the abuse was observed by the African servants of the house. One Rhodesian family extended an open invitation for six aircraftsmen to have sundowners with them and to give them the opportunity to meet white girls. The party went well, all enjoyed themselves, but when it came to bidding their hosts goodnight, the latter were flabbergasted to find the necks of beer bottles sticking out of pockets. Worse still, when clearing up, the houseboy reported some of the silver to be missing. And that was not an isolated incident.

In the immediate post-war years, the Southern Rhodesia Government became anxious, for political reasons, to expand the white population very appreciably and very fast. They did that by encouraging and assisting the immigration of artisans from Britain and from South Africa. In issuing visas for entry, preference was given to artisans over intellectuals and persons with money and business acumen. The intention was to foster a gigantic building programme and, in doing that, they were indeed successful. At breakneck speed, new suburbs were mushrooming and the skylines of Salisbury and of Bulawayo were displaying multi-storey buildings where, hitherto, there had been only single and double-storey buildings.

Unfortunately, once again, many of those immigrants were the wrong type of settler for an African country only decades removed from the primitive. Whether or not the blame could be laid squarely on their shoulders, the fact remained that no longer could people leave their houses for even an hour without locking doors and windows. The African was not slow in learning wrong practices, particularly when life was made easy for black thieves by whites becoming receivers of stolen goods.

Late one evening, Alfeyo, who was now doubling as car-attendant and houseboy, rushed into the house to tell Gordon that he and the Mashona cook, Kennis, had caught two natives prowling around the premises. Gordon rushed out and, sure enough, there was slimly built Kennis, armed with a pick-axe, holding at bay in the garage a man armed with a long pole. Gordon stepped forward to grab it, when Kennis called out 'Don't, sir. It is sharp.' Sure enough, it was!

Razor blades had been inserted along its length.

A new method of stealing had gained popularity – the fishing method, ideal for a country where warm temperatures at night made it necessary to keep windows open.

For protection, the windows were generally fitted with ornate wrought-iron screens or by metal bars, but these were not a great obstacle to the new brand of thief on the search for clothes left on a chair or for jewels lying on top of a dressing table. All he had to do was fish the items out with a pole fitted with a hook at the end. Should the occupant waken at the wrong moment and grab at the pole, he or she stood a good chance of having their fingers amputated because, here again, razor blades had been inserted in it.

Employers of house servants in Europe seldom invite them to join them at table, but in Southern Rhodesia many of the newcomers were doing just that, and familiarity bred contempt. While white Rhodesian women took an interest in the welfare of their native servants, they didn't visit them in their living quarters, except, perhaps, to doctor them in time of illness, and that task was left, generally, to their husbands to do. But among the newcomers, quite a few of the women thought nothing of paying social calls, and some went even so far as to loan their husband's pyjamas when they saw the 'boys' going to sleep in their day-time shorts. Familiarity of that sort caused the uneducated African to lose respect for white women and undermined discipline.

A European couple in Salisbury ran a hot-dog stall to cater for late-night revellers. Usually, when the rush was over, at around about midnight, the wife returned home to go to bed. In order not to disturb her, the husband, when he closed the stall and went home, usually went to sleep in another room.

In the early hours of one morning, she was roused by a movement in the bed. Drowsily she called out: 'What's the matter? Are you alright?' The only response was an arm being tightened around her and pressure being extended against her back. On opening her eyes she was horrified to find a native in bed with her. At the first shriek he bolted. At that time, the sentence for a black man raping a white woman was death, so the culprit had taken a very great risk.

There stood a very large tree right in the middle of North Avenue in Salisbury, which divided the two lanes of traffic. Legend had it that when all the other trees in the locality had been uprooted to make way for the road, it had been spared, deliberately, as an undertaking that no white person would ever be hanged in Southern Rhodesia for any offence whatsoever. Be the legend true or false, the fact was that white persons sentenced to death were always sent to South Africa for the privilege of being hanged there.

The introduction of so many whites – with many of them being the wrong type for settling in a black country – resulted in the breakdown of what had come to be regarded as a stable and mutually understood, and mutually respected relationship between the two races. Just as in Kenya where the African regarded the Asian as a stumbling block to his progress by being employed in all the medium-range jobs, such as masons, carpenters, clerks and sales staff, so, in Southern Rhodesia, he came to feel shut out by the new class of immigrant artisan.

The situation was being worsened by visits by left-wing politicians and by trade unionists from Britain, voicing their opinions and ideologies, in a country about which they knew precious little. A classic example was the case of a leading member of the United Kingdom Trade Union movement expressing dismay and horror at finding that black artisans were receiving lower rates of pay than their white counterparts. He called straight away for equal pay for equal work and was more than astonished to find he was being supported by the local white artisan's union. The reason, of course, being that if an employer was required to pay a black and less experienced artisan the same rate he was to pay an experienced white, who was going to be silly enough to employ a black?

Development soon outstripped the economy in Southern Rhodesia, so the politicians started to cast covetous eyes on the neighbouring British territories of Northern Rhodesia and Nyasaland. The economy of Southern Rhodesia was based mainly on flue-cured Virginia tobacco and to a lesser extent on the export of chrome, mica, asbestos, maize and a small quantity of gold. She was not only short of cash to race along with her aspirations, but also of labour, and for this she had to rely on a flow of manpower from Nyasaland, the Portuguese territory of Mozambique and, to a lesser extent, from Northern Rhodesia. If only she could be assured of a controllable source of money and of labour, the country could develop even more rapidly, and continue to provide the population with a comfortable standard of living – or so thought the politicians.

Northern Rhodesia had only a comparatively small white population and was very wealthy, thanks to a flourishing copper mining industry. Also, there was no shortage of native labour; much of it was already making its way to the gold and diamond mines of South Africa. Unfortunately, being so land-locked, for the export of her goods she was entirely dependent on rail traffic, and the railways were owned by Southern Rhodesia and the Union of South Africa.

Nyasaland also had a small white population, with its economy dependent mainly on the export of flue-cured and fire-cured Virginia tobacco and oil-producing nuts. In terms of finance, she was the smallest and poorest of the three countries, but she was rich in manpower. Because of a lack of demand for labour within the country, much of it found its way to Southern Rhodesia for service on farms and in industry, and to South Africa for work in the mines. The country was very dependent upon the cash regularly remitted by these men to their families back in the homeland.

Southern Rhodesia was a self-governing colony, but both Northern Rhodesia and Nyasaland were British protectorates, having, of their own free will, sought the protection of 'The Great White Queen who loves the black people'. In these two territories, whites could own land in only very restricted areas, the rest being reserved for the indigenous inhabitants. If the three countries could be unified under one government, a great nation could be created, but this would only be possible if the British Government abrogated its responsibility of protectorship and that, of course, it couldn't rightly do, and was not prepared to do.

The next best thing in the eyes of the white politicians was federation, and so, in 1953, there came into being the Federation of Rhodesia and Nyasaland, which was to be administered from Salisbury, the capital of Southern Rhodesia. Right from the start its lifespan was doomed to be a short one. Firstly, it had to support, financially, not one but four governments – the Federal parliament plus local legislatures in each of the three territories. Then there was the question of representation in those governments. In the two northern territories, blacks had seats in their legislatures, and there was also direct black representation in the Federal Parliament, but in the Southern Rhodesia legislature there were no seats for blacks, their interests being taken care of by a white Minister for African Affairs.

Another major stumbling block was the difference in scope for the development of the African in the two protectorates and their southern partner, and, more specially, the difference in lifestyles and outlook. In the south, there were different counters in a post office for blacks and whites, so that Europeans would not have to jostle for a place in a queue with houseboys, garden boys and messengers.

There was no such segregation in Nyasaland and in Northern Rhodesia. There, too, Africans were often employed as clerks and as typists, but in the South those duties were carried out mainly by Europeans.

A farcical situation arose in Southern Rhodesia. Black railway workers wished to become firemen, but that was a post reserved for whites – surely an unenviable post in a warm climate for anyone! The Rhodesia Railways Union – a whites only body – voiced strong opposition. Mr Daubi Yanga, an African representative in the Federal Parliament, pressed a strong case for blacks. He claimed that the job didn't require any particular skill and he was prepared to support that contention by doing the work himself for a day.

The Union protested and ruled: 'Before he can mount the footplate, and thus become the first African in the history of the railways to do so, Mr Yamba will have to sign a form of indemnity. He will then be provided with a pass endorsed "Available on locomotives" from the General Manager's Office.'

Happily, the railway management stepped in to stop that silly wrangle. Because of his age, fifty, they wouldn't agree to let Mr Yamba proceed with his challenge, and were 'delighted to announce that from September 1960, Africans would be trained as firemen and be given opportunity on the footplate'.

The political atmosphere throughout most of Africa, south of the

Sahara, was astir. It was particularly tense in Kenya, the Belgian Congo, Mozambique, and the Rhodesias and Nyasaland. The tension was heightened by Harold Macmillan, a very senior member of the British Parliament, racing the length of the African continent proclaiming a much publicised pronouncement: 'The Winds of Change'.

Without any doubt, it was the most obvious hint to African leaders in areas already simmering with discontent, that they could count on the support, clandestine or otherwise, of the British Government. In effect, it was a passport to instability and disruption.

To the settlers in the British territories, the writing was on the wall, clear and distinct. Few had ever banked on any support, at any time, from the British Labour Party which seemed to be ashamed of the words 'empire' and 'colony'. But now the majority came to realise they could no longer count on any backing from the British Conservatives – Macmillan was their leader.

Settlers of long-standing were being faced with the imponderable. Could they continue to live in a country to be governed by blacks? And, more to the point, by blacks, who, only a few decades past were still living a primitive lifestyle. When the Second World War broke out, white Rhodesians had rushed to Britain's aid. For them, there had been no need for conscription – they had volunteered in large numbers. To many who had never put foot in Britain, it was even 'home'. How much longer could those bonds of loyalty be expected to last when a senior conservative politician, like Macmillan, was hinting, broadly, to the African, that the tide was running in his favour. White Rhodesians were feeling very let down.

The calamitous situation in the Belgian Congo, resulting from the Belgians literally scooting out of the country, without caring about what was to happen to law and order once they were gone, had an unsettling effect on the neighbouring territories. African politicians in Rhodesia began to feel that if the whites could be driven out of the Congo quite so easily, there was hope for them to be able to do the same.

Soon, trouble began to brew. In Nyasaland, Matthew Phiri, the African vice-chairman of the United Federal Party in Blantyre, the capital, was attacked in the main street by a mob of about two hundred Africans shouting party slogans. He had offended them by preaching patience and common sense. He only escaped with his life by running into a European-owned chemist shop. The unruly mob was eventually persuaded to disperse by the police using tear gas after the white Provincial Commissioner had tried, unsuccessfully, to persuade them to do so. The only response to his pleas had been shouts of 'kwacha' (freedom).

Gordon had been a witness to the proceedings, and had seen and heard reporters and photographers of United Kingdom tabloids actually paying and encouraging African youths to join the fracas, by shouting insults and throwing stones at cars and premises owned by Europeans.

In Northern Rhodesia, street gangs of black youths had adopted an anti-white campaign. Cars were their main target, but particularly their occupants. Matters had reached such a pitch that the police warned drivers not to stop at the scene of any accident, but to drive on, and when safely away, to report the incident to the nearest police station.

On the Ndola-Mufulira main road, a crowd stopped a car being driven by Mrs Lillian Burton, a housewife with no political connections. As she had tried to drive on, they poured petrol over the car and over her and her two young daughters, and set them alight. As Mrs Burton and the girls struggled to get out of the car they were kicked and beaten to death.

Happy to relate, at about the same time, but at a separate location, an African police inspector, Rejoice Lubesha, rescued a European from a hostile crowd of Africans. He had carried the man away on the carrier of his bicycle despite the injuries and insults to himself, and was proud to receive a letter of commendation from the Governor of Northern Rhodesia, Sir Evelyn Hone.

It is nice to be able to recount a reciprocal act of kindness, which took place at about the same time, but many miles away. A white farmer, driving home, found, by the side of the road, an elderly

African being savaged, brutally, by a gang of five natives, so he stopped the car and went over to intervene. They immediately turned their fury onto him and called him all sorts of white filth. Fortunately, he had had the good sense to take his metal shooting stick with him, and flayed that around to protect himself. But while dragging the victim away, he himself was badly beaten, although miraculously, he managed to get the victim into the car. As he was starting up, the hooligans shattered the windscreen and two windows and badly damaged the bodywork.

In Southern Rhodesia, serious trouble broke out in both Salisbury and Bulawayo, amounting to actual rioting – the worst disturbances since the Matabele rebellion. The irony of it was that while the essential aim had been to damage white-owned property, the persons who suffered most were moderate-minded Africans.

The extent of the troubles in all three territories of the Federation was as child's play compared with what was happening in the adjacent Belgian Congo. There, not only were the lives of the white community made almost untenable and put at grave risk, but African tribe was fighting African tribe, and faction against faction. One moment the army was supporting the Government, the next it was taking the law into its own hands, looting, pillaging and going on the rampage.

At Mnono in the north, Europeans living in outlying places such as farms were ordered to leave their homes and converge on the town, because Baluba tribesmen were murdering and creating havoc.

The political party, Abako, was in favour of a federal system of black rule, but the Prime Minister, Mr Lumumba was in favour of a unitary republic of which he would be president. Supporters of the two parties took to the streets against each other, using as weapons whatever came to hand.

The situation had become so bad that Dag Hammarskjoeld, Secretary General of the United Nations, warned the security council that UN troops had been unable to disarm Congolese soldiers in the Kivu province and elsewhere, and that the presence of UN troops was becoming impossible.

A small unit of Canadian signallers was about to leave by plane for

Luluabourg, when they were forced to lie on the ground, some being stripped down to their underwear. Identification cards, weapons and other belongings were stolen. The captain was knocked unconscious by a blow to his head with a rifle butt. Other Congolese troops jumped up and down on the men's backs.

Once again, it is encouraging to find loyalty and courage in the most unexpected places. An ordinary houseboy saved the lives of a European woman and her small son who were living on a lonely plantation near Kamina. When he saw truckloads of army mutineers driving towards the house, he put the woman and her child in the boot of her car and courageously drove towards the soldiers. When they stopped him, he explained that he had purloined his employer's car for himself and was driving it to his home. He was congratulated for his enterprise!

Another African, Father Perre, a priest, saved the lives of a large community of whites who were sheltering in a hall, while several hundred mutineers were rampaging through the town, looting, burning and murdering. He calmly took his stand in the middle of the street, held up his hand to stop the onrush, reasoned with them, and eventually persuaded them to spare the lives of the people in the hall.

Belgian refugees were flocking into the Federation on their way back to Europe or to South Africa; at one time their number was estimated at 10,000. Small wonder that the Federal Government was alerted to its own security – especially after the riots in Salisbury and Bulawayo. It decided to form a volunteer unit, on the lines of the Home Guard established in Britain during the War, and to call it the 'Local Defence Volunteers' – the actual name by which the Home Guard first came into being. That move was criticised immediately by the African leadership, who claimed it belied the proclaimed aim of the Federal and Territorial legislatures to establish full partnership between the races. They themselves, on the other hand, gave no pledge to abstain from violence.

There can be no doubt that during those troubled times, the leaders of the white communities in all three territories were making very real efforts to give tangible proof of their determination to do away with the colour-bar completely, and to establish full partnership. The position was excellently clarified in an editorial in the *Rhodesia Herald* of 18 August 1960:

> For seven years the finger was pointed at Southern Rhodesia. The Colony's racial policies and practices, it was charged, were a major stumbling block to acceptance of Federation by the majority of the people in the northern territories. And African nationalists there made much of the point even (while their followers) continued to flock south for work.
>
> In a seeming rush that is slightly breath taking, Southern Rhodesia in the past few days has begun to take man-sized steps along the path to implementing that partnership which, at the time of Federation, was as implicitly promised for the territorial fields as the Federal.
>
> The measures, adopted and operating as it is hoped they will be, will indeed provide very tangible evidence of racial goodwill.
>
> A redelimitation of constituencies will mean that Africans elected by their own people will sit in the highest councils of the land.

There was rather a touching story and a true one, of the elderly, uneducated African, who had been in his company's employ for many years and now wished to improve his status from labourer to ticket clerk. To understand the story, one must realise that the ordinary, man-in-the-street African always refers to a coat as a jaycket (jacket). The examination simply required the aspirant to spell from a primer with, for added simplicity, a picture illustrating each word; for instance DOG with a picture of a dog. All had gone well with B.A.T = bat; C.A.T = cat, but when it came to C.O.A.T, he called out jaycket! He was not made a ticket clerk, but was given a rise in pay and a measure of authority over his work mates.

Although the white politicians were pressing ahead with changes in law and attitude as fast as one can expect politicians to go in a democratic society, the African leadership deemed progress to be too slow. They were getting restive. The trouble was that under pressure from vociferous activists, the more moderate-minded leaders were losing influence. There was, however, one moderate who by his very personality and charm was able to withstand the pressure – he was

Kenneth Kaunda, leader of the United Independence Party in Northern Rhodesia. He was content to achieve his aspirations by passive resistance and not through violent demonstration.

In Southern Rhodesia the prospect was not looking at all good. Every move made by whites to create a greater measure of partnership between the two races was being regarded by Africans, not as a gesture of goodwill, but of weakness. They were not demanding just the proverbial mile for each inch given, but several miles! Each concession met, invariably, with an even greater demand. To make matters worse, Britain was seen to be appeasing the United States of America by ignoring her white settlers and not even calling on the African leadership to exercise patience. By now, white South Africans were able to see what the granting of concessions to the black man meant.

White Rhodesians who had fought for Britain and who had created the most advanced and prosperous country, barring South Africa, south of the Sahara, were being thrown, literally, to the dogs. Britain appeared to be closing her eyes, deliberately, to the bloodshed, anarchy and the economic disasters which were occurring in the African countries being 'liberated' from their colonial powers.

In course of time the patience of the European community in Southern Rhodesia wore thin. Many sold their houses, farms and possessions on a very poor seller's market and left the country. There was no light at the end of the tunnel. Settlers of long standing, who had made the country their home, could see no hope of a decent future. They couldn't face the prospect of becoming underdog to people they had once employed.

The upshot of it all was that the Federation was dissolved in December 1963. Northern Rhodesia was granted independence and became the independent state of Zambia, with Kenneth Kaunda as its first president with executive authority. Nyasaland was also granted independence and became the Republic of Malawi with Dr Hastings Banda as executive president.

Southern Rhodesia, the only self-governing colony among the three, also sought independence, but the British Government was prepared to accede to this request only if the majority of the population were in favour of it and that majority rule would prevail. Very obviously, Africans would vote in favour only if they were assured of becoming the governing body. And that, of course, was something to which the whites would not agree. They were quite prepared for Africans to have seats in Parliament and govern in partnership, but they were not prepared to cede their majority in the House.

In face of the impasse, Southern Rhodesia forged ahead on her own against great odds – particularly the opposition from the African and Asian members of the United Nations. As usual, the United States was well to the fore, as she had always been, in her attempts to damage the British Empire. When one frequently hears complaints of unfair treatment by her own Indian, black and Hispanic citizens, it was rather incongruous to find her suddenly championing the demands of the blacks in Southern Rhodesia. More surprising still, was Australia becoming a supporter of black rights, while blatantly overlooking the misery she had inflicted on the Aborigines.

Two Africans emerged as leaders: Joshua Nkomo whose base was in Matabeleland, and Robert Mugabe, a Mashona. Isolated cases of sabotage turned into guerrilla warfare which lasted several years. Ian Smith, Prime Minister and leader of the Rhodesian Front – a man who was very badly wounded while serving with the Royal Air Force during the War – made his famous declaration of UDI (Unilateral Declaration of Independence), a declaration which Harold Wilson, Prime Minister of Great Britain, preferred to regard as IDI (Illegal Declaration of Independence). The white community were regarded as rebels, but, be it understood most fully, they continued to profess their loyalty to the British Crown.

The British Government responded to UDI by embarking on a policy of graduated economic sanction. The small white community replied, bravely, by manufacturing many of the commodities denied by the embargo – commodities they had never thought of producing before the sanctions. They tightened their belts, flexed their industrial muscle to beat the embargo and the white farmers, the most vulnerable section of the community, strengthened their schemes for mutual assistance in times of emergency, converting their lonely homesteads into fortresses.

The British public, if not their politicians, felt a sense of pride in their own kith and kin facing tremendous odds with great courage. Then, unfortunately, Ian Smith blundered badly – he insulted the Queen's representative, the Governor, Sir Humphrey Gibbs, himself born in Rhodesia, by confining him to the Governor's Residence and cutting off supplies of electricity and water.

The British don't mind being attacked and criticised, in fact they have become used to it, but attack their sovereign and you strike at their very heart. From that moment, Smith lost a valuable and crucial asset – the backing of the man in the street, and therefore of many of his supporters.

The farmers were the ones to face the brunt of the guerrilla attacks which by then had become frequent. Like their counterparts in Kenya during the Mau Mau rebellion, they stood up to it well, despite the many barbarous and cowardly atrocities that were committed against them. A special salute for their wives!

The sad and lengthy saga was brought to a close at Lancaster House in London with Southern Rhodesia being granted independence as the Republic of Zimbabwe. A little-known personality, the Reverend Banana, became the first President with Robert Mugabe, a Mashona, the first Prime Minister. On 1 January 1988 Banana stepped down and Mugabe became president with executive authority over a one-party state: 'Zanu-PF.'

It is said that Robert Mugabe is a Marxist-Leninist. Fortunately, for quite a few years now, he has had the good sense to temper those leanings in his dealings with the white community. He has realised that the economy, as well as the stability of the country, is very dependent upon the expertise and the achievements of the Europeans.

The new regime has been given a very strong base on which to build. It has inherited well-established towns with beautiful multi-storey buildings, good schools, fine hospitals, splendid shops, excellent farms, good roads, an efficient railway system, first-class telecommunications, the marvellous Kariba Dam, many smaller dams, freedom from the dreaded tsetse fly and from the even more dreaded rinderpest.

Chapter XVII

The ordinary black Zimbabwean has become disillusioned by the President not fulfilling the promises he made at the time of the country achieving independence from British rule. Apart from the President's cronies, very few black citizens have been settled on the land taken from white farmers, food stocks are in short supply and prices have risen drastically; there are long queues at the pumps for petrol and diesel; editors and journalists on local newspapers have been imprisoned for not towing the political party line; roads are falling into disrepair and even street lights are dimmed early to economise on electricity. However, a palatial residence has been built and maintained for the President's new wife who patronises the most expensive haute couture in Europe.

Unemployment among the black community is assessed at 50 per cent; inflation at the end of 1999 was running at 60 per cent and was rising steadily. Between 20,000 and 30,000 Matabele lost their lives at the hands of Mugabe's brutal 5th Brigade, whose members were trained in communist North Korea. The only logical reason for those vile and sadistic murders was as revenge for the atrocities committed more than a hundred years earlier, by Mziligazi, the first Matabele king and overlord, on his disobedient Mashona vassals. Mugabe, of course, is a Mashona. Despite the economic crisis which is afflicting the country, Mugabe has committed Zimbabwean ground troops and air force to the civil war raging in the Congo. His country's dwindling exchequer is being saddled with the heavy cost of that adventure while, it is believed, his own purse is swelling with diamonds and gold from the Congo's rich mines.

Mugabe received his first shock when he lost the vote in a referendum calling for a change in the constitution to enhance his power and to make him President for life. To his surprise, he found that the black labour movement under Morgan Tsvangarai had formed a new political party, the MDC (the Movement for Democratic Change). It calls on Mugabe either to change his ways or to resign. It has grown so fast and so strong that Zanu-PF is employing bully-boy tactics against anyone found wearing an MDC emblem or T-shirt.

One youth found wearing such a shirt was made to put his head on a block by a Mugabe supporter wielding an axe – the boy was not killed, but was left petrified. The incident was a grim warning to anyone else supporting the new party. On another occasion, an elderly woman, the grandmother of several children, was so badly beaten in front of them that she was crippled for life. The onlookers won't forget that lesson either.

In an endeavour to regain the loss he has suffered in the popularity stakes, Mugabe has taken to playing the race/land card. At the time of coming to power in 1980 he promised to acquire five million hectares of white-owned farmland on which to settle 160,000 black landless families within a period of five years. The British Government undertook to help finance the project provided the white owners who were to be displaced would receive fair compensation.

However, all that has happened by July 2000, is that some 40,000 hectares, forcibly purchased in 1996, are either lying idle or have been given to the President's cronies or to those on whom he has to rely for protection and power, such as heads of the army and the police and some senior civil servants. Few of them have had any farming experience and have no real desire to farm but only to own the land. As a result, the economy suffers.

The new strategy to curry favour with the populace is to encourage the landless, or anyone else who chooses, to take the law into their own hands and force their way onto white-owned farms and squat on them. To do this is a simple matter because each farm, being 1,500 to 2,000 acres in extent, is virtually an isolated island separated by quite a distance from its nearest neighbour. The farmer and his black staff are left to their own devices. They cannot resort for protection to the use of a firearm for fear of being charged with manslaughter or murder. There is no point in calling in the police because the answer is bound to be 'Sorry, we have no vehicles', or 'We have no petrol'. Ironically, the vehicles and the petrol are often being used to transport the squatters on to the property and, to add insult to injury, the squatters receive a daily rate of pay from the Government.

The usual drill is for a mob armed with axes, machetes, iron bars and clubs to break into the owner's house, ransack it in search of weapons, money and food, purloin what they want and destroy what they don't. Often the white womenfolk are forced to dance and sing while their menfolk are being beaten and clubbed. The farm labourers are rounded up and are forced to swear allegiance to Mugabe and to denounce the MDC party. Any who are suspected of being members of that party are beaten savagely and their dwellings set alight. Some have even been killed. The mob even goes to the foolish length of destroying the tobacco crop on which the country's economy is so dependent.

In April 2000, two white farmers were murdered. David Stevens was abducted from his farm at Marondera in Mashonaland, driven away in his own vehicle and murdered by a bullet in the head on a dusty track several miles from his home. His body was then thrown on top of two other white men who had been beaten brutally, but not killed.

A few days later, Martin Olds, who was born in Zimbabwe, or Rhodesia as it was then called, was killed in a gun battle on his isolated ranch in Matabeleland He had sent his family away for security reasons and was alone in the farm house when a mob attacked with firearms and axes. Though severely wounded, he fought on bravely until a petrol bomb set the building alight. As he struggled to get out of the inferno, he was hacked to death. Oddly enough, several years earlier he had been awarded a medal for bravery by President Mugabe himself, for saving a black man from attack by a crocodile.

That was the first case of a white farmer being attacked in Matabeleland during the current disturbances. The fear among both Matabeles and whites now in Matabeland was that the dreaded 5th Brigade might be back in the province. It was rumoured that large groups of Mugabe supporters, among them 5th Brigade personnel, had been spotted in the countryside.

To the chagrin of British settlers in Zimbabwe, the British Government under Tony Blair as Prime Minister, is doing nothing to help them on the grounds that Zimbabwe is no longer a colony but an independent state. However in April 2000 it extended an invitation to Mugabe to go to London for talks with Robin Cook the Foreign Secretary and with Peter Hain, the Minister for African Affairs and a personal friend of Mugabe.

Mugabe did attend, but no one had high expectations of a successful accord being reached – because he has no respect for Prime Minister Blair and has described his government as a band of homosexuals and lesbians. As far as can be seen the main outcome of the talks was for Mugabe, on his return to Zimbabwe, to declare in a radio broadcast that the white farmers are the 'enemies of the country'. In other words, he was inciting violence!

It is incongruous that in the years gone by, Peter Hain campaigned for the end of white rule in Rhodesia and for the installation of his friend Mugabe as President. One wonders what his feelings were at the London conference.

It would also be interesting to know how another veteran politician in the (British) New Labour Party feels when he refers back to what he recorded in his diary on 4 March 1980: 'Robert Mugabe has won the Rhodesian elections outright. It is a fantastic victory and I cannot think of anything that has given me such pleasure for a long time. When I think of the systematic distortions of the British press, it is an absolute disgrace.' (That quote is an extract from an article by Stephen Glover in the *Spectator*. He qualified it by adding 'the Thatcher government, but not Thatcher herself, emitted its own squeaks of optimism about Mugabe, if not in such lunatic terms.')

By early 2000 a distinct change could be seen. In parliamentary elections the MDC party secured the majority of urban seats but did not do so well in the rural constituencies However, the result put an end to one-party rule. All will depend on how Mugabe and his thugs will treat the new members of parliament and whether bribery will play an important role.

An extraordinary feature is that despite all the problems besetting the country the Zimbabwean parliament remains modelled on Westminster, the main difference being that the members address each other as 'honourable comrade'. Portraits of the Queen and the white speakers of the old colonial regime still adorn the walls.

Perhaps the day will come when President Mugabe will recall the advice given him at the time of his installation as President, by his friend Sammora Machele, President of Mozambique. 'Don't make the mistake I made.' Referring, of course, to the mistake he made in getting rid of the Europeans when Mozambique gained independence.

Bhayte Zimbabwe!

Bibliography

Baines's Gold Fields Diaries, Vol I.

Baines's Gold Fields Diaries, Oppenheimer Series III, edited by J.P.R. Williams.

Bullock, Charles, 'The Mashona and the Matabele', paper read to the Royal Colonial Institute.

Carbutt, C.L. (1948), 'A Brief Account of the Rise and Fall of the Matabele', NADA No. 25.

Colquhon, Archibald R. 'Matabeleland', paper read to the Royal Colonial Institute on 28 November 1893, Proceedings of the Royal Colonial Institute, Vol XXV, 1893-4.

Doyle, Dennis, *The Rise and Fall of the Matabele Nation.*

Jones, Rev. Neville (1946), 'More Sindebele Proverbs', NADA No. 23.

Livingstone, Dr, 'Narrative', a paper.

Mackenzie, Rev. J., *Ten Years North of the Orange River.*

Marshall Hole, H., 'The Passing of the Black Kings', paper read to the Royal Scientific Association.

Marshall Hole, H., 'The Rise of the Matabele', paper read by H.J. Taylor at a meeting of the Rhodesia Scientific Association on 8 May 1913, RSA Proceedings, Vol XII.

Moffat, Rev. Dr Robert, sundry papers and notes.

Nielson, P., 'The Manners and Customs of the Matabele', papers read by P. Nielson on 25 September 1912 at a meeting of the Rhodesia Scientific Association, RSA Proceedings, Vol XII.

Posselt, F.W.T., 'Mziligazi: The Rise of the Amandabele', paper read by F.W.T. Posselt at a meeting of the Rhodesia Scientific Association held on 2 July 1919, RSA Proceedings, Vol XVII, Part I.

Selous, F.C., 'The History of the Matabele and the Cause and Effect of the Matabele War', paper read to the Royal Colonial Institute on 13 March 1894, Proceedings of the Royal Colonial Institute, 1893-4.